John Stuart Blackie

Life of Robert Burns

John Stuart Blackie

Life of Robert Burns

ISBN/EAN: 9783337056391

Printed in Europe, USA, Canada, Australia, Japan

Cover: Foto ©Raphael Reischuk / pixelio.de

More available books at **www.hansebooks.com**

LIFE

OF

ROBERT BURNS

BY

JOHN STUART BLACKIE

———

LONDON

WALTER SCOTT

24 WARWICK LANE, PATERNOSTER ROW

———

1888

CONTENTS.

CHAPTER I.

PAGE

Mission of poets; Burns's birth and parentage; born at
Doonholm, Ayrshire, 25th January 1759; farm at Mount
Oliphant, 1766; at Tarbolton, 1777; education; literary
culture; early loves and love songs; love of country;
debating society; flax dressing at Irvine; despondency;
death of his father, 1784 1

CHAPTER II.

His brother Gilbert; joint farm at Mossgiel; early struggles;
Epistle to David Sillar; freemasonry; Burns and the
Church; Moderates and Evangelicals; personal piety;
Holy Willie; Epistle to the Rev. J. M'Math; "The
Holy Fair"; politics; "Birthday Ode"; power of sar-
casm; dramatic power; "The Jolly Beggars"; Mauchline
loves; Bonnie Jean; Highland Mary; proposed emigra-
tion to Jamaica; poems published; first edition, Kilmar-
nock, 1786; introduction to Edinburgh; Dr Laurie; Dr
Blacklock; Professor Dugald Stewart 29

CHAPTER III.

Journey to Edinburgh; Covington; Edinburgh society; "The
Caledonian Hunt"; critical notices of his poems; Harry
Erskine; the Duchess of Gordon; Miss Burnet of Mon-
boddo; "Ode to Edinburgh"; law and lawyers in Edin-

burgh; Roslin; Jacobitism; monument to Fergusson;
description of Burns's personal appearance in Edinburgh,
by Professorr Walker and Sir Walter Scott; Edinburgh
edition of his poems, April 1787; tour in the Lowlands;
Robert Ainslie; Duns; Coldstream; Kelso; Jedburgh;
Miss Lindsay; Selkirk; Earlston; Warkworth and
Alnwick; Sanquhar; Mossgiel and the Armours; short
excursion to the south-west Highlands; Loch Lomond;
Inverary; Highland tour, August 1786; William Nicol;
Linlithgow; Borrowstouness; Stirling; Carron; Duni-
pace; Harvieston and Miss Chalmers; Taymouth; Ken-
more; Aberfeldy; Dunkeld; Neil Gow; Killiecrankie;
Blair Athole; Professor Walker; Falls of Bruar; Lord
Lynedoch; Fall of Foyers; Inverness; the Findhorn;
Gordon Castle; Nicol; Lochaber; Aberdeen; Rev.
John Skinner; Stonehaven; in Edinburgh, 16th Septem-
ber; in October revisits Harvieston; Castle Campbell;
Peggie Chalmers; Ramsay of Ochtertyre; Murray of
Ochtertyre; Glenturit; Dunfermline; preparations for
leaving Edinburgh; love affair with Mrs M'Lehose;
Clarinda correspondence; takes lease of Ellisland on the
Nith from Miller of Dalswinton   74

CHAPTER IV.

Installed at Ellisland, March 1788; gives £200 to his family;
his marriage with Jean Armour publicly acknowledged,
August 5th; passes examination for the excise; Mrs
Burns detained at Mauchline; song in view of her
coming to Ellisland; she arrives in December; local
library at Ellisland; convivialities on the Nith; Captain
Riddell and "The Whistle"; theological polemics; "The
Kirk's Alarm"; electioneering verses; "The Five Car-
lines"; Grose, the antiquarian; "Tam o' Shanter";
"Highland Mary"; the farming business at Ellisland
abandoned, November 1791; Burns an excise officer in
Dumfries   .   .   .   .   .   :   .   .   . 109

CHAPTER V.

PAGE

Burns as an exciseman ; **Dumfries** society ; drinking ; farewell
to Clarinda ; four Dumfries fair ones—bonnie **Lesley,**
Chloris, **Lucy Oswald,** Mrs Riddell ; explosion at **Wood-**
ley Park ; **despondency** and despair ; lyrical activity ;
contributions to Thomson's " Scottish Melodies " ; life in
Dumfries ; vigorous performance of his duties as an exciseman ; " **The Deil's awa' wi' the Exciseman** " ; political
excitement ; Burns a reformer, but opposed to extreme
French ideas ; joins the **Dumfries** Volunteers ; ill of
rheumatic fever, January 1796 ; **his** last lyrical pieces ;
4th July, at Brow ; visit of Mrs Riddell to the sick poet,
5th July 1796 ; death, 21st July ; public funeral . . 127

CHAPTER VI.

The mission of Burns ; his realism ; **his characteristic** excel-
lencies as a lyric poet of **the first rank** ; his complete and
well-rounded manhood, intelligence, shrewdness, sagacity,
sense, humour, wit, and patriotism ; great zest of life ;
social electricity ; immense force of passion ; sociality and
conviviality ; great self-respect and sense of honour ; pride,
independence, and manliness ; " **A Man's a Man for** a'
that ; " contempt for money ; intellectual ambition ;
literary culture ; **his** letters ; his **appreciation of Scotch**
as the musical **dialect** of English ; **religion ;** defends the
Covenanters ; want **of self-control ;** the Bard's epitaph ;
his mission fulfilled ; **wise** counsel **to young men entering**
on life 155

INDEX 177

GLOSSARY 181

NOTE.

THE Life of ROBERT BURNS has employed the pen
of so many biographers of acknowledged ability,
that little remains for a new writer but to make a judicious
selection from existing materials, and to pronounce an
equitable judgment on a remarkable man, the complex
character of whose genius and life demands a calm consideration, equally remote from patriotic idolatry on the
one hand, and Pharisaic severity on the other. In the
choice of the materials so richly provided by Currie,
Walker, Cunningham, Chambers, Douglas, and others, I
have been guided by a desire to combine variety of situation with strongly pronounced aspects of character ; and,
as a matter of course also, have allowed the poet, both
in his verse and in his prose, to be as much as possible
his own portrait painter.

J. S. B.

LIFE OF BURNS.

CHAPTER I.—1759-1784.

BANKS OF DOON AND TARBOLTON.

"The boy is father of the man."—WORDSWORTH.

MAN is of all animals the most variable and the most incalculable. Why? Simply because, though within certain limits his course is as imperatively prescribed for him as for the other living creatures, beyond these limits it is his destiny and his privilege to shape his own course, and make the best he can of the manifold and ever-varying circumstances by which he is surrounded. He is thus, as it were, a god in a secondary sense, a being created in the image of God (Gen. i. 27), with the mission, as a deputy from the supreme Creator, to make a world of order and beauty out of any chaos into which he may find himself flung. He starts, in fact, with his proper manhood, only where the other animals end; their instincts are, like all manifestations of vital force, miraculous; but they are uniform, and as calculable in their changes as the tides or the seasons. Some animals of the highest type no doubt manifest certain emotions, which are among the best that humanity can boast. The dog, for instance, shows a worshipful

A

regard to man, who is to him as a god; but here he
stops. His reverence produces no church, no creed,
and no religion. Man, as Socrates long ago taught, is the
only religious animal. Out of our divine gift of freedom
proceed our churches and our creeds, our social politics,
and our constitutions, our schools and universities, our
academies of literature and art,—in fact the whole structure of our social existence, the rich and various display
of what we call our civilisation. In this civilisation, therefore, as the product of our own constructive liberty, we
justly rejoice. But we must rejoice with trembling; because, grand as the product unquestionably is, and most
specifically human, it is the product of a finite creature,
—a creature who can safely exercise his divine gift of free
construction only in a continual spirit of loyalty to the
primal source of all healthy energy, the original νοῦς or
λόγος, mind or reason, which, from a masculine point of view
we wisely call GOD, and in its feminine aspect NATURE.
By this divine unchanging standard, all institutions, creeds,
systems, conventions, and fashions of every kind come to
be measured; so far only as they have shaped themselves
in reverential conformity to Nature, have they any root
of soundness in them, and any guarantee of permanence.
Now, all history shows plainly, that whether from some
original defect at the start, or from the overculture of
some favourite feature, or from the mere feebleness of
senility to which all growth is subject, civilisation in
all its forms has a tendency to deflect from that Nature
of which its only value is to be the expression; and of
this evil, ever as it shows itself, the only cure lies in a
revolt against everything arbitrary and conventional, with
a recurrence of the spoiled children to good old mother

Nature in all her freedom, in all her healthiness, and in all her harmony. To bring about this restoration of society to its normal type, the great Architect of the universe sends forth from time to time specially authorised messengers to rouse, to stimulate, and to lead into the right way, the erring sons of men.

These messengers may appear as legislators, prophets, philosophers, poets, according to the want of the hour; but under whatever guise, their function is always the same, to call back to Nature and truth the spoiled children of convention and affectation. Of these messengers, the most wide in his range, and the most generally accepted, is the poet; for, while the legislator is often cramped in his efficiency by the hardness of the materials with which he has to deal, and the prophet too often has his influence confined and bound by the very forms of a church which owed its existence perhaps to his catholicity, the great poet in his honest utterances is hampered by no forces external to his own genius.

The works of such great poets—for we do not speak here of mere dressers of pretty fancies—are a real evangel of Nature to all people who have ears to hear. Such were Homer and Pindar to the Greeks; Horace and Virgil to the Romans; to the English, Shakespeare and Wordsworth; to Scotland, Walter Scott and Robert Burns,—both largely human, and at the same time, though in very different fashion, characteristically Scotch, and therefore eminently worthy of being hung up prominently in the great gallery of human notabilities. On the present occasion our business is with the latter.

It is a notable feature of the Divine procedure in the sending forth of these messengers of eternal truth, that

they are often chosen from the lower ranks of society,
and from men fitted out with the scantiest amount of
educational appliances, as if to show to the mighty movers
of the hereditary machinery of society how little Providence has need of their titles, dignities, training schools,
and social agencies of all kinds, in order to trumpet forth
the stirring summons of her great primal truths. This
was specially seen and triumphantly noted by St Paul
(1 Cor. i. 26) in the original preaching of the Gospel. If
on any notable occasion, then certainly in the promul-
gation of the Christian Church, God chose the weak
things of the world to confound those that are mighty;
and if we wish for an example of the same feature of
Divine procedure in the history of literature, we can find
no illustration more apt than the life of Robert Burns.

At a time when all the world was possessed with the
idea that without Latin and Greek, and the so-called
classical culture of the schools and universities, no
man could enunciate great moral truths, or turn a
pointed sentence with efficiency, the Creative Power sent
forth a peasant ploughman from the green slopes and
the brown clods of Ayrshire, to achieve a reputation as
a lyric poet, which the most cunning combination of
Athenian learning and Parisian polish would have spurred
itself in vain to produce. Great is Nature, and will
prevail; and she delights in showing that she needs no
outfitting and outrigging from man to put forth her most
miraculous forces in the most attractive guise. Robert
Burns was a ploughman, and the son of a ploughman.
His ancestors for several generations had been farmers
in Kincardineshire, a district of Scotland where, at the
present day, the name of Burns, or Burness, as it was

originally written, shows a good face ; but his immediate
father, William Burness, having fallen into reduced cir·
cumstances, had been obliged to leave his northern
home, and turn his steps southward in quest of a liveli-
hood. He found work first at Edinburgh, in the capacity
of gardener, a profession in which the Scotch people
have been forward to show the faithfulness and the
fruitfulness of their characteristic power of hard work ;
and afterwards proceeded to Ayr, where he engaged
himself as a gardener to the Laird of Fairly, with whom
he lived two years ; and then took service under Crawford of Doonside. Shortly afterwards, with the view of
advancing himself in life, he took a lease of seven acres
of land in Doonside, intending to carry on business as
a nurseryman ; but from that undertaking he was with-
drawn by Mr Ferguson of Doonholm, in the immediate
neighbourhood, who engaged him as a gardener and
overseer. Here he built with his own hands a clay cottage, of a most humble description, but not in anywise
without a certain neatness. "It consisted of a kitchen
in one end, and a room in the other, with a fireplace
and chimney, and there was a concealed bed in the
kitchen, with a small closet at the end ; and when
altogether cast over inside and outside with lime, it had
a neat and comfortable appearance."[1] While living in
this humble tenement, the poor Kincardineshire gardener
married Agnes Brown, the daughter of a Carrick farmer ;
and of this marriage the first-fruit was our poet Robert,
born on the 25th day of January 1759,—a year forming
a starting-point also in the history of German literature,
as being the year of the birth of Schiller. He was thus

[1] Gilbert Burns, the poet's brother, in Chambers, I. 16.

ten years posterior to Goethe, who was born in 1749, and twelve years anterior to his great compatriot Sir Walter Scott, who was born in 1771. In the year 1766, when the poet was seven years old, his father, having approved himself as a faithful workman in Mr Ferguson's service, was advanced to the dignity of tenant in the small upland farm of Mount Oliphant, a few miles above the mouth of the Doon. In this farm he remained for ten years, and then (1777) removed to a larger farm a little further north, in the parish of Tarbolton,—transplanted thus from the banks of one bonnie stream, the Doon, to the banks of another, the Ayr, scarcely less redolent of the picturesque charm so distinctive of Scottish lowland scenery. In the possession of this farm he continued for seven years ; and then, under the pressure of bad seasons, and in the midst of some unpleasant disputes with his landlord's factor, as to the terms of the lease,[1] his health began to decline, and on the 13th February 1784 he died.

So much for the outward scaffolding, so to speak, and material supports of our poet's parentage. Let us now take a peep into the bosom of the family, and, as in the case of the hardy mountain heather, when we look into the delicate purple blossom, admire the miraculous beauty that is spreading forth its vital mysteries there. And

---

[1] This affair of the factor, no doubt, served as moral for the verses in the genial idyll of the " Twa Dogs,"—

> " Poor tenant bodies, scant o' cash,
>   How they maun thole a factor's snash," &c.,—

and also very appropriately forms the first scene in the dramatic sketches from the life of Burns (Edinburgh, 1878) from the pen of the distinguished metaphysician Dr Hutchison Stirling.

here, in the first place, we encounter a principle of the widest operation in biographical history, that, though great genius is seldom or never hereditary, yet it is observable that men of great original powers generally come of a good stock, both by the father and mother, and that they owe to that stock not a few of those good qualities which do not indeed constitute genius, but supply the firm root out of which it may grow, and the healthy atmosphere which it may breathe. So Goethe, in an often quoted stanza, refers with gratitude to the severe love of systematic work which he inherited from his father, and the habitual cheerfulness and easy play of words which was the gift of his mother. In like manner the father of our poet is described as a Scottish peasant of the first class, of physical stature above the common, thoughtful, serious, and intelligent, and withal full of kindliness and cheerful enjoyment of life; and, though devoutly religious, not at all tinged with that severe awfulness which makes, or used to make, the piety of some Scottish heads of families so ungenial and so unsocial. His mother, though not boasting any particular intellectual gifts, was adorned with all those graces which make a good wife and a good mother; and it is not easy, especially in reference to the lower ranks of society, to overrate the value of the home culture, which, more than the best formal school drill, gives a healthy tone to the green sprouts of early manhood. We must bear in mind too that the parents were not only made of sound physical and moral stuff as individuals, but that they carried with them the superior instincts and habits which, by general admission, belong to the Scottish peasant, as contrasted with the peasantry of many other countries.

This superiority, we believe, he owes in a great measure
to the republican form of church government under
which he has been brought up, and to the principle of
popular education connected with it, which made every
church necessarily demand a school as its complement,
and which, for a blind reliance on sacerdotal functions
and priestly ceremonies, substituted a personal study of
the Bible, and formation of character under Bible influences. It has been said, and well said, that a sympathetic study of the Bible, which comes so naturally to
Scotsmen in the serious repose of a Scottish Sabbath,
is an education in itself; and, if to this we add the
appliances of the parochial school, and the personal
influence of a schoolmaster generally not without some
tincture of the higher culture which universities afford,
we shall have no difficulty in believing that the son of
a small Ayrshire farmer a hundred and thirty years ago
may have enjoyed those stimulants to culture, which
come in the shape of books, though without the for-
mality of Greek and Latin, virtually in as high a
degree as the best educated of the sons of English
gentlemen at Eton and Harrow about the same period.
The poet himself, in an autobiographical sketch printed
by Currie, gives the following short summary of the
range of his youthful reading at the time when his father
resided in the farm of Lochlea :—

"It is during the time that we lived on this farm that my little
story is more eventful. I was, at the beginning of this period,
perhaps the most ungainly, awkward boy in the parish ; no *solitaire*
was less acquainted with the ways of the world. What I knew of
ancient story was gathered from 'Salmon's' and 'Guthrie's' geographical grammars; and the ideas I had formed of modern

manners, of literature, and criticism, I got from the 'Spectator.'
These, with 'Pope's Works,' some plays of 'Shakespeare,' 'Tull
and Dickson on Agriculture,' the 'Pantheon,' 'Locke's Essay on
the Human Understanding,' 'Stackhouse's History of the Bible,'
'Justice's British Gardener's Directory,' 'Bayle's Lectures,' 'Allan
Ramsay's Works,' 'Taylor's Scripture Doctrine of Original Sin,'
'A Select Collection of English Songs,' and 'Hervey's Medita-
tions,' had formed the whole of my reading. The collection of
songs was my *vade mecum*. I pored over them driving my cart,
or walking to labour, song by song, verse by verse : carefully noting
the true, tender, or sublime, from affectation and fustian. I am convinced I owe to this practice much of my critic craft, such as it is."[1]

Young Burns, in addition to what stores the cottage
library or the kindness of intelligent neighbours might
supply, had the advantage from his early years of the
guidance of a very intelligent teacher, Mr Murdoch, from
whose account the reader will be pleased to see the following extract :—

"My pupil, Robert Burns, was then between six and seven years
of age ; his preceptor about eighteen. Robert, and his younger
brother Gilbert, had been grounded a little in English before they
were put under my care. They both made a rapid progress in reading, and a tolerable progress in writing. In reading, dividing
words into syllables by rule, spelling without book, parsing sentences, &c., Robert and Gilbert were generally at the upper end of
the class, even when ranged with boys by far their seniors. The
books most commonly used in the school were, the Spelling Book,
the New Testament, the Bible, Mason's Collection of Prose and
Verse, and Fisher's English Grammar. They committed to memory
the hymns, and other poems of that collection, with uncommon
facility. This facility was partly owing to the method pursued by
their father and me in instructing them, which was, to make them
thoroughly acquainted with the meaning of every word in each sen-

---

[1] Currie, 3rd edition, London, 1802, p. 43.

tence that was to be committed to memory. By the by, this may be easier done, and at an earlier period, than is generally thought. As soon as they were capable of it, I taught them to turn verse into its natural prose order ; sometimes to substitute synonymous expressions for poetical words, and to supply all the ellipses. These, you know, are the means of knowing that the pupil understands his author. They are excellent helps to the arrangement of words in sentences, as well as to a variety of expressions.

"Gilbert always appeared to me to possess a more lively imagination, and to be more of the wit, than Robert. I attempted to teach them a little church-music. Here they were left far behind by all the rest of the school. Robert's ear, in particular, was remarkably dull, and his voice untunable. It was long before I could get them to distinguish one tune from another. Robert's countenance was generally grave, and expressive of a serious, contemplative, and thoughtful mind. Gilbert's face said, ' Mirth, with thee I mean to live,' and certainly, if any person who knew the two boys had been asked which of them was the most likely to court the Muses, he would surely never have guessed that Robert had a propensity of that kind." [1]

These two interesting notices we may supplement with the following note from the poet's brother, Gilbert :—

"With Murdoch we learned to read English tolerably well, and to write a little. He taught us, too, the English Grammar. I was too young to profit much by his lessons in grammar, but Robert made some proficiency in it, a circumstance of considerable weight in the unfolding of his genius and character ; as he soon became remarkable for the fluency and correctness of his expression, and read the few books that came in his way with much pleasure and improvement, for even then he was a reader when he could get a book. Murdoch, whose library at that time had no great variety in it, lent him ' The Life of Hannibal,' which was the first book he read (the school books excepted), and almost the only one he had an opportunity of reading while at school ; for ' The Life of Wallace,

---

[1] Currie, I. 88.

which he classes with it in one of his letters to you, he did not see for some years afterwards, when he borrowed it from the black-smith who shod our horses." [1]

After this, those who are acquainted with the large opportunities afforded by the parish school in those days will naturally expect to find that the young ploughman poet, besides having had an early taste of the great English classics, such as Shakespeare, Pope, and Addison, had also been subjected to some elementary drill in Latin. But it was not so. That exercise, which some scholastic persons suppose essential to the formation of a good English style, he escaped, and wrote very good English nevertheless. To a lady who asked him whether he had not enjoyed the benefit of drill in the language of the Romans, he replied promptly and politely, "All he knew of Latin was contained in three words—OMNIA VINCIT AMOR!" He seems, however, under the forward help of Mr Murdoch, to have appropriated as much French as might be serviceable to give point to a sentence in fashionable society; but, so far as his higher culture was concerned, the glib smoothness of Parisian saloons had as little to do with it as the robust majesty of the Roman forum.

Burns attended more schools than one in the course of his boyhood and youth; and when he was in his nineteenth year he resided some time at Kirkoswald, in the district of Carrick, the native county of his mother, and at the time made studies of mensuration, surveying, drilling, &c., under the parish schoolmaster, named Rodger. Of an intellectual encounter between this mathematical

[1] Currie, I. 59.

pedagogue and the young song-writer, Chambers gives
an interesting account :—

"While attending the school Burns had formed an intimate
acquaintance with a young man called 'Willie,' and with this young
friend, as eager for intellectual improvement as himself, instead of
playing at ball or shinty with the other boys of the school, he was
accustomed to take a walk in the neighbourhood of the village, and
exercise himself with him in such speculations and discussions as
young Scotsmen love. By and by they fell upon a plan of holding
disputations or arguments on speculative questions, one taking one
side, and the other the other, without regard to their respective
opinions on the point, whatever it might be, the whole object being
to sharpen their intellects. They asked several of their companions
to come and take a side in these debates, but not one would do so ;
they only laughed at the young philosophers. The matter at length
reached the ears of the master, who, however skilled in mathe-
matics, possessed but a narrow understanding and little general
knowledge. With all the bigotry of the old school, he conceived
that this supererogatory employment of his pupils was a piece of
absurdity, and he resolved to correct them in it. One day, therefore, when the school was fully met, and in the midst of its usual
business, he went up to the desk where Burns and Willie were sitting opposite to each other, and began to advert in sarcastic terms
to what he had heard of them. They had become great debaters,
he understood, and conceived themselves fit to settle affairs of importance which wiser heads usually let alone. He hoped their disputations would not ultimately become quarrels, and that they
would never think of coming from words to blows : and so forth.
The jokes of schoolmasters always succeed amongst the boys, who
are too glad to find the awful man in anything like good humour,
to question either the moral aim or the point of his wit. They
therefore, on this occasion, hailed the master's remarks with hearty
peals of laughter. Nettled at this, Willie resolved he would
'speak up' to Rodger ; but first he asked Burns if he would sup-
port him, which Burns promised to do. He then said that he was
sorry to find that Robert and he had given offence ; it had not been
intended. And indeed he had expected that the master would be

rather pleased to know of their endeavours to improve their minds. He could assure him that such improvement was the sole object they had in view. Rodger sneered at the idea of their improving their minds by such nonsenical discussions, and contemptuously asked what it was they disputed about. Willie replied that generally there was a new subject every day; that he could not recollect all that had come under their attention; but the question of to-day had been, 'Whether is a great general or a respectable merchant the most valuable member of society?' The dominie laughed outrageously at what he called the silliness of such a question, seeing there could be no doubt for a moment about it. 'Well,' said Burns, 'if you think so, I will be glad if you take any side you please, and allow me to take the other, and let us discuss it before the school.' Rodger most unwisely assented, and commenced the argument by a flourish in favour of the general. Burns answered by a pointed advocacy of the pretensions of the merchant, and soon had an evident superiority over his preceptor. The latter replied, but without success. His hand was observed to shake; then his voice trembled; and he dissolved the school in a state of vexation pitiable to behold." [1]

This anecdote is certainly eminently characteristic of the independence of spirit, manly courage, and ready wit which distinguished the poet through his whole career. We shall now let his formal schoolmastering drop, and turn our eyes to what concerns us more directly, the stirrings of soul which mother Nature was raising within him, in order to prepare him for his special mission as the great song-writer and chosen patriotic minstrel of the Scottish people. Burns was emphatically the lyric poet of love, love in its purest and best form, among a class of unsophisticated people, who have no temptation either to poison its purity by secondary respects, or to let it run riot in fields of unreal and unhealthy imagination. Mar-

[1] Chambers, I. 33.

riages in high life, and political marriages, are most apt to
have the fountain-heads of love from which they ought
to flow tainted with considerations that remove them
into the region of a splendidly decorated prose; but in
the simple relations of peasant life, love, which is the
true poetry of youth, is allowed to show itself with all
that native grace and unencumbered charm which we
admire in the modest bloom and tender leafage of the early
spring. So old a poet-theologer as Hesiod, wishing to
teach how the unformed chaos was shaped into the orderly
beauty of a cosmos, found no more significant power
than that of Ἔρος or Love, by which to achieve so glorious a transmutation; " Ἔρος, he says, the most beautiful
of the immortal gods, which dissolves the limbs, and
subdues the souls of the fiercest men." Greek mythology,
ever true to Nature, was eminently true here; and if it
be the function of the scientific man to expound the
truth simply because it is true, and of the apostolic man
to preach the doing of right simply because it is right,
there remains for the poet the special function of com
pleting the divine triad, by painting the beautiful simply
because it is beautiful; and this he can only do by the
potent agency of Love. The field of love, of course, is as
wide as the universe; in all cases where the soul is not
overwhelmed by the majestic and the sublime, it is the
beautiful that attracts us, that is, so to speak, the daily
food of our spiritual nature; and so love, by which we
appropriate the beautiful, becomes the fulfilling of the
law in an æsthetical as well as in a moral sense; and the
amount of the poetry of life which belongs to any man
can be estimated by no more certain test than by the
intensity and the range of his capacity of loving. This

test applies to the ordinary inarticulate man, as well as
to the speechful poet; the only difference being, that,
while the ordinary man may enjoy all the rapture of the
passion, the poet has the superadded privilege of harmonious plastic form and pictorial imagination. Well,
the poet is distinctively a lover; a poet without love being
in fact as much an anomalous monster as a bird without
wings, or a fish without fins. But what shall he love, and
whom? All nature of course, in the first place, which,
as Goethe finely expresses it, is spread out before us as the
living vesture of the Godhead,—every green leaf and every
blooming flower, every creature of God, from the moth that
sports in the sunny beam to the whale that spouts in the
ocean wave. But the divine affection of love, to be felt in
all its delicious intensity, like other forces, must not be
allowed to squander itself largely; like steam, it must be
concentrated and confined to a single object. Hence,
from the general cosmic principle is evolved the individual love betwixt man and man which we call friendship, and the individual love betwixt man and woman,
lad and lass, where from various causes, it is most highly
potentiated. That like draws to like is a universal truth
as well in the moral as in the physical world; but that
contraries attract and unite is equally true in its own
sphere; and if a man loves a woman in a higher degree
than he loves a favourite dog or a horse, simply because
she is a being of his own kind and kinship, who can
respond to every pulse of his human nature in a way that
no most lovable dog or most serviceable horse can do;
so, over and above this kinship and mutual appreciation
in the case of persons of different sexes, there is the
manifest contrast which Nature has intended in the

attitude, and in the tissue, and the endowment of the male and the female. The man is pre-eminently the strong animal, the woman the beautiful; and so each seeks the other by way of complement to its own defect. Now, in the love of lad and lass, which is the great subject of all love poetry, there is the element of youth and puberty, which is one of the great mysteries of Nature, and of novelty and surprise, which is one of the most powerful stimulants of all dormant affections. Let it be borne in mind also, that the beauty of a young woman is not the mere physical beauty that may belong to a lily or to a birch tree. She cannot boast genuine womanly beauty without the soul that belongs to a woman; she must observe nicely; she must feel finely; she must think nobly. She need not be of such capacious brain, or of such potentiated energy, as her male admirer; but she must not be silly, she must not be stupid; and, if she be a little more clever than ordinary, and able to cope with the male on his own ground, she will be so much the more attractive. Let us now hear what Burns says of himself in reference to this love of women, which was so strong a constituent of his nature, and so prominent a feature of his poetry:—

"But far beyond all other impulses of my heart, was *un penchant à l'adorable moitié du genre humain.* My heart was completely tinder, and was eternally lighted up by some goddess or other; and as in every other warfare in this world my fortune was various, sometimes I was received with favour, and sometimes I was mortified with a repulse. At the plough, scythe, or reap-hook, I feared no competitor, and thus I set absolute want at defiance; and as I never cared farther for my labours than while I was in actual exercise, I spen the evenings in the way after my own heart. A country lad seldom carries on love adventures without an assisting confidant.

I possessed a curiosity, zeal, and intrepid dexterity, that recommended me as a proper second on these occasions; and I daresay, I felt as much pleasure in being in the secret of half the loves of the parish of Tarbolton, as ever did statesman in knowing the intrigues of half the courts of Europe. The very goose-feather in my hand seems to know instinctively the well-worn path of my imagination, the favourite theme of paragraphs on the love adventures of my compeers, the humble inmates of the farm-house and cottage; but the grave sons of science, ambition, or avarice, baptize these things by the name of follies. To the sons and daughters of labour and poverty, they are matters of the most serious nature; to them, the ardent hope, the stolen interview, the tender farewell, are the greatest and most delicious parts of their enjoyments." [1]

Here we are at once admitted into the inner shrine of the poet's erotic workshop; and we cannot do better, being here, than take a look at some of his earliest, most pleasant, and most popular productions, under this potent inspiration.

" Behind yon hill, where Lugar flows,
  Mang moors an' mosses many, O !
The wintry sun the day has clos'd,
  And I'll awa' to Nannie, O !

The westlin' wind blaws loud an' shrill ;
  The night's baith mirk and rainy, O !
But I'll get my plaid and out I'll steal,
  An' owre the hills to Nannie, O !

My Nannie's charming, sweet, an' young ;
  Nae artfu' wiles to win ye, O !
May ill befa' the flattering tongue
  That wad beguile my Nannie, O !

---

[1] Paterson, IV. 11.

Her face is fair, her heart is true,
   As spotless as she's bonnie, O !
The opening gowan, wat wi' dew,
   Nae purer is than Nannie, O !

A country lad is my degree,
   An' few there be that ken me, O !
But what care I how few they be,
   I'm welcome aye to Nannie, O !

My riches a's my penny-fee,
   An' I maun guide it cannie, O !
But warl's gear ne'er troubles me,
   My thoughts are a' my Nannie, O !

Our auld guidman delights to view
   His sheep an' kye thrive bonnie, O !
But I'm as blithe that hauds his pleugh,
   An' has nae care but Nannie, O !

Come weel, come woe, I care na by,
   I'll take what Heaven will sen' me, O !
Nae ither care in life have I,
   But live, an' love my Nannie, O !"

" It was upon a Lammas night,
   When the corn rigs are bonnie,
Beneath the moon's unclouded light,
   I held awa to Annie :
The time flew by wi' tentless heed,
   Till, 'tween the late and early,
Wi' sma' persuasion she agreed
   To see me thro' the barley.

The sky was blue, the wind was still,
   The moon was shining clearly :
I set her down, wi' right good will,
   Amang the rigs o' barley.

I ken't her heart was a' my ain ;
 I lov'd her most sincerely ;
I kiss'd her owre **and owre again,**
 Amang the rigs of barley.

I lock'd her in my fond embrace,
 Her heart was beating rarely ;
My blessing on that happy place
 Amang the rigs o' barley !
And by the moon and stars so bright
 That shone that hour so clearly,
She aye shall bless that happy night
 Amang the rigs o' barley !

I hae been blythe **wi' comrades dear,**
 I hae been merry drinkin' ;
I hae been joyfu' gath'rin' gear,
 I hae been happy thinkin' ;
But a' the pleasures e'er **I saw,**
 Tho' three times doubled fairly,
That happy night was worth them **a'**
 Amang the rigs o' barley.

   CHORUS.
Corn rigs an' barley rigs,
 An' corn rigs are bonnie ;
I'll ne'er forget that happy night
 Amang the rigs **wi' Annie.**"

In these poems, **which were composed at** Tarbolton,
while his father still **lived, and before the young** lyrist
had attained what the Scotch law calls the perfect age of
five-and-twenty, we discover all the genuine warmth, un-
affected simplicity, and easy grace of truthful Nature, which
will often be sought for in vain in the lyrical productions
of the most accomplished poets of the most refined ages
of all countries. Nothing conventional, nothing artificial,
nothing affected or overstrained, here interferes to disturb

the harmonious impression made by the utterance of the most finely modulated emotions, in an atmosphere and amid a scenery in which they seem to repose as naturally as a child in the bosom of its mother. They are a picture of rural nature, as much as they are the outpouring of an impassioned singer; they are not only eminently poetical and musical, but strikingly biographical; and stand here, therefore, as a scene in the life of the greatest love poet of modern times, with a more vivid portraiture than the pen of the most finished master of descriptive eloquence could achieve.

But we must not imagine that the love of fair women, —or bonnie lasses rather, to use his native style,—though it was the strongest element in his moral constitution, was the only one of which his early youth gave a decided indication. There is another passion also, the love of country, in which, had he been deficient, he would certainly have failed to have been recognised by his countrymen all over the world as their typical representative. Scotchmen, always and everywhere, Lord Macaulay remarks, have been distinguished for the ardent love of a country which, though not basking in the brightness of an Italian sky, is in every way worthy of their love; and indeed, it is as natural and as normal for a well constituted man to love the land in which he was born, as the mother by whose milk he was nursed. We may say, with all truth, that a cosmopolitan man, who has no preference for one land more than another, is an anomaly in nature, or rather a nonentity; and that, as Southey somewhere has it, the man who has not a strong root of patriotism in his nature, is deficient in one of the main elements, not only of poetical excellence but of all social greatness. And, if this is true of all countries, it is specially true of Scotland; a country which grew strong through centuries in a series of stiff struggles for national independence, and on two special occasions—the one in the contest for civil liberty against the land greed of the Plantagenets, and the other for religious liberty against the priestly despotism of the Stuarts—knew to assert its independence in such fashion as to leave a significant stamp on the general history of European civilisation. Unfaithful to the names of Bruce and Wallace the favourite poet of Scotland could not be; and accordingly we find in his letters to his confidential friend, Mrs Dunlop of Dunlop, the following account of his communings with the soul of the great champion of Scottish liberty, on the lonely green braes about Tarbolton :—

"The first book I met with in my early years, which I perused with pleasure, was 'The Life of Hannibal;' the next was 'The History of Sir William Wallace;' for several of my earlier years I had few other authors; and many a solitary hour have I stole out after the laborious vocations of the day, to shed a tear over their glorious but unfortunate stories. In those boyish days I remember in particular being struck with that part of Wallace's story where these lines occur—

> 'Syne to the Leglen wood, when it was late,
> To make a silent and a safe retreat.'

I chose a fine summer Sunday, the only day my line of life allowed, and walked half a dozen of miles to pay my respects to the Leglen wood, with as much devout enthusiasm as ever pilgrim did to Loretto; and, as I explored every den and dell where I could suppose my heroic countryman to have lodged, I recollect (for even then I was a rhymer) that my heart glowed with a wish to be able to make a song on him in some measure equal to his merits." [1]

---

[1] Paterson, IV. 157.

How nobly the poet realised his youthful aspirations in this regard, the national song of "Scots wha hae wi' Wallace bled," which stirs the hearts of all true sons of Caledonia from utmost East to utmost West, as strongly as the memory of Marathon did the Greeks, stands to this day, and will continue to stand, while Scotland holds its place among the nations, as a convincing proof.

We have now to notice a sphere of intellectual activity which the ambitious young ploughman fast carved out for himself at Tarbolton. Those who are acquainted with the discipline of the Scottish universities, which are the great engine of a broadly popular education in that country, will no doubt be aware that an important part in the academic teaching of the Caledonian youth is performed by debating societies of various kinds, under the direction of the students, without any control on the part either of professors or tutors. The freedom of utterance encouraged by these associations, the stimulus which they afford to intellectual adventure, and the lessons of self-correction, self-proving, and self-estimate which, as in a miniature parliament, they inculcate, have been universally acknowledged ; as, indeed, most of our distinguished Scotsmen—Adam Smith, David Hume, Francis Jeffrey, Leonard Horner, and Lord Brougham—have registered their indebtedness to this arena of free and unfettered intellectual gymnastics. Whether moved by the contagion of some academical campaigners returned from Edinburgh or Glasgow, or, as we may rather suppose, on his own impulse, Burns, in the year 1780, when he was completing his twenty-first year, took the lead in establishing a debating society of this kind at Tarbolton ; from the meetings of which, in an humble country village there can be no doubt that the rising young intellect of the district received as beneficial a spur as it could have done under the venerable roof of a learned university. The rules, from the poet's own hands, laid down for the conduct of debate in this Tarbolton academy, are given at length by Dr Currie, in the appendix to his first volume; but, however judicious and sensible, they contain nothing in the main but what the necessities of profitable discussion, and the laws of good order, plainly suggest. Only one rule of the Association, No. 10, is altogether singular, and smells so strongly of the most marked features of the poet's character, that it cannot be omitted here :—

"Every man proper for a member of this society must have a frank, honest, open heart; above anything dirty or mean; and must be a professed lover of one or more of the female sex. No haughty, self-conceited person, who looks upon himself as superior to the rest of the club, and especially no mean-spirited, worldly mortal, whose only wish is to heap up money, shall upon any pretence whatever be admitted. In short, the proper person for this society is a cheerful, honest-hearted lad, who, if he has a friend that is true, and a mistress that is kind, and as much wealth as genteelly to make both ends meet, is just as happy as this world can make him." [1]

But now, in his twenty-third year, we find the poet entering upon a field of education much more important, in some respects, than the intellectual jousting and tilting of a club of ambitious young villagers, bound to write learned essays, to discuss profound philosophies, and to be devoted admirers of the fair sex. This was his transplantation to Irvine, a small seaport town, a little north

[1] Currie, I. 367.

of Ayr, for the purpose of getting some hint of a start in
life beyond the range of an Ayrshire ploughman or a
petty farmer. Hitherto he had been content to follow
the plough, or to wield the scythe as a willing assistant
to his old father, and in this rustic work he was as dex-
terous as willing, notable for the sweep of weighty arm
with which he levelled the falling sheaves ; so industrious,
indeed, in this sturdy vocation, as to have contracted—
so his brother notes—a slight stoop of the shoulder,
making his apparent height somewhat less than his real
stature, which, like his father's, was considerably above
the average. But now, whether it was from a natural
desire in an ambitious young poet to see a little more of
men and manners, a poet's great training school, or that
he had seen enough of the hard conditions and incalculable chances of a small farmer's life, to make him
averse from trusting to that one string to his bow in the
slippery warfare of life,—or, what is more likely, from a
combination of both these motives,—certain it is that at
the age mentioned he removed to Irvine, and appren-
ticed himself to a flaxdresser, not a very pleasant occupation one should think for a young poet. The plough
seemed much more poetical ; but the young poet had to
make his bread, and bread is not made by poetry. His
object in attempting some trade of this kind, where
opportunity offered, was doubtless highly praiseworthy ;
but it turned out, as he says, altogether an "unfortunate
affair," and did him more harm than good, in one important respect, as he was honest enough to confess, and
as Carlyle has strongly emphasised in his admirable essay
on Burns. No doubt it was a necessary step in the education of a great poet to fling himself out of the narrow

sphere in which his youth had been spent, and, as we say, to see the world; but the knowledge of the world is only valuable in so far as it teaches us to appreciate the good, and to shun the evil that is in it; and it may often be better to remain in a clean lane, however narrow, than to march out into a broad highway to defile yourself with mud, and to make acquaintance with persons the purity of whose principles has not been improved by the amplitude of their range. At Irvine, among the marine people who frequent that place, our poet met with a sailor who had a knowledge of the world vastly superior to his, and who was in the main a lad of a manly character and great nobility of spirit. And, adds Burns, "he was the only man I ever saw who was a greater fool than myself where woman was the presiding star; but he spoke of illicit love with the levity of a sailor, which hitherto I had regarded with horror. Here his friendship did me a mischief, and the consequence was that soon after I resumed the plough I wrote 'The Poet's Welcome.'" [1] This was a consummation indeed most devoutly to be lamented; and in connection with it, we find that the poet, while thus initiated into a low class of pleasures from which his nobler nature revolted, was at the same time the victim of a terrible nervous depression, which inward self-dissatisfaction and outward disharmony had combined to create. At the end of December 1781, we find, in a letter from Irvine to his father, utter-

---

[1] "Rab the Rhymer's Welcome to his Bastard Child," one of those poems which profess a jaunty indifference to what in his better moments stung him with a manly sorrow, and, as Mr Lockhart expresses it, paraded before a fellow-sinner a pseudo-heroism by "glorying in his shame."

ances of a broken spirit, to whom life had become an intolerable burden, and which had to look for relief only to a state of bliss beyond the grave. He contemplates with inward satisfaction the speedy approach of the time "when he shall bid an eternal adieu to all the pains, uneasiness, and disquietude of this weary life, of which he is heartily tired;" and is so enraptured with the promise of celestial bliss in the Apocalyptic words (Rev. vii. 15, 16), that "he would not exchange the noble enthusiasm which they inspire for all this world has to offer." And at the very moment when he stood on the threshold of one of the greatest fields of moral influence, and one of the greatest literary reputations that have been made in modern times, we find him talking like a misanthropic religionist, or a world-renouncing devotee, in the following terms :—"As for this world, I despair of ever making a figure in it. I am not formed for the bustle of the busy world, nor the flutter of the gay. I foresee that poverty and obscurity probably await me; and I am in some measure prepared, and daily preparing, to meet them." This is very strong language, and no doubt sincerely felt at the moment; but the humours of the soul are, like the humours of the weather, the more violent in their expression the more likely soon to pass into the contrary. However strongly his weariness of life is expressed here, Burns had too much manhood, and too much sincere thoughtful piety, to dream of putting a sudden end to the painful pang of the moment by the violent revenge of the moment; and nothing could be more worthy of a good Christian, and a true philosopher, than the following lines, written either at the Irvine visitation of the evil genius, or on some similar occasion :—

" Oh Thou Great Being ! what Thou art
 Surpasses me to know :
Yet sure am I, that known to Thee
 Are all Thy works below.

Thy creature here before Thee stands,
 All wretched and distrest ;
Yet sure those ills that wring my soul
 Obey Thy high behest.

Sure Thou, Almighty, canst not act
 From cruelty or wrath !
Oh, free my weary eyes from tears,
 Or close them fast in death !

But if I must afflicted be,
 To suit some wise design ;
Then man my soul with firm resolves,
 To bear and not repine."

The man who could feel and write thus was not far
from the best piety of the psalms of David ; and so, after
a three months' experience of *de profundis clamavi*, the
Father of all good brought him out of the pit of darkness, and caused the light of His countenance to shine
upon him. But the dawn of the new day was not yet
come, and a dark cloud from the valley of the shadow of
death was destined to pass over his soul, before he was
to be ushered into the unexpected splendour of a new
intellectual life. Shortly after his return from Irvine he
found that his beloved father, to whom he owed the best
part of his education as a man, had begun to show alarm-
ing symptoms of the decrease of vital energy, to which
he ultimately succumbed. On the 13th February 1784,
the worthy old man died. Of the closing scene, Mrs

Begg, the poet's sister, gives the following interesting and instructive account :—

"Mrs Begg remembers being at his bedside that morning, with no other company besides her brother Robert. Seeing her cry bitterly at the thought of parting with her dear father, he endeavoured to speak, but could only murmur a few words of comfort, such as might be suitable to a child, concluding with an injunction to her 'to walk in virtue's paths, and shun every vice.' After a pause, he said there was one of his family for whose future conduct he feared. He repeated the same expression, when the young poet came up and said, 'Oh, father, is it me you mean?' The old man said it was. Robert turned to the window, with tears streaming down his manly cheeks, and his bosom swelling as if it would burst from the very restraint he put upon himself." [1]

An angel from heaven, specially commissioned for the purpose, could not have launched the young poet forth on the brilliant career for which he was destined, with a more prophetic text than these words of warning from the good old father.

[1] Chambers, I. 82.

MOSSGIEL.

" The star that rules my luckless lot
  Has fated me the russet coat,
  And damned my fortune to the **groat** ;
        But, in requit,
  Has blessed me wi' a **random shot**
        O' countra wit ! "

—BURNS.

THE death of his father, and the breaking up of the
family establishment at Lochlea, is the starting
point of a new era in the poet's life. The ship, so to
speak, was now fairly out of port, master of its own
course, and lord of its own pilotage. The prospect was
on the whole very fair, as things go. Burns had been
trained in farming, and was a good ploughman; the
flax-dressing adventure had thrown him back a wiser
man on his natural vocation; and he had as his partner
in any economical concern his brother Gilbert, a man,
though less brilliant than Robert, more sober and staid,
and better fitted for the steady routine of daily life.
Accordingly, we find that the brothers, as soon as they
had shaken themselves clear from the entanglements of
the Lochlea lease, took from Mr Gavin Hamilton the farm
of Mossgiel, in an upland country, about one hundred and
eighteen acres in extent, close to the village of Mauchline ;
and we have the brother's testimony to the steadiness and

industry with which the poet, so long as the concern
lasted, performed his part in the daily duties of the
partnership. Every member of the family, he says, was
allowed seven pounds per annum for the labour he performed on the farm. The accounts were kept with the
utmost accuracy by his brother, and his temperance and
frugality were everything that could be desired. This
sounds well; and there can be no doubt also that the
out-of-door life of a small farmer, though not without its
share of the frets and fags that human flesh is heir to, is
by no means an unfavourable situation for a man who,
like our poet, at intervals of ease from the pressure of
business, must have his heart open for the visitations of
the Muse. At the same time, it must be confessed that
a lyrical poet of fervid temperament and strong passions,
whatever car he was yoked to in the daily drudgery of
life, would be apt to kick, and to do his weekly taskwork
not quite so sweetly and contentedly as ordinary mortals.
Of this we find the strongest evidence in the detailed
doings of these Mossgiel years. All the while that he was
following the plough or wielding the flail,—though sometimes a field mouse or a field daisy might touch him to
a pleasing key,—there was a god within, or it might
be a devil occasionally, that gave him trouble. He was
longing for a loftier and a larger field in which to disport freely. Accordingly when he came home in the
evening, after the sweaty toil of the day, he would sit
down in the garret closet of his wee wee house at
Mossgiel, and dash off a playful letter to some sympathetic soul in the neighbourhood. These epistles,
besides being among the most characteristic and original
of the poet's works not falling under the strict category

of song, are of inestimable value for their biographical material, and admit us, in fact, into the inner life of the writer with an honesty and a nakedness that no confessions of a private diary could excel. In fact, he was too proud and too boastful a man to conceal anything ; and if he had done some not altogether respectable things, which with a person of his passions was but natural, he either tries to put a playful face upon it, or drops a penitential tear which did not always mean reformation. Of the friendly good fellows to whom these epistles were addressed, one of the best known was David Sillar, the son of a small farmer at Tarbolton, and, like Burns, a devotee of the Muse, but not with wing enough to help him to a niche in the top ridge of the Caledonian Parnassus ; he was, however, successful in business, first as a grocer, then as a schoolmaster, and eventually even as a councillor and magistrate in the good town of Irvine, where his friend Burns had made the unfortunate experiment of flax-dressing.[1] To this David Sillar, in the Kilmarnock edition of the poems, there appeared a poetical epistle, dated January 1785, headed, "An Epistle to Davie, a brother poet, lover, ploughman, and fiddler." In this production the following verses present a vivid picture of a mind alternating between fits of fretful discontent, and pious acquiescence in the lot which Providence had assigned him :—

> " It's hardly in a body's pow'r
> To keep at times frae being sour,

---

[1] Of Sillar, and the other Ayrshire contemporaries of Burns, a detailed biography will be found in " The Contemporaries of Burns," Edinburgh, Paton, 1840.

To see how things are shar'd ;
How best o' chiels are whiles in want,
While coofs on countless thousands rant,
  An' ken na how to wair't ;
But, Davie, lad, ne'er fash your head,
  Tho' we hae little gear,
We're fit to win our daily bread,
  As lang's we're hale and fier :
    Mair speir na, nor fear na,
      Auld age ne'er mind a feg,
    The last o't, the warst o't,
      Is only for to beg.

It's no in titles nor in rank ;
It's no in wealth like Lun'on bank,
  To purchase peace and rest ;
It's no in making muckle mair ;
It's no in books, it's no in lear,
  To mak us truly blest !
If happiness has not her seat
  And centre in the breast ;
We may be wise, or rich, or great,
  But never can be blest !
    Nae treasures, nor pleasures,
      Could make us happy lang ;
    The heart aye's the part aye
      That makes us right or wrang.

Then let us cheerfu' acquiesce ;
Nor make our scanty pleasures less,
  By pining at our state ;
And, even should misfortunes come,
I, here wha sit, hae met wi' some,
  An's thankfu' for them yet.
They gie the wit of age to youth ;
  They let us ken oursel' ;
They make us see the naked truth,
  The real guid and ill.

Tho' losses, and crosses,
    Be lessons right severe,
There's wit there, ye'll get there,
    Ye'll find nae ither where.

But tent me, Davie, ace o' hearts !
(To say aught else wad wrang the cartes,
    And flatt'ry I detest ;)
This life has joys for you and I,
And joys that riches ne'er could buy,
    And joys the very best.
There's a' the pleasures o' the heart,
    The lover, an' the frien' ;
Ye hae your Meg, your dearest part,
    And I my darling Jean !
    It warms me, it charms me,
        To mention but her name ;
    It heats me, it beets me,
        And sets me a' on flame ! "

This is beautiful ; but Burns, like Coleridge, was a
man of moods, and we cannot expect to find him in his
worst moments harmoniously consistent with his best.
In a second epistle to Davie, we are grieved to encounter
a certain tone of recklessness and devil-may-care-ishness,
and a helmless surrender to fitful plunges of passion, not
ominous of good. He says of himself, indeed, in his
letter to Dr Moore, that, though he entered on the farm
at Mossgiel with the full resolution, " *Come, go, I will be
wise,*" bad seasons, and other untoward circumstances,
" overset all his wisdom; and he returned *like a dog to his
vomit, and the sow that was washed to her wallowing in
the mire.*" No doubt this is strong language, and as it
was his fashion to deal in strong phrases, we need not
understand it in its worst sense ; still it must mean some-

thing, and what it does mean seems sufficiently indicated in the following verses from the "Second Epistle to
Davie ":—

" Hale be your heart, hale be your fiddle,
Lang may your elbuck jink and diddle,
Tae cheer you through the weary widdle
 O' warl'ly cares,
Till bairns' bairns kindly cuddle
  Your auld gray hairs.

For me, I'm on Parnassus' brink,
Rivin' the words tae gar them clink ;
Whyles daez't wi' love, whyles daez't wi' drink,
 Wi' jauds or masons ;
An' whyles, but aye owre late, I think,
  Braw sober lessons.

Of a' the thoughtless sons o' man,
Commen' me to the bardie clan ;
Except it be some idle plan
 O' rhymin' clink,
The devil hae't, that I sud ban,
  They ever think.

Nae thought, nae view, nae scheme of livin',
Nae cares to gie us joy or grievin',
But just the pouchie put the nieve in ;
 An' while ought's there,
Then, hiltie skiltie, we gae scrievin',
  An' fash nae mair.

Leeze me on rhyme ! it's aye a treasure,
My chief, amaist my only pleasure ;
At hame, a-fiel', at wark or leisure,
 The Muse, poor hizzie,
Tho' rough an' raploch be her measure,
  She's seldom lazy.

> Haud to the Muse, my dainty Davie :
> The warl'. may play you mony a shavie ;
> But for the Muse, she'll ne'er leave ye,
>   Tho' e'er sae poor,
> Na, even tho' limpin' wi' the spavie
>   Frae door tae door."

The most brilliant poet in the world in such company and in such a humour never can be an object of admiration. So far as bad seeds or bad harvests were the cause of it, he justly claims our human pity and our brotherly sympathy, as many a poor farmer too often does in our days; but even then the wise moralist will feel himself compelled to say, in the words of the preacher, "If thou faint in the day of adversity thy strength is small." But it is only too plain that the bad seasons were not the only or the principal cause of that wallowing in the mire, and those "stabs of remorse" to which, in another place, he so feelingly alludes; it was his own impetuous passions, which he had never brought under control, and it was his ill-starred intimacy with the loose sailor moralist at Irvine that first taught him to overstep the bounds that separate a legitimate freedom from an unholy license.

It will be observed in this second letter to Davie there is special mention made of "masons," and there can be little doubt that not a few of the masons in those days were not much better than the "jauds" with whom they are coupled. Of course there is a good side in Freemasonry; so far indeed as it means humanity and good fellowship and brotherly recognition, and kindly help in need, there cannot be a better thing; but in the latter part of the last century, in such a village as Tarbolton or Mauchline, it practically meant only a convivial meeting of jolly good fellows, which might often be without wit, but never could be without drink. Into the mystical brotherhood at Tarbolton, the poet had flung himself with all the ardour of the social enjoyment which, next to love, supplied the most potent steam of his soul. But steam requires regulation; and where there is no regulation, explosion is nigh. As an essentially social being, beating in every vein with an intense pulse of human kinship, Burns entered heart and soul into the best company he could find at the time and place; and if he did not always escape the contagion of unworthy companionship, he could at all events boast for himself that he strangled blue devils in the most brilliant style, and for his fellow-boosers that he turned the commonplace level of their convivial compotations into an intellectual treat of the highest order.[1]

It will be pleasant to turn from these jovial exercitations, in which the Muse of Coila cannot always appear in a dress consistent with her character and dignity, to a field of spiritual encounter in which the most brilliant master of Scottish wit could not fail to find adversaries worthy of his steel. We allude to the part which Burns took, and an active part it was, in the religious movements of his time, a matter which may justly claim a few pages of more serious consideration. From the Reformation downwards the Scotch have been notably a religious people, a feature no doubt springing originally from a strong root of earnestness in their character, but intensified partly by the engrafting of Genevan theology in the

[1] Of the sort of conversation that would take place at these masons' meetings, see a vivid sketch in Stirling's book, above quoted, Act III. Sc. 2.

person of John Knox, and partly by the noble stand
which they made for liberty of conscience against the
sacerdotal despotism of the Stuarts. A similar struggle
was made by the English Puritans, but it was successful
only for a year and a day under the presidency of
Cromwell; and the return of the Stuarts in 1662 was
not merely a restoration of the monarchy, but a rehabi-
litation of a form of Church government and creed which
had not been fought out by the people, but dictated
by the Crown and the hierarchy. But in Scotland, not
only was the national religion, declared by public act
of Parliament in 1560, essentially democratic and republican, but the constant purpose of the despotic
monarch to undermine the foundations of a popular
Church, and his repeated attempts to impose on the
country the ritual of the Anglican Church, could only
strengthen in the hearts of the people their zeal for a
religion which had grown out of the national conviction,
and was identified with their national character. Thus
patriotism and piety combined to impress on the Scottish
nationality a character of serious religious conviction,
which for accentuation and prominence had no parallel
in the southern half of the island. So long as the
struggle against the Episcopal intrusionists lasted, that
is about fifty years, from the throwing of the famous
stool of Dame Geddes against the head of the officiating
Dean in St Giles' Cathedral to the final settlement of all
liturgical and sacerdotal differences, the assertion of the
scriptural right of Presbytery, as against the claims of the
Anglican hierarchy, naturally stood as a prominent feature
in the religious physiognomy of the Scottish Church.
But when all danger from that quarter ceased, the in-

herited religiousness of the people began to act in bringing to light certain not unimportant internal differences,
which during the great struggle for liberty of conscience
had found no field for display. The matters of dis-
sension which stirred the Church with no quiet ferment
during the greater part of the eighteenth century were
two. First, the dispute about patronage, frequently
alluded to by Burns, whether the pastor of a Christian
church was to be elected by a civil authority, the Crown,
or great man of the district,—or by the church, that is
the individual congregation; and again, the dispute
about certain points of doctrine to which the somewhat
metaphysical theology of the Scottish Confession had
attached an exaggerated importance. The dispute about
patronage issued, as is well known, in the creation of
two formidable protesting bodies, the Relief secession
in 1761, and the great Free Church separation in 1843;
while that about doctrine came to a head in the so-
called "Marrow controversy," and lay at the root of
the earlier secession of the famous Ebenezer Erskine
in 1740. The nature of the dispute will be seen at a
glance from the formula put forth by the Presbytery
of Auchterarder, which they required all candidates
for the ministry to sign, viz. :—" I believe that it is
not sound and orthodox to teach that we must forsake
sin in order to our coming to Christ;" a proposition
no doubt intended innocently enough on the part of
expounders to magnify the pardoning grace of God in
the gospel, but which at the same time was very liable
to be misunderstood, and did not seem at all to
harmonise with the preparatory watchword of John
the Baptist, "Repent! for the kingdom of heaven is

at hand!" Connected with this point were various extreme dogmas about original sin, inherited guilt, sovereign grace, election, reprobation, eternal damnation, and the whole array of the five points of the Synod of Dort, which had raised such a commotion in Holland against poor Grotius in the first quarter of the previous century. The importance given to these doctrines ranged the whole Church of Scotland into two parties, known by the names of Evangelical and Moderate; of whom the Evangelical, or thorough-going Calvinists, looked upon themselves as the only orthodox proclaimers of gospel truth, and in this view were the favourite party with the mass of the people, who in every country delight to have their theological nutriment seasoned with a stimulant spice of exaggeration; while the Moderates were looked upon not only as dangerous doctrinal innovators, but as deficient in evangelising zeal, and more secular than spiritual in their social attitude. The fact of the matter is, that, as in the political so in the religious world, the adverse parties, which by a necessity of human nature always display themselves, are composed of persons who, while agreeing to act together on some common ground, allow much variety of opinion and great diversity of fibre. If amongst the Evangelicals there were always a few who delighted to revel in the exaggeration of Calvinistic phraseology, and to entangle their wits in the subtleties of a metaphysical theology, we may charitably suppose that the great majority were men of a fervid temperament, who what they believed firmly felt themselves bound to express strongly, and thus with good reason became more popular with the people than those who incurred the suspicion of coolness in the advocacy of a serious cause ; on the other hand, if among the Moderates there were some who seemed out of place in a spiritual body,—men who had more head than heart, whom Nature had intended rather for lawyers or professors than preachers, and who were altogether in the pulpit like a rose without the smell of a rose,—there were not a few others whose only fault was that they knew how to temper zeal with discretion, and who, if they professed to turn the ethical rather than the doctrinal face of the gospel to the public, had as good a right to shield themselves under the ægis of the Apostle James, as the adverse party had to draw their swords under the leadership of Paul. But there is yet another feature in the antagonism of these two parties which must be distinctly envisaged before we can understand the full significance of the part which Burns played in these spiritual encounters. With a more pronounced doctrinal orthodoxy, and a more fervid moral appeal, was united, in the Evangelical party, a severe and stern morality, coupled sometimes with a Pharisaic punctiliousness about matters indifferent, and a certain sanctimonious awfulness of tone which refused all communion with a healthy gaiety of soul, and looked upon innocent recreation as a sin. So much for the moral diagnosis of the Church in the year of grace 1784, when our poet took his station as a farmer beneath the spiritual wing of what, in the language of St Paul (Titus i. 5–7), would be called the presbyter or bishop of the church at Mauchline. Let us now inquire in what spirit, with what vocation, and in what connection he entered into the theological lists.

In the first place, we have to bear in mind that Burns

was not only a Scotsman breathing the religious atmosphere of the west, and brought up with pious care in
a religious family, but he was personally a religious man,
to a degree which the cursory reader of his works would
never suspect. Of this there is the strongest evidence
scattered through various parts of his correspondence,
but appearing with special emphasis in the concluding
words of his commonplace book, bearing date October
1785, and which run thus :—

" If ever any young man, on the vestibule of the world, chance
to throw his eye over these pages, let him pay a warm attention to
the following observations, as, I assure him, they are the fruit of a
poor devil's dear-bought experience. I have, literally, like that great
poet, and great gallant, and, by consequence, that great fool Solomon,
' turned my eyes to behold madness and folly,'—nay, I have, with all
the ardour of a lively, fanciful, and whimsical imagination, accompanied with a warm, feeling, poetic heart, shaken hands with their
intoxicating friendship. In the first place, let my pupil, as he tenders
his own peace, keep up a warm, regular intercourse with the Deity." [1]

The young man of six-and-twenty who penned these
words, without the slightest notion of their ever seeing
the public eye, could not have been other than personally
religious, or at least under strong religious convictions ;
and any youth who wrote such words, even though he
had not been a Burns, could not but feel a warm interest
in the religious life and Church controversies of the
district where he resided. But Burns was a young man
of eminently social instincts, with keen human feelers
stretching out in all directions, with a catholicity of

[1] Robert Burns's Commonplace Book ; from the original MS. in
the possession of John Adam, Esq., Greenock. Edinburgh, 1872,
privately printed.

sympathy such as belongs only to men like Shakespeare, Goethe, Scott, and all the most richly endowed representative types of our species. Independently, therefore, of his personal piety, wherever the pool of human passions was troubled, he would walk into it,—whether it were a revel among jolly beggars, or a fray amongst irate gospellers, it was a human business, and he would be there. Rightly too. There are human oysters that can slip through life contentedly within their own narrow shell, political, academical, or ecclesiastical, pecuniary or domestic,—

" Et contenta suam habitans amat ostrea valvam."

But not so a true poet. Burns must be there; and if there, with the passionate fervour that belonged to him as a lyric poet, he must take a part, and a very emphatic part. He sided with the Moderates; and for this there was both a cause and an occasion, which must be well noted. The cause was twofold. To a man, like Burns, thrilled all through with a strong zest of life, and especially to a song-writer, the tendency to a severe and somewhat ascetic morality visible in some prominent members of the Evangelical party, must have rendered them peculiarly odious; then, as a man of strong brain and great common-sense, he could not but perceive that the points of dogmatic theology to which the same party had attached so much importance, were really of very little practical value, and that the Moderates were right in keeping them in the background, or dropping them altogether in their pulpit ministrations. And yet a third reason lies plainly enough on the surface; if the Evan-

gelical preachers had been sometimes too strict in their
injunctions, the poet had been perhaps too loose in his
practice; he stood before them as a man marked, with fair
show of reason, for ecclesiastical censure; he had been a
poacher on their special domain (*see* "Epistle to Rankine"),
and had no reason to look with special favour on the game-
keepers. He took his side, therefore, heart and soul, with
that party in the Church which seemed most marked by
broad thinking, and was at the same time kindly inclined
to look with a more human eye on the besetting sins of
his perfervid temperament. The occasion was as follows :
From the time of the Covenanters downwards, the kirk-
session, or subordinate bodies of ecclesiastical government
in Scotland, had been accustomed to exercise a severe,
and as one would say now, a pedantically and oppres-
sively minute, discipline over the members of the Church.
This was no doubt nothing worse in principle than the
Elizabethan enactments which imposed a fine on all
persons who did not attend public worship at the stated
diets; nay, it seemed only natural, when the State had
retired from the field of compulsory piety, that the Church
should exercise her powers of supervision in matters of
sacred observance with so much the greater strictness.
But times were changing; and occasions easily arose, when
strict disciplinarians of the Calvinistic type might feel
themselves called upon to acts of interference with the
religious practice of individuals, which enlightened public
sentiment could not but regard as impertinent and in-
solent. Mr Gavin Hamilton, Burns's kind landlord, a
legal practitioner in Mauchline, had fallen under the
censure of the elders of the parish in session assembled,
on the ground of his alleged irregular attendance on

Church ordinances. This led to a rejoinder by the accused gentleman, to the effect that there were no legal grounds of procedure against him, and that the censure was founded on some of those private grounds of offence, and motives of petty jealousy, such as are apt to spring up in small village communities. The kirk-session persevered in their charge; but this only led the alleged culprit to bring his case successively before the superior tribunals, from which at last he got a triumphant verdict of acquittal in July 1785. Burns was not a man to stand quietly by when he saw his friend maligned and persecuted, by a set of men whom he believed to be the representatives, not of evangelical piety, but of Pharisaic formalism, and he picked out one of them, whom he held for the worst of the lot, and posted him before the Ayrshire churches as a hollow hypocrite, and an incarnation of sanctimonious spite, under the name of "Holy Willie."

" Oh Thou, wha in the heavens dost dwell,
　　Wha, as it pleases best thysel',
　　Sends ane to heaven, and ten to hell,
　　　　A' for thy glory,
　And no for ony guid or ill
　　　　They've done afore thee !

　I bless and praise thy matchless might,
　When thousands thou hast left in night,
　That I am here afore thy sight,
　　　　For gifts and grace,
　A burnin' and a shinin' light
　　　　To a' this place.

　What was I, or my generation,
　That I should get sic exaltation,

I wha deserve sic just damnation,
      For broken laws,
Five thousand years 'fore my creation,
      Thro' Adam's cause !

When frae my mither's womb I fell,
Thou might hae plungèd me in hell,
To gnash my gums, to weep and wail,
      In burnin' lake,
Where damnèd devils roar and yell,
      Chain'd to a stake.

Yet I am here a chosen sample,
To show thy grace is great and ample ;
I'm here a pillar in thy temple,
      Strong as a rock ;
A guide, a buckler, and example
      To a' thy flock.

O Lord ! thou kens what zeal I bear,
When drinkers drink, and swearers swear,
And singin' there, and dancin' here,
      Wi' great and sma',
For I am keepit by thy fear
      Free frae them a'.

Lord ! mind Gaw'n Hamilton's deserts,
He drinks, and swears, and plays at cartes,
Yet has sae mony takin' arts,
      Wi' gret and sma',
Frae God's ain priests the people's hearts
      He steals awa'.

Lord ! in the day of vengeance try him,
Lord ! visit them wha did employ him,
And pass not in thy mercy by 'em,
      Nor hear their pray'r ;
But for thy people's sake destroy 'em,
      And dinna spare.

> But, Lord ! remember me and mine,
> Wi' mercies temp'ral and divine,
> That I for gear and grace may shine,
>   Excell'd by nane,
> And a' the glory shall be thine,
>   Amen ! Amen ! "

One can lightly imagine into what a state of amazed concern the explosion of such a bombshell must have thrown the good people of the presbytery of Ayr. That a small farmer in a small country parish should lift up his voice in public castigation of an elder of holy kirk, immediately beneath the nose of the local bishop, was an action as unknown and inconceivable to the religious mind of the time, as it would have been to have seen the horse-hair wig of a lord of session at the county assizes publicly plucked from his head by the criminal at the bar. But if the great majority stood aloof in petrified astonishment, there were not a few who applauded ; and not only those who knew the contemptible character of the individual thus splendidly pilloried, and those also who, while they disapproved of the assault could not but admire the courage of the assaulter; but with much more prominence, and more cordial sympathy, the churchmen of the Moderate party, who were only too glad, in face of the sharp arrows of the zealous Evangelicals, to place themselves under the broad shield of such an Ajax. Burns was soon the declared advocate and publicly recognised champion of the Moderate party in the Church ; and the temper and attitude with which he assumed this advocacy, are so important in his career both as a man and a poet, that we make no apology for inserting here at full length his rhymed epistle to one of

its members, the **Rev.** John M'Math, **in which the merits**
of the cause, from the pleader's point **of view, are set**
forth with unexampled vividness and vigour :—

" While at **the** stook the shearers cow'r
    To shun the bitter blaudin' show'r,
    Or in gulravage rinnin' scow'r
            To pass the time,
To you I dedicate the hour
            In idle rhyme.

My Musie, tir'd wi' mony a sonnet
On gown, and ban', and douse black bonnet,
Is grown right eerie now **she's done it,**
            Lest they should blame her,
And rouse their holy thunder on it,
            And **anathem her.**

I own 'twas rash, and rather hardy,
That I, a simple countra bardie,
Should meddle wi' a pack sae sturdy,
            Wha, if they ken me,
Can easy, wi' a single **wordie,**
            Loose hell upon me.

But I **gae mad at their grimaces,**
Their sighin', cantin', **grace-proud faces,**
Their three-mile prayers, and hauf-mile graces,
            Their raxin' conscience,
Whase greed, revenge, and pride disgraces
            Waur nor their nonsense,

There's Gaw'n, misca't waur than a beast,
Wha has mair honour in his breast
Than mony scores as guid's the priest
            Wha sae abus't him,
And may a bard no crack his jest
            What way they've used him ?

See him, the poor man's friend in need,
The gentleman in word and deed ;
And shall his fame and honour bleed
    By worthless skellums,
And not a Muse erect her head
    To cowe the blellums ?

Oh, Pope, had I thy satire's darts
To gie the rascals their deserts,
I'd rip their rotten, hollow hearts,
    And tell aloud
Their jugglin' hocus-pocus arts
    To cheat the crowd.

God knows I'm not the thing I should be,
Nor am I even the thing I could be,
But twenty times I rather would be
    An Atheist clean,
Than under gospel colours hid be
    Just for a screen.

An honest man may like a glass,
An honest man may like a lass,
But mean revenge, and malice fause,
    He'll still disdain,
And then cry zeal for gospel laws,
    Like some we ken.

They take religion in their mouth ;
They talk o' mercy, grace, and truth ;
For what ?—to gie their malice skouth
    On some puir wight,
And hunt him down, o'er right and ruth,
    To ruin straight.

All hail, Religion ! maid divine !
Pardon a Muse sae mean as mine,

Who in her rough imperfect line,
   Thus daurs to name thee ;
To stigmatise false friends o' thine
   Can **ne'er defame** thee.

Tho' blotch't and foul wi' mony a stain,
And far unworthy of thy train,
With trembling voice I tune my strain,
   To join with **those**
Who boldly daur thy cause maintain,
   In spite of foes :

In spite o' crowds, in spite o' mobs,
In spite o' undermining jobs,
In spite **o'** dark banditti stabs
   At **worth and** merit,
By scoundrels, even wi' holy robes,
   But hellish spirit.

Ah Ayr ! my dear, my native ground,
Within thy presbyterial bound
A candid, lib'ral band is found
   Of public teachers,
As men, as Christians too, renown'd,
   And manly preachers.

Sir, in that circle you are nam'd ;
Sir, in that circle you are fam'd ;
And some, **by whom your doctrine's blam'd**
   (Which gies you honour),
Ev'n, sir, by them your heart's esteem'd,
   And winning manner.

Pardon this freedom I have ta'en,
And if impertinent **I've been,**
Impute it not, **good sir, in ane**
   Whase heart ne'er wrang'd ye,
But to his utmost would befriend
   Ought that belang'd ye. "

       D

But the crowning achievement of the poet's outbreak of sarcastic humour in the great Church controversy, is undoubtedly the well-known " Holy Fair," a composition of some length, in which he allows himself to exercise his brilliant powers of playful humour and scathing sarcasm in holding up to ridicule the most holy sacramental rite of the Christian Church as it was then celebrated in Ayrshire. This was a much more serious business than helping the willing part of the public to laugh at the squabble of two irate presbyters set by the ears, or the insolence of one or two parish officials comporting themselves like gods; and it must be confessed that it requires a considerable amount of charity altogether to vindicate the piety or the prudence, or the good taste, of such an exercise of the sarcastic Muse. That Burns as a man, if not of consistent religious practice, certainly of true religious sentiment, should have allowed his Muse to run riot in the humorous handling of certain incidental abuses connected with the local celebration of so sacred a rite, can be explained only on the supposition that the abuses were more than commonly gross,— that the poet, once in the heat of the fray between the Moderates and Evangelicals, had lost the natural reverence which in his normal temper would have withheld him from treading so ruthlessly on holy ground ; and again, that whatever Burns did he could do not otherwise than boldly and fearlessly, tossing his horns, and swinging his tail lustily with a luxurious enjoyment of the sport. As for prudence and policy, neither in religion nor in any other sphere were they his marked virtues. Speaking the truth in love generally, sometimes in sportive wrath, was his only craft; and when he had once made up

his mind that some pretentious individual or inflated
corporation required the whip, he, Robert the rhymer,
was there to administer it, without respect of persons;
neither fond mother, nor sober brother, nor wise sister,
nor even some dear Annie or Peggy or Jeanie, could
have prevailed to make him retreat one step. What
they looked upon as unseemly to proclaim, he would
have considered it cowardly to withhold.

So much for this notable escapade of the poet's
tremendous lust for moral raillery, as a significant
exponent of his character. As a matter of fact, in the
history of Scottish literature and religion, this caricature
of the Holiest, as some might be inclined to call it,
did no harm, but rather good; for the caricature lay
undoubtedly to no small extent in the real facts of the
case, not in the mere treatment of the poet.[1] Harm to
Burns it certainly did do; for it tended to raise a wall of
partition between him and the reverential sentiment
of the country, which stands in the way of his acceptance
with not a few of the most worthy of his countrymen
even at the present hour. Harm to the people it could
not do; for so far as it was overcharged, the roots of
the popular piety had struck too deep to be shaken by a
rude hand; and so far as it was true, the reproof has
been so effective that not a shadow of the abuse remains.
Had it not been for the polemical relation in which he
found himself to the zealous party in the Church, and for
the glaring nature of the abuse of sacred ceremonies
that forced itself on his observation, I feel certain that

---

[1] But that the abuses so severely lashed by Burns were far from
being common in Scotland may be seen in various quarters, and
specially in M'Farlane's "Life of Professor Lawson of Selkirk," p. 84.

Burns was the last man in the world to have wantonly held so sacred a rite up to public ridicule. Had it been the good fortune of the bard to be present at the celebration of the sacrament at one of those autumnal gatherings common to the north of the Grampians, his soul would undoubtedly have been stirred to a lyrical out-pouring, which would have gone down to the latest ages, as a companion picture to "The Cottar's Saturday Night," among the choicest gems of British sacred poetry. How finely would he have contrasted the worship, where

> "The weird untutored psalm is borne
> Far resonant o'er the purple-breasted hills,"

with the organed hymn that swells beneath proud halls vaulted with gold in the cultured services of our cathedral churches. These no doubt have their poetry; but while the grandest displays of artistic worship are apt to suggest the idea of artifice and effort, the simple devotions of rustic worshippers savour only of the quiet growth and majestic repose with which they are surrounded. This may be called sentimental; but the man who does not feel it has never caught a breath from the soul of Robert Burns.

But we must not suppose that the Presbyterian Bethesda of Ayrshire was the only pool in which our fearless frolicking satirist loved to splash. The Scottish bard who could walk up before the general eye and pluck venerable church elders and doctors of divinity by the beard, was not likely to shrink from an encounter with princes and politicians, and even with royalty on the throne, when opportunity might offer. Nor was the

opportunity **long of showing** itself. June 4, 1786, was
his Majesty George III.'s birthday, and, **as** usual, in St
James's **a** grand birthday levee was held on that day, and
a birthday **ode** presented by the laureate. **Compositions**
of this kind everybody knows are apt **to** be **amongst**
the most meagre productions of the court minstrel, **as**
not springing from the strong inspirations of **spontaneous**
passion, but **from the tame** dictation of a graceful propriety. The Mauchline minstrel had caught **the text
of these** courtly contributions from the newspapers, and
thinking the laureate's **verses** rather weak, and the whole
business looking more like **a** gilded parade than an
honest reality, he felt himself violently moved to **present**
himself before Majesty, with his other loyal **subjects**
and royal retainers, in the shape of "A Dream." **In this**
production, even more marked than **his** clerical **tiltings**
with the manly independence **and gay** freedom **of the
born enemy** of all convention, **not** only **are** birthday
odes, with their fair-faced flatteries, shown up in all their
hollowness **by the** exhibition of the contrary, but his
most gracious Majesty individually, and his most
gracious **Consort,** the Prince of Wales, and **the whole**
array of royal dukes, are spoken **to, and preached to, with**
an **easy** unconcern, **as** if, with **all their royal state and**
high social position, **they** had **been nothing** better **than**
the town's officer at Kilmarnock, or the minister's **man at**
Mauchline. Here it is:—

"A DREAM.

'Thoughts, words, and deeds, the statute blames with reason;
But surely *dreams* were ne'er indicted treason.'

[On reading, in the public papers, the *Laureate's Ode*, with the other parade
of June 4, 1786, the author had no sooner dropt asleep, than he imagined himself
transported to the birthday levee; and in his dreaming fancy, made the following
Address.]

Guid-mornin' to your Majesty !
  May Heaven augment your blisses,
On every new birthday ye see,
  A humble poet wishes !
My bardship here, at your levee,
  On sic a day as this is,
Is sure an uncouth sight to see,
  Amang the birthday dresses
        Sae fine this day.

I see ye're complimented thrang,
  By mony a lord an' lady ;
"God save the King !" 's a cuckoo sang
  That's unco easy said aye ;
The poets, too, a venal gang,
  Wi' rhymes weel turn'd an' ready,
Wad gar you trow ye ne'er do wrang,
  But aye unerring steady,
        On sic a day..

For me ! before a monarch's face,
  Ev'n there I winna flatter ;
For neither pension, post, nor place
  Am I your humble debtor :
So, nae reflection on your grace,
  Your kingship to bespatter ;
There's monie waur been o' the race,
  An' aiblins ane been better
        Than you this day.

Far be't frae me that I aspire
  To blame your legislation,
Or say, ye wisdom want, or fire,
  To rule this mighty nation !
But faith ! I muckle doubt, my Sire,
  Ye've trusted ministration
To chaps, wha, in a barn or byre,
  Wad better fill'd their station
        Than courts yon day.

I'm no mistrusting Willie Pitt,
   When taxes he enlarges,
(An' Will's a true guid fallow's get,
   A name not envy spairges,)
That he intends to pay your debt,
   An' lessen a' your charges ;
But God sake ! let nae saving fit
   Abridge your bonnie barges
      An' boats this day.

Adieu, my Liege ! may freedom geck
   Beneath your high protection ;
And may ye rax Corruption's neck,
   An' gie her for dissection !
But since I'm here, I'll no neglect,
   In loyal, true affection,
To pay your Queen, with due respect,
   My fealty an' subjection
      This great birthday.

Hail, Majesty Most Excellent !
   While nobles strive to please ye,
Will ye accept a compliment
   A simple poet gies ye ?
Thae bonnie bairntime Heav'n has lent ;
   Still higher may they heeze ye,
In bliss, till fate some day is sent,
   For ever to release ye
      Frae care that day.

For you, young potentate o' Wales,
   I tell your Highness fairly,
Down pleasure's stream wi' swelling sails
   I'm tauld ye're driving rarely ;
But some day ye may gnaw your nails,
   An' curse your folly sairly,
That e'er ye brak Diana's pales,
   Or rattl'd dice wi' Charlie,
      By night or day.

Yet aft a ragged cowte's been known
  To make a noble aiver ;
So, ye may doucely fill a throne,
  For a' their clish-ma-claver :
There him **at Agincourt** wha shone,
  Few better were or braver ;
And yet wi' funny queer Sir John
  He was an unco **shaver**
      For monie a day.

For you, right rev'rend Osnaburg,
  Nane sets the lawn-sleeve sweeter ;
Altho' a ribbon at your lug
  Wad been a dress completer :
As ye disown yon paughty dog
  That bears the keys of Peter,
Then, swith ! an' get a wife to hug,
  Or, troth ! ye'll stain the mitre
      Some luckless day.

Young royal Tarry-breeks, I learn,
  Ye've lately come athwart her,
A glorious galley stem and stern,
  Well rigg'd for Venus' barter ;
But first hang out, that she'll discern
  Your hymeneal charter,
Then heave aboard your grapple airn,
  An' large upo' her quarter
      Come full that day.

Ye, lastly, bonnie blossoms a',
  Ye royal lasses dainty,
Heav'n make you guid as weel as braw,
  An' gie you lads a-plenty :
But sneer na British boys awa',
  For kings are unco scant aye ;
An' German **gentles are but sma',**
  They're better just than want aye
      On ony day."

The man who wrote this was stamped by Nature for a truth-speaker and a public reprover, in a field where the preacher and prophet would either be silent, or deliver their message with a tone more than half ashamed of its audacity.

Once recognised in all the region of Ayrshire as a man of bright genius and of fearless adventure, who could handle the well-flourished whip to make an offender . smart, and paint a vivid picture to make the public smile, there was no sphere of life that could escape a sharp reproof or a sly glance from his keen observance. So in the case of Dr Hornbook, a village schoolmaster, who conceited himself to vend simples because he could spell sentences, he came down against the whole race of quack doctors with a scourging lash; while the tramps and tinkers, and worthless waifs of city life, with the lowest scum of the village, and general floating wreck of unprosperous humanity, came not under his lash, but under the rampant sweep of his kindly brush, in the *Cantata* called "The Jolly Beggars." This poem, which is a sort of lyrical drama, or " Beggars' Opera," did not appear in the original edition of the. poet's works, nor indeed in any edition during his lifetime, but was first published in a pirated edition of his works by Stewart in 1801. And there was very good reason for the reticency. The poet says, in one of his letters, that he had always "felt a peculiar pleasure in the company of blackguards;" not that he had any ambition to be taken for one,—as we have known characters who for some foolish pride wished to make themselves appear worse than they are,—but simply he had a divine rage for humanity in every shape, and liked to have a taste of it even in its lowest forms. This vagrant love for human beings simply because they are human beings, is the natural outcome of the catholic sympathy which is the essence of the poetical character; and it is this sympathy which enabled Shakespeare to plant his drunken Trinculos and Stephanos alongside of the pure innocence and serene idealism of the leading characters of his play of the Enchanted Island; and it was this same human fellow-feeling which caused the wise Goethe, in his sketches of Venetian life, to give prominence to those picturesque groups of low and worthless characters, for which he was reprimanded by the prim critics of polite Weimar, whom he represents as asking him whether he had ever seen good society, and gives the answer thus :—

> "Oh yes! your good society, in the mint
>   Of courts 'tis coined, and very well I know it;
> So fine and featureless, it leaves no hint
>   For smallest touch of Nature to a poet."

Every person who has the least sympathy with dramatic genius will at once acknowledge this. But in the musical drama of "The Jolly Beggars," Burns has so identified himself with the congregation of vagrants assembled in a low tippling shop in Mauchline, kept by a hospitable dame called "Poosey Nancy," that it requires an exertion in the mind of a common prosaic person not to suspect that the poet, on some occasions when the old Adam might be strong within him, was as great a blackguard as the congregation of scamps whom he delineates. A regard for the very natural feelings of these persons sufficiently accounts for the non-appearance of this singular production in a volume, where the "Holy Fair" and the

"Dream" had not been ashamed to show their faces.
It was a freak of that faculty of imaginative transmutation, that makes a poet become any other man for the
moment into whose skin it may list him to jump, and
only proves that bountiful Nature had endowed the song-
writer with a greater capacity for the drama or the novel
than he ever dreamt of realising.[1]

So far one sees plainly that this Mossgiel act of the
poet's life showed a capacity of expansion in various directions, which his early melodies on the banks of the Doon
might not have led us to expect. But we must in no-
wise suppose that the more public arena into which his
theological, political, and social sympathies led him, had
shaken him loose from the original theme which had
prompted the earliest utterances of his Muse. The keynote of his lyre, in the cradle of his fame, was the love of
fair women, and was destined so to remain. And in this
regard two notable figures stand out with marked prominence, to give a pathetic significance and a tragic close to
the four years' farming work at Mossgiel. We mean, of
course, "bonnie Jean," and "Highland Mary," of whom
a somewhat more detailed narrative must now be given.

Jean Armour was a comely country lass, full of sweetness and grace, by no means so brilliant as some of the
Mauchline belles whose charms had power to call forth

---

[1] His friend Mr Ramsay of Ochtertyre, whom the poet visited in
one of his Highland tours, in one of his letters, seriously pressed
upon him the idea of writing a rustic drama, on the model of the
"Gentle Shepherd;" but I imagine the Muse of Burns had been too
long accustomed to the pleasant sport of jumping like a fish to the
fly, to relish the persistent continuity of constructive architecture
which such a composition implied.

their special mention in his rhymes;[1] but there she was,
somewhere in the year 1785, as we have seen in his confidential epistle to David Sillar :—

> " Ye hae your Meg, your dearest part,
>   And I my darling Jean.
>   It warms me, it charms me,
>   To mention but her name ;
>   It heats me, it beets me,
>   And sets me in a flame."

She was the daughter of a master-mason in Mauchline ;
and Burns had picked up an acquaintance with her at
one of those village balls, which are apt to shoot themselves
spontaneously into shape, out of the vagrant humour of
lads and lasses, at the country fair, or the country races.
On one of these occasions Burns and Jean happened to
be in the same dance, when the poet's dog, as dogs will
do, leapt into the middle of the figure, causing not a
little offence to the legs of some of the performers, and
not a little merriment to the rest of the company. On
this Burns playfully remarked to his partner, that he
wished he could get any of the "lasses to like him as
well as his dog did." A short while afterwards, as Jean
was bleaching the clothes in the washing green of the
village, the poet, with his ramping little attendant, hap-

---

[1] Of her personal charms the poet, in a letter to Mrs Chalmers,
September 16, 1788, says :—" She has got the handsomest figure,
the sweetest temper, the soundest constitution, and the kindest
heart in the county. She is also well acquainted with her Bible,
and with all the ballads of the country side, and has the finest wood
notes ye ever heard."—Paterson, V. 158. Bonnie Jean has also had
the honour to secure a niche in Mrs Jamieson's " Romance of Biography," London, 1837.

pened to pass by, somewhat dangerously near to the cincture of her scouring operations, on which she called out to him to call back his dog, asking him at the same time, if he had got any of the lasses to like him as well as his dog.[1] This of course was an oblique female way of saying, that in point of affection to such a master she could vie with the dog herself. And at that moment the spark was kindled, that we have seen grown to a flame in the "Epistle to Davie." This was all as it should be; but Burns was a man who—partly from the ardour of his temperament, partly from opportunities too easily found in the intercourse of the sexes in rural life, partly also no doubt from the loose notions with which he had been infected by his sailor society at Irvine—was only too much inclined to abuse the confidence which might be placed in him by a fond confiding young woman; and so the man became a husband, and the woman a wife, in a fashion which religious principle, social propriety, and legal sanction disdain to recognise. This was a bad business; and here for the first time the poet was condemned, in the shape of public shame and private vexation, to reap the fruits which never fail to grow from the seeds of unregulated passion and unchastened desire. But Burns, though inconsiderate and light in such matters, was not base. When it was discovered that the master-mason's fair daughter was in the way of becoming a mother, the poet, conscious of the fault he had committed, was prevailed on to save the honour of the object of his affection by giving her a letter of acknowledgment of their conjugal relation, in a form

---

[1] This anecdote is from Chambers, I. 98, and has been seized on for dramatic purposes by Dr Stirling, in the work above quoted, Act III. 1.

which the Scotch laws recognise as valid. So far well.
But the course was not yet clear. A plain principle of
honour in the gentlemanly conduct of courtship, is that
no man is entitled to present himself in the character of a
suitor to any woman, when it is not in his power from
his own means, or hers, or both together, to keep her
comfortably and respectably in the position of society to
which she naturally belongs. Now Burns, at the time
when the necessity of acknowledging Jean as his lawful
wife was pressed upon him, was not in a condition to sup-
port her; from bad seasons the farming business had
failed so completely, that our rising star was looked on by
many people in the country as a person, socially considered, of unhappy retrospects and of worse prospects;
and, in fact, so hopeless did his condition appear to
himself, that at the very time when this legalisation of the
connubial relation took place, he had actually taken the
resolution of migrating to Jamaica, and was making terms
with a planter for service as a book-keeper on his estate.
No wonder, therefore, that from the Armour point of view,
the bit of paper legitimating the expected offspring of the
irregular intimacy was viewed as anything but a satisfactory repentance for the wrong done. The old father,
legal or illegal, would hear nothing about the document;
he would not have his daughter ruin her social prospects
by marriage with a wandering waif of a village rhymer,
without ballast and without substance; so with all the
imperious urgency of an injured father, he prevailed on
the poor girl to renounce the marriage which she had
forced the poet to own, and to cleave to a respectable
father rather than to a questionable husband. One step
only remained to put what at the time appeared to be

the finishing stroke to this unhappy business. The poet himself came forward, and in the face of the church received a public rebuke for his irregularities, and marched back into the world "with a bachelor's certificate in his pocket." Of this strange humiliation an account is given in a letter to Mr David Brice, shoemaker, Glasgow, dated Mossgiel, 17th July 1786, which runs as follows :—

"Poor Armour is come back again to Mauchline, and I went to call for her, and her mother forbade me the house, nor did she herself express much sorrow for what she had done. I have already appeared publickly in church, and was indulged in the liberty of standing in my own seat. I do this to get a certificate as a bachelor, which Mr Auld has promised me. I am now fixed to go for the W. Indies in October. Jean and her friends insisted much that she should stand along with me in the kirk, but the minister would not allow it, which bred a great trouble, I assure you, and I am blamed as the cause of it, though I am sure I am innocent; but I am very much pleased, for all that, not to have had her company."[1]

Of course the poet, here and elsewhere, in his letters written at this time, threw no measured blame both on Jean and her father for their conduct in rendering this humiliation necessary; but he was willing to forget that it was the blind haste of his own passion that gave the start to all this tissue of unpleasant complications. How fondly he loved her, and how sharply he felt the sting of the separation, the following extract from another letter to the same individual amply proves :—

"Poor ill-advised, ungrateful Armour came home on Friday last. You have heard all the particulars of that affair, and a black affair it is. What she thinks of her conduct now, I don't know; one thing I do know, she has made me completely miserable. Never man loved,

---

[1] Paterson, IV. 134.

or rather adored, a woman, more than I did her; and to confess a
truth between you and me, I do still love her to distraction after all,
although I won't tell her so if I were to see her, which I don't want
to do. My poor, dear, unfortunate Jean, how happy I have been in
thy arms! It is not the losing her that made me so unhappy, but
for her sake I feel most severely; I foresee she is in the road to—
I am afraid—eternal ruin. May Almighty God forgive her ingratitude and perjury to me, as I from my soul forgive her; and may His
grace be with her and bless her in all her future life! I can have no
nearer idea of the place of eternal punishment than what I have felt
in my own heart on her account. I have tried often to forget her.
I have run into all kinds of dissipation and riots, mason meetings,
drinking matches, and other mischief, to drive her out of my head,
but all in vain. And now for a grand cure: the ship is on her way
home that is to take me out to Jamaica; then farewell, dear old
Scotland; and farewell, dear, ungrateful Jean, for never, never, will
I see you more."[1]

So much for bonnie Jean. Contemporary with this
affair, and so closely interwoven with it that it has been
called "an episode," is the romantic and tragic story
of the poet's love for "Highland Mary." The most
natural, as well as the most charitable, way of interpret-
ing the interlineation of these two loves, is to suppose,
with Chambers, that while his heart was bleeding sorely
from what appeared to him the ungenerous and ungrateful disownment of their connubial bond by bonnie
Jean, one of his old flames—for their name was legion
—who had formerly fluttered about him in an easy way,
now came to the front, with the healing power, so strong
in woman, and poured the balm of tender sympathy into
his wounds. It is difficult for any man, especially a man
like Burns, to resist the thrill that passes through him at
the touch of a loving hand on such an occasion. Mary

[1] Paterson, IV. 131.

Campbell, a Highland girl from the neighbourhood of
Dunoon on the Clyde, "a most sprightly blue-eyed
creature of great modesty and self-respect," had been in
the service of his friend Gavin Hamilton, and was still
in the neighbourhood of Mauchline when that unfortunate affair with Jean was setting the village in a blaze ;
and in administering comfort to the widowed heart of
the Robert who had lost his Jean, she presented him
as a more than worthy surrogate for the loss with Mary
her beautiful self ; and this Mary had so much faith in
the unfortunate young farmer, that she agreed to plight
herself to him for life, and follow him to the Indies or
whithersoever his broken fortunes might lead him. It
was agreed between them that she should give up her
place, go to the Highlands, where her father was a
sailor in Campbeltown, and arrange matters there for
her formal union with the poet. The poetical union
had already been completed in a most sentimental and
pious fashion. On the banks of the Ayr, or in the adjoining valley of the Faile, the lovers had a meeting on the
second Sunday in May 1786, where they made the most
solemn vows of faithful adherence. Standing on each
side of a slow-running brooklet, and holding a Bible
between them, the two swore themselves to be one till
death. Mary presented her lover with a plain small Bible
in one volume, while Burns responded with a more dainty
one in two volumes. These two volumes have been
preserved, and may be seen in the Burns Monument at
Alloway, near Ayr. They are inscribed by the hand of
the poet with two texts of Scripture in the most solemn
style,—the one from the Old Testament, Leviticus xix. 12,
"Ye shall not swear by my name falsely, I am the Lord ;"

E

and the other from the New Testament, Matthew v. 33, "Thou shalt not forswear thyself, but shalt perform unto the Lord **thine oaths.**" And the day of this solemn act of devout self-dedication was the last time that Burns saw his Highland Mary. No wonder that it remained in his soul for life a picture of pure affection more sacred than any with which his large experience of female favours had furnished him. Mary Campbell, after visiting her parents in Campbeltown, was returning to Glasgow, where she had obtained a place, when, stopping on the road at Greenock to attend a sick brother, she caught fever from him, and died. This was early in the month of October of the same year in which her faith was plighted to the poet. She was buried in the West kirkyard of the town, a spot where all who love the Scottish Muse never fail to drop their fervent tear.

The fortunes of the poet were now to all appearance at the lowest possible ebb. Economical destitution in the present, regretful memories of the past, and uncertain prospects for the future, combined to fling him into a purgatory which seemed much nearer to a madhouse than to any possible heaven that might shoot a gleam into its gloom. One slight alleviation of his bitter sorrow from his connection with Jean came to him by the birth of twins, pledges of his ill-starred love; an event which brought about an agreement between the poet's family at Mossgiel and the Armours, with regard to the nurture of the children, which caused the threatened legal prosecution from the side of the offended old father to cease. But permanent hope from that quarter in the meantime there could be none; he must make a new start altogether, or flounder for ever

in the mire into which his own folly had plunged him.
And that new start came,—a start which was to raise
him at once from the provincial notoriety of a village
rhymer to the full blaze of popular recognition and
literary distinction. Of course the man who, without
any of the usual social advantages, had written such
poems as "The Cottar's Saturday Night," "Hallowe'en,"
and "The Holy Fair," must have been conscious to
himself of the possession of talents which entitled him
to claim a place among the acknowledged literary ex-
ponents of his country's best; but from the writing of
poetry to its publication there is always a difficult step,
and from the publication to the probable recognition of
its value a step yet more difficult, and a third step, the
most slippery of all the steps, from the sympathetic
recognition to the pecuniary sequence which to a poor
rhymer is often more valuable than the popular applause.
And all these difficulties lay directly in the way of
Burns, with the additional one, as it naturally appeared
to him, that the critic of learning and of culture might
brand him "as an impertinent blockhead obtruding his
presence on the world; and who, because he can
make shift to string a few doggerel Scotch rhymes together, looks upon himself as a poet of no small consequence." Nevertheless, his ambition, of which he had
a fair stock, made him determined to run the risk;
besides a position in the literary world, he might even
hope, by a successful publishing adventure, to put a few
pounds in his pocket, which would pay his passage to
Jamaica, and help him to a more dignified settlement
there. His first vague intentions of venturing on print
are announced to one of his most intimate Mauchline

cronies, James Smith, in anything but hopeful tones, as
follows :—

> " The star that rules my luckless lot,
> Has fated me the russet coat,
> An' damned my fortune to the groat ;
> But in requit,
> Has blessed me wi' a ramdom shot
> O countra wit.
>
> This while my notion's ta'en a sklent
> To try my fate in guid black prent ;
> But still the mair I'm that way bent,
> Something cries ' Hoolie !
> I red you, honest man, tak tent !
> Ye'll shaw your folly.
>
> ' There's ither poets much your betters,
> Far seen in Greek, deep men o' letters,
> Hae thought they had ensured their debtors
> A' future ages ;
> Now moths deform in shapeless tatters
> Their unknown pages.'
>
> Then fareweel hopes o' laurel-boughs
> To garland my poetic brows !
> Henceforth I'll rove where busy ploughs
> Are whistling thrang,
> An' teach the lanely heights and howes
> My rustic sang.
>
> I'll wander on, with tentless heed
> How never-halting moments speed,
> Till fate shall snap the brittle thread ;
> Then, all unknown,
> I'll lay me with th' inglorious dead,
> Forgot and gone ! "

But the poet, who, with all his faults, was at bottom a
good fellow, and a noble-minded man, had not a few

friends, who would **not allow him** to indulge these melancholy notions; **so,** with their good **advice** and patronage, there came forth to public light, **at the end of** July,

POEMS

Chiefly in the Scottish Dialect

by

ROBERT BURNS.

[1] Kilmarnock : 1786,

a volume which will ever remain a precious rarity in the **select** libraries of the best British literature. **The** result was quite satisfactory, and **surprising** perhaps to no **one** but the poet, who, with **all** his pride, **had** sense enough to know the slippery chances **of the game, and** modesty enough to underrate rather than overestimate his **own intellectual** merits. The edition had been one of **six** hundred copies, more than the half **of** which had been subscribed for before publication. **In** two months the **whole** impression **had** disappeared; and **after payment** of all expenses, the sum of £20 had found its way into the pocket of the successful author. This success, of course, made the outlook towards Jamaica for the moment a little more doubtful; but only for the moment. The engagement with Highland Mary **was still** pending. With only £20 in his purse, and no visible means **of** subsistence, it was **not** easy to **see** how **he** could carry out his solemn transaction with her; and **when a second** edition **of** the poems **was** proposed **and** abandoned,

---

[1] Of this original edition an exact facsimile has been published at Kilmarnock, Wilson, 1886.

there seemed nothing for him but expatriation. But the expatriation did not come. Never, as the Hebrew psalmist sings again and again, is light nearer than when darkness is deepest. A reverend gentleman, Dr Laurie, of Loudon, who had a just appreciation of the good qualities of the poet, sent a copy of the Kilmarnock volume to Dr Blacklock, the well-known blind poet and preacher, then residing in Edinburgh. The native human kindness, Christian sympathy, and fine literary appreciation of this gentleman were not slow in educing that striking testimony to the merits of the poet, which, as being the first note of the trumpet that ushered him into a new and brilliant career in the metropolis of his native land, justly claims a prominent place in his biography. Here it is :—

" *To* Dr GEORGE LAURIE,
" St Margaret's Hill, Kilmarnock.

" REV. AND DEAR SIR,—I ought to have acknowledged your favour long ago, not only as a testimony of your kind remembrances, but as it gave me an opportunity of sharing one of the finest, and perhaps one of the most genuine, entertainments of which the human mind is susceptible. A number of avocations retarded my progress in reading the poems ; at last, however, I have finished that pleasing perusal. Many instances have I seen of Nature's force or beneficence exerted under numerous and formidable disadvantages, but none equal to that with which you have been kind enough to present me. There is a pathos and delicacy in his serious poems, a vein of wit and humour in those of a more festive turn, which cannot be too much admired nor too warmly approved ; and I think I shall never open the book without feeling my astonishment renewed and increased. It was my wish to have expressed my appreciation in verse ; but whether from declining life, or a temporary depression of spirits, it is at present out of my power to accomplish that intention.

"Mr Stewart, Professor of Morals in this University, had formerly read me three of the poems, and I had desired him to get my name inserted among the subscribers ; but whether this was done or not I never could learn. I have little intercourse with Dr Blair, but will take care to have the poems communicated to him by the intervention of some mutual friend. It has been told me by a gentleman to whom I showed the performances, and who sought a copy with diligence and ardour, that the whole impression is already exhausted. It were therefore much to be wished, for the sake of the young man, that a second edition, more numerous than the former, could immediately be printed, as it appears certain that its intrinsic merit, and the exertions of the author's friends, might give it a more universal circulation than anything of the kind which has been published in my memory. . . . .

"T. BLACKLOCK." [1]

This letter threw Jamaica more and more into the background ; the name of Blacklock was sufficient of itself to enable the poet to take his place in the literary society of the Modern Athens, with that amount of respect which his pride always demanded, and that hope of economical aid which his necessities required. But besides Blacklock, he came to Edinburgh under the wing of one of the most accomplished and popular academical men of his time, Professor Dugald Stewart, well known to England as having presided at the youthful studies of Lord Palmerston, Lord John Russell, and other distinguished ornaments of English life at the close of the past and the first half of the present century. This gentleman had a lovely country residence at Catrine, on the river Ayr, a few miles from Mossgiel, and could not live there and remain ignorant of the rising reputation of the village songster and satirist. He accordingly, with

[1] Chambers, I. 303.

the kindness of a fellow-mortal, and the large sympathy
of a moral philosopher, invited the poet to dine with him
in his villa.   This of course was an altogether different
sort of society from that in which Burns had revelled at
the Whitford Arms, or Poosey Nancy's in the village ;
for not only was an Edinburgh professor somewhat of
an awful character to dine with in the eyes of a jingler of
Scottish rhymes, but, as it chanced, there was also a
lord, a veritable lord there, whose convivial proximity
worked so potently on the imagination of the poet, that
he expressed the novelty of his sensations in the following characteristic lines :—

> " This wot ye all whom it concerns :
> I, Rhymer Robin, alias Burns,
>   October twenty-third,
> A ne'er-to-be-forgotten day,
> Sae far I sprachled up the brae,
>   I dinner'd wi' a Lord.
>
> I've been at drucken writers' feasts ;
> Nay, been bitch-fou 'mang godly priests,
>   Wi' rev'rence be it spoken ;
> I've ev'n join'd the honour'd jorum,
> When mighty squireships of the quorum,
>   Their hydra drouth did sloken.
>
> But wi' a Lord !—stand out my shin !
> A Lord—a Peer—an Earl's son !
>   Up higher yet my bonnet !
> And sic a Lord !—lang Scotch ells twa,
> Our Peerage he o'erlooks them a',
>   As I look o'er my sonnet.
>
> But, oh, for Hogarth's magic pow'r !
> To show Sir Bardie's willyart glow'r,

And how he star'd and stammer'd,   .
When goavan, as if led wi' **branks**,
And stumpin' on his ploughman shanks,
     He **in** the parlour hammer'd.

I sidling shelter'd in a nook,
And at his Lordship stealt a look,
     Like some portentous omen : .
Except good sense and social glee,
And (what surprised me) modesty,
     I markit nought uncommon.

I watch'd the symptoms o' **the** Great,
The gentle pride, the lordly state,
     The arrogant assuming ;
The fient a pride, nae pride **had he,**
Nor sauce, nor state, that I could see,
     Mair than an **honest** ploughman.

Then from his Lordship I shall learn,
Henceforth to meet with unconcern
     One rank as weel's another ;
Nae honest worthy man need care
To meet with noble youthful Daer,
     For he but meets a brother."

In **this good** humour, and with this happy introduction
to a higher **platform of** social adventure, the ploughman
poet enters on the **third act of his** life **drama. The**
scene now closes on Mossgiel, and, when the curtain
rises, we find ourselves in Edinburgh.

CHAPTER III.—1786-1788.

EDINBURGH.

"The town is at present agog with the ploughman poet, who receives adulation with native dignity."

—Mrs COCKBURN of Fearnilee.

OUR poet is now on the road to the metropolis of his dear native land, trotting on a pony; and having passed through the country of the Covenanters in the north-west of Ayrshire and the south-west of Lanarkshire, finds himself hospitably entertained by a sympathetic farmer at Covington,—a district well known to the general traveller, as being on the main line of the Caledonian Railway from Carlisle to the north, a little south of the junction where the ways part, on the west to Glasgow and on the east to Edinburgh. And it was not only a comfortable lodging and a warm welcome that he met with here; it was a grateful ovation in honour of his past performances, and a prophetic overture of his future success. Mr Prentice, his kind-hearted landlord, had sent a flying message through the district, to convene all patriotic sympathisers, from Tintock Hill and Culter Fell on the south to Carstairs on the north, to meet the poet. A white sheet attached to a pitch-fork had been perched on the top of a corn stack to

signal the approach of the wonderful stranger; and when
the object of their admiring welcome entered the farm-
yard, he found all the notables of Covington and the
adjoining parishes arranged in blithe circles to receive
him. Of course the shaking of hands was followed by
the more substantial honour of a rural banquet, and the
flash of wit and the play of humour with which the
poet never failed to season the flow of Scotch drink.
Next morning, after lunching at Carnwath with a family
of the name of Stodart, well known for generations in
that district, he remounted his Rosinante, and reached
Edinburgh on the evening of the 28th November. Here
he took up his abode with one of his old Mauchline
cronies, John Richmond, now a clerk in a lawyer's office,
who lodged in Baxter's Close in the Lawnmarket, or
upper part of the High Street, in a house still shown to
imaginative and patriotic tourists, as one of the most
interesting stone memorials of a city whose streets may
literally be said to be paved with story at every turn.[1]

We have already said that Burns did not come to
Edinburgh as an unknown adventurer; but Dr Blacklock
and Professor Stewart were not the only men ready to
herald his approach with words of good omen, and to
introduce him to the best circles of literary society in the
metropolis. The Earl of Glencairn, who, as an Ayrshire
man, had taken note of the rising star of Mauchline, and
some other Ayrshire friends, were at hand to usher him.
Edinburgh was at that time the centre of a circle of
men of wit, learning, and various accomplishments, and

---

[1] "Memorials of Edinburgh in the Olden Time," by Dr Daniel
Wilson. Edinburgh, 1847, p. 165.

distinguished for easy and brilliant sociability, with some sprinkling of the nobility also, who had not yet learned to desert the kindly haunts of their historic homes for the pretentious state of the overgrown capital on the Thames. Accordingly, not more than a fortnight after his settlement in Baxter's Close, we find him thus announcing to one of his early Ayrshire patrons the flattering details of his first appearance on the Edinburgh stage :—

" EDINBURGH, *13th December 1786.*

" To JOHN BALLANTYNE, Esq.,
   Banker, Ayr.

" I arrived · here on Tuesday was se'nnight, and have suffered ever since I came to town with a miserable headache and stomach complaint, but am now a good deal better. I have found a worthy, warm friend in Mr Dalrymple of Orangefield, who introduced me to Lord Glencairn, a man whose worth and brotherly kindness to me I shall remember when time shall be no more. By his interest, it is passed in the Caledonian Hunt, and entered in their books, that they are to take each a copy of the second edition, for which they are to pay one guinea. I have been introduced to a good many of the *noblesse*, but my avowed patrons and patronesses are the Duchess of Gordon, the Countess of Glencairn, with my Lord and Lady Betty, the Dean of Faculty, Sir John Whitefoord. I have likewise warm friends among the literati :—Professors Stewart, Blair, and Mr Mackenzie, the ' Man of Feeling.' An unknown hand left ten guineas for the Ayrshire bard with Mr Sibbald, which I got. I since have discovered my generous unknown friend to be Patrick Miller, Esq., brother to the Justice-Clerk, and drank a glass of claret with him by invitation at his own house yesternight. I am nearly agreed with Creech to print my book, and I suppose I will begin on Monday. I will send a subscription bill or two next post, when I intend writing my first kind patron, Mr Aitken. I saw his son to-day, and he is very well.

" Dugald Stewart, and some of my learned friends, put me in the periodical paper called the *Lounger*, a copy of which I here enclose you. I was, sir, when I was first honoured with your notice, too obscure ; now, I tremble lest I should be ruined by being dragged too suddenly into the glare of polite and learned observation.

" I shall certainly, my ever-honoured patron, write you an account of my every step ; and better health and more spirits may enable me to make it something better than this stupid matter-of-fact epistle.—I have the honour to be, good sir, your ever-grateful humble servant,

" R. B." [1]

The Caledonian Hunt here mentioned, is a society of Scottish nobility and gentry for the purpose of patronis- ing those field sports, the culture of which naturally arises from the occupations and interests of a country gentle- man. Their names in the front page of a new edition of his poems were of as great importance to the poet as if Majesty itself had stooped from the throne to patronise him. The mention of the *Lounger* alludes to a very favourable notice of his poems by Mackenzie, the author of the book called " The Man of Feeling," a writer than whom no literary man at that time was more quick to discover literary excellence, or more influential to give it notoriety. In this notice the critic did not hesitate to place the peasant bard, in some points of his genius, on the same platform with Shakespeare. Not only in his pathos and passion, the strong points of purely lyrical poetry, does he recognise the hand of a master, but the power of his genius, he says, is not less admirable in tracing the manners of men, in catching the hues of life, with that intuitive glance which we admire in Shakespeare and other first-class dramatists. The Duchess of Gordon, who figures in this same letter as an avowed patroness of the poet, seems to have been a person peculiarly fitted

---

[1] Paterson, IV. 175.

for performing that function; for in an age when conviviality was largely indulged, not seldom to the extent
of what might be called dissipation, with her good sense,
and her light heart, she was ready to take the lead in all
the gaieties of the season, be a never-failing foot at dancing,
and a never-failing hand at cards, and able to go to bed
at four in the morning, and rise at nine without any
apparent diminution of her flow of spirits. Among the
advocates, a body of men who had always shown a
worthy ambition to clothe the dry skeleton of the statute
book with the rich vesture and the fragrant flowers of
literature, Harry Erskine, brother to the Earl of Buchan,
was at that time pre-eminent for wit and grace and manly
independence, and, above all, for a pure flow of the milk
of human kindness, and as such the very man to exchange
a glance of true brotherhood, whether it might be at a
Freemasons' meeting in John Street, where the Kilwinning
Lodge were wont to assemble, or at any of those genial
dinner parties or supper parties where nature found free
vent unfettered by convention, and the flash of wit had
nothing to fear from the frowns of a strait-laced propriety.
The ingenious and eccentric Lord Monboddo, well known
for his metaphysical and philological speculations, does
not appear in this letter; it is certain, however, that he
belonged to the brilliant circle into which Burns was now
familiarly admitted. But what the poet admired in the
atmosphere of this learned judge, was neither his meta-
physics nor his philology, but his daughter, an apparition
of female beauty of an altogether different type from any
that had fired the heart of the poet among the Jeans and
Jennies and Maries of the Ayrshire village, and which
was powerful to strike from the poet the strongest

language that he has ever used in describing the charms of his favourite sex. She is called "the heavenly Miss Burnet, to whom there has not been anything nearly like, in all the combinations of beauty, grace, and goodness which the Great Creator has formed, since Milton's Eve on the first day of her existence." [1] A lady whose presence was potent to call forth such a flash of transcendental admiration from such a devotee of the sex, could scarcely fail to appear prominently in his first impressions of life in Edinburgh, which we here insert at length, as the best possible description of what he saw and felt in that most beautiful, most picturesque, and most interesting of modern cities :—

> " Edina ! Scotia's darling seat !
>   All hail thy palaces and towers,
> Where once beneath a monarch's feet
>   Sat Legislation's sovereign powers !
> From marking wildly-scatter'd flowers,
>   As on the banks of Ayr I stray'd,
> And singing, lone, the ling'ring hours,
>   I shelter in thy honour'd shade.
>
> Here wealth still swells the golden tide,
>   As busy Trade his labour plies ;
> There Architecture's noble pride
>   Bids elegance and splendour rise ;
> Here Justice, from her native skies,
>   High wields her balance and her rod ;
> There Learning, with his eagle eyes,
>   Seeks Science in her coy abode.

---

[1] See some account of Elizabeth Burnet, with portrait, in "The Land of Burns," Edinburgh, 1840, Vol. I., p. 77.

Thy sons, Edina ! social, kind,
   With open arms the stranger hail ;
Their views enlarg'd, their lib'ral mind,
   Above the narrow, rural vale ;
Attentive still to sorrow's wail,
   Or modest merit's silent claim ;
And never may their sources fail,
   And never envy blot their name !

Thy daughters bright thy walks adorn
   Gay as the gilded summer sky,
Sweet as the dewy milk-white thorn,
   Dear as the raptur'd thrill of joy !
Fair Burnet strikes th' adoring eye,
   Heav'n's beauties on my fancy shine :
I see the Sire of Love on high,
   And own his work indeed divine !

There, watching high the least alarms,
   Thy rough, rude fortress gleams afar ;
Like some bold vet'ran, grey in arms,
   And mark'd with many a seamy scar :
The pond'rous wall and massy bar,
   Grim-rising o'er the rugged rock,
Have oft withstood assailing war,
   And oft repell'd th' invader's shock.

With awe-struck thought, and pitying tears,
   I view that noble, stately dome,
Where Scotia's kings of other years,
   Fam'd heroes ! had their royal home :
Alas ! how changed the times to come !
   Their royal name low in the dust !
Their hapless race wild-wand'ring roam,
   Tho' rigid law cries out, 'twas just !

Wild beats my heart to trace your steps,
  Whose ancestors, in days of yore,
Through hostile ranks and ruin'd gap
  Old Scotia's bloody lion bore :
E'en I who sing in rustic lore,
  Haply my sires have left their shed
And faced grim danger's **loudest roar,**
  Bold-following where your fathers **led !**

Edina ! Scotia's darling seat !
  All hail thy palaces and towers,
Where once beneath a monarch's feet
  Sat Legislation's sovereign powers !
From marking wildly-scatter'd flowers,
  As on the banks of Ayr I stray'd,
And singing, lone, the ling'ring **hours,**
  I shelter in thy **honour'd shade.**"

Of his experience of the lawyers and their high
mettled wranglings, he has left us the following short but
characteristic account :—

LORD ADVOCATE.

" **He clench'd** his pamphlets in **his fist,**
  He quoted and he hinted,
Till in a declamation-mist
  His argument he tint it :
He gap'd for't, he graip'd for't,
  He fand it was awa', man ;
But what his commonsense came **short,**
  He eked it out wi' **law, man.**

MR ERSKINE.

Collected, Harry stood a wee,
  Then open'd out his **arm, man :**
His lordship sat wi' ruefu' e'e,
  And eyed the gathering storm, man ;

F

> Like wind-driven hail, it did assail,
> Or torrents owre a linn, man ;
> The Bench sae wise lift up their eyes,
> Half-wauken'd wi' the din, man."[1]

Burns, of course, in that age of prolonged conviviality and Bacchanalian revelry, was not always to be found in his bed at John Richmond's, in Baxter's Close, at the hour when ordinary mortals think it time to be sleeping. So one evening, having with his friend Nasmyth, the artist, the painter of his well-known portrait, protracted his social potations to an early hour, the two friends determined not to go home at all, but by taking a ramble to the Pentland Hills, at once enjoy the freshness of the morning breeze and dash off any bad effects that the evening's diversions might have left in their seat of reason. In the course of this matutinal excursion they came down upon the village of Roslin to breakfast; and here the poet, with a sharp appetite, found himself so pleasantly regaled in a little inn kept by Mrs David Wilson, that before leaving he left the following rhymed note of thanks inscribed on a wooden platter :—

> " My blessings on you, sonsy wife ;
> I ne'er was here before :
> Ye've wealth of gear for spoon and knife,
> Nae heart could wish for more.

---

[1] An interesting memorial of the brilliant society in which the poet moved in Edinburgh, will be found in a picture of his inauguration into the Edinburgh Kilwinning Lodge, as poet-laureate of the lodge, on the 1st March 1787, executed by brother Stewart Watson, R.I.A., from which a limited number of engravings was thrown off. This interesting picture may now be seen in the Freemasons' Hall,

> Heaven keep you free frae sturt and strife
>   Till far ayont fourscore ;
> And while I toddle on through life,
>   I'll ne'er gang by your door."

We mention this chiefly as an instance of a practice which he had of leaving on the wall or the windows of the various places which he visited some rhymed memorial of his entertainment ; a practice altogether characteristic of the man, whose poems were struck out directly from the life, and in whose experience no event elevating him a little above the daily routine of existence could occur without leaving a speaking record in his song.

It will have been observed, that in the concluding stanzas of the verses to Edinburgh, there is an allusion to the exiled family of the Stuarts ; and it is notable also, that on the last day of December, shortly after his arrival in Edinburgh, he attended, in the capacity of poet-laureate for the nonce, a meeting to celebrate the birthday of the unfortunate Charles Edward, the lineal descendant of our Scottish race of kings. From this it has been hastily concluded, by some superficial observers, that Burns was a Jacobite, or, as we may phrase it otherwise, a poetical Tory in principle. Quite a mistake. So far as he was a politician at all, he was, by mental constitution, by nurture, by social position, and specially by the instincts of his genius, a man of the people,—a poetical democrat,

George Street, Edinburgh. The publication of the engraving naturally demanded an explanatory account of the persons represented in the picture, which appeared under the name of "A Winter with Burns, Edinburgh, 1846."

as one may see it plainly set forth in his deservedly popular song, "A man's a man for a' that." His Jacobitism, so far as it appears in his works, is merely a whiff of loyal sentiment, such as any well-constituted mind might feel at the contemplation of the sad fate of that handsome young prince, and the series of romantic adventures through which he passed; but the poet, besides being naturally a Liberal, and wearing in Edinburgh the well-known colours of the buff and the blue, had far too much sense to mistake the brilliant dash of a romantic adventure for the sober march of a reasonable policy.

One only other strong impression made on the poet's mind by his residence in Edinburgh, and which issued in a worthy deed, must not be omitted. Edinburgh had been the residence of Allan Ramsay and Robert Fergusson, the poet's two great forerunners as masters of the Muse of their country; and the latter of these, specially akin to Burns both in the good and bad of his temperament, had been dead only twelve years before the poet's arrival in Edinburgh. With this poet, as to an elder brother and a fellow-sufferer, Burns had felt and expressed a sympathy, more honourable perhaps in some respects to his feelings than to his judgment; but however great the distance might be that the verdict of posterity was to establish between the position of the two poets, it was more creditable to the noble nature of Burns to overrate than to underrate the merits of his predecessor. Finding, therefore, on his visit to the Canongate Kirkyard, to drop a tear over the green sod where his brother lyrist lay, no memorial of his name, the poet forthwith wrote to the managers of the kirk and kirkyard with a request "to be allowed to place a simple stone over the revered ashes" of the bard. The request was granted; and the stone erected with the inscription, as follows :—

> " Here lies Robert Fergusson, poet,
> Born Sept. 5, 1751 ; died 16 October 1774.

> No sculptured marble here, nor pompous lay ;
> No storied urn, nor animated bust ;
> This simple stone directs pale Scotia's way
> To pour her sorrow o'er her poet's dust."

And on the reverse side we read :—

> " By special grant of the managers to Robert Burns, who erected this stone, in a burial place to remain for ever sacred to the memory of Robert Fergusson."

Thus far of the new and brilliant scene into which the poet found himself so suddenly transplanted. Let us now see what Edinburgh thought of the actor ; and here we have the good fortune to encounter, on the threshold, the evidence of two men in every way well calculated to give a true and vivid portrait of the new-comer. The first is Josiah Walker, a countryman and intimate friend of the poet himself, not guiltless of flirtation with the Muse, and afterwards Professor of the Latin Language and Literature in the University of Glasgow. This gentleman first met Burns at breakfast with his early patron, Dr Blacklock, and writes as follows :—

> " I was not much struck with his first appearance, as I had previously heard it described. His person, though strong and well knit, and much superior to what might be expected in a ploughman,

was still rather coarse in its outline. His stature, from want of setting up, appeared to be only of the middle size, but was **rather above** it. His motions were firm and decided, and though without any pretensions to grace, were at the same time so free from clownish restraint as to show that he had not always been confined to the society of his profession. His countenance was not of that elegant cast which is most frequent among the upper ranks, but it was manly and intelligent, and marked by a thoughtful gravity which shaded at times into sternness. In his large dark eye the most striking index of his genius resided. It was full of mind, and would have been singularly expressive under the management of one who could employ it with more art for the purpose of expression.

"He was plainly but properly dressed, in a style midway between the holiday costume of a farmer and that of the company with which he now associated. His black hair, without powder, at a time when it was very generally worn, was tied behind, and spread upon his forehead. Upon the whole, from his person, physiognomy, and dress, had I met him near a seaport, and been required to guess his condition, I should have probably conjectured him to be the master of a merchant vessel of the most respectable class.

"In no part of his manner was there the slightest degree of affectation, nor could a stranger have suspected, from anything in his behaviour or conversation, that he had been for some months the favourite of all the fashionable circles of a metropolis.

"In conversation he was powerful. His conceptions and expression were of corresponding vigour, and on all subjects were as remote as possible from commonplace. Though somewhat authoritative, it was in a way which gave little offence, and was readily imputed to his inexperience in those modes of smoothing dissent and softening assertion which are important characteristics of polished manners."[1]

Our next witness is even more important. Sir Walter Scott was at the time a young man of sixteen, undergoing his apprenticeship to the law in the office of his

[1] Chambers, II. 60.

father, a writer to the signet. Through a son of Dr
Adam Ferguson, one of his youthful companions, the
greatest Scottish poet and novelist in embryo had the
opportunity of meeting the greatest living master of the
Scottish lyre in full bloom at the house of his friend's
father ; and the impression made on his youthful fancy
at that early period, was afterwards communicated to his
son-in-law and biographer, J. G. Lockhart, as follows :—

"Of course," says he, "we youngsters sat silent, looked, and
listened. The only thing which I remember as remarkable in
Burns's manner, was the effect produced upon him by a print of
Bunbury's, representing a soldier lying dead on the snow, his dog
sitting in misery on one side, on the other his widow with a child
in her arms. These lines were written underneath :—

> 'Cold on Canadian hills, or Minden's plain,
> Perhaps that parent wept her soldier slain,—
> Bent o'er her babe, her eye dissolved in dew,
> The big drops mingling with the milk he drew,
> Gave the sad presage of his future years,
> The child of misery baptized in tears.'

Burns seemed much affected by the print, or rather the ideas
which it suggested to his mind. He actually shed tears. He
asked whose the lines were, and it chanced that nobody but myself
remembered that they occur in a half-forgotten poem of Lang-
horne's, called by the unpromising title of the 'Justice of Peace.'
I whispered my information to a friend present, who mentioned it
to Burns, who rewarded me with a look and a word which, though
in mere civility, I then received, and still recollect, with great
pleasure. His person was strong and robust ; his manners rustic,
not clownish ; a sort of dignified plainness and simplicity, which
received part of its effect perhaps from one's knowledge of his extraordinary talents. His features are represented in Mr Nasmyth's
picture ; but to me it conveys the idea that they are diminished, as
if seen in perspective. I think his countenance was more massive

than it looks in any of the portraits. I would have taken the poet, had I not known what he was, for a very sagacious country farmer of the old Scotch school,—that is, none of your modern agriculturists who keep labourers for their drudgery, but the *douce guidman* who holds his own plough. There was a strong expression of sense and shrewdness in all his lineaments; the eye alone, I think, indicated the poetical character and temperament. It was large, and of a cast which glowed (I say literally *glowed*) when he spoke with feeling or interest. I never saw such another eye in a human head, though I have seen the most distinguished men of my time. His conversation expressed perfect self-confidence, without the slightest presumption. Among the men, who were the most learned of their time and country, he expressed himself with perfect firmness, but without the least intrusive forwardness; and when he differed in opinion, he did not hesitate to express it firmly, yet at the same time with modesty. . . . I have only to add, that his dress corresponded with his manner. He was like a farmer dressed in his best to dine with the laird. I do not speak in *malam partem*, when I say I never saw a man in company with his superiors in station and information more perfectly free from either the reality or the affectation of embarrassment. I was told, but did not observe it, that his address to females was extremely deferential, and always with a turn either to the pathetic or humorous, which engaged their attention particularly." [1]

The new edition of the poems, published by Creech, appeared on the 21st of April, under the best possible auspices, and with the certainty of a splendid success, about five months after the author's first appearance on the Edinburgh stage. All concern about pecuniary matters being now removed, Burns, before settling down to the ordinary routine of his future life, whatever that might be, determined to make a series of tours through his native country; wisely, both for himself and for the

[1] Chambers, II. 64.

public,—for himself, because being now one of the literary notabilities of Scotland, it was proper that he should make himself acquainted in a living fashion with the country of whose virtues he was the acknowledged interpreter; for the public, because to a man of such quick sensibilities and such impassioned realism of character, new scenes were sure to open up new sources of inspiration; while at the same time, such a lover of the pure Scottish Muse, could not fail, when wandering from glen to glen, to pick up fragments of traditional song, which without his sympathetic touch would certainly have been lost. As his companion in the first of these tours he took Mr Robert Ainslie, afterwards a respectable member of the legal fraternity in the city of lawyers, but at that period a pleasant light-hearted and intelligent young man, and an admirable travelling companion. They started on Saturday, May 5, 1787, and proceeded on horseback over the dreary slopes of the Lammermuir Hills, in a south-easterly direction, to Berry Well, near Duns, the residence of Mr Ainslie's father. At Duns, on Sunday, the poet attended church service with the Ainslie family, and had an opportunity of indulging his favourite amusement of writing impromptu verses, while sitting beside Miss Ainslie in the family pew. The clergyman had chosen a text containing a strong damnatory denunciation of obstinate sinners. The poet observed the young lady, who is described as handsome and full of sweetness and good humour, fumbling in the leaves of her Bible for the text. With his usual obedience to the whim of the moment, he took out a pencil from his pocket, and on a slip of paper wrote the lines :—

> " Fair maid, you need not take the hint,
>   Nor idle texts pursue ;
>   'Twas guilty sinners that he meant,
>   Not angels such as you ! "

From Duns he proceeded to Coldstream, and crossing
the beautiful bridge of the Tweed at that place, set his
foot for the first time on English ground, and in a fit of
patriotic enthusiasm repeated there the two concluding
stanzas of " The Cottar's Saturday Night " :—

" O Scotia, my dear, my native soil," &c.

Thence he advanced to Kelso, one of the most beauti-
fully situated towns in Britain, admired there the old
abbey, so familiar in the border history of the country,
and visited the ruins of Roxburgh Castle in the immediate
neighbourhood, where the second of the ill-starred race of
Stuart was killed by the accidental bursting of a cannon.
The next halt was Jedburgh ; but here, as usual, it was
not the splendid remains of sacred architecture that
attracted him, it was the living beauty of the ladies with
whom he took a walk up the romantic little stream
the Jed; and to one of these, called Miss Lindsay,
with "beautiful hazel eyes, full of spirit and sparkling
with delicious moisture, he attached himself, and some-
how or other got hold of her arm, and felt his heart
thawed with melting pleasure, after having been so long
frozen up in the Greenland Bay of indifference amid the
noise and nonsense of Edinburgh." The civic dignitaries
of the good old burgh waited on the poet, and in the
most flattering terms presented him with the freedom of
the town. This no doubt was highly gratifying ; but when

he leaves the good Border burgh, as he must in the morning, it is neither the rare old town nor the civic honours that he thinks of, but sweet Isabella Lindsay,—" May peace dwell in thy bosom, uninterrupted, except by the tumultuous throbbings of rapturous love ! That love-kindling eye must beam on another, not on me ; that graceful form must bless another's arms, not mine." From Kelso the two travellers proceeded up the Tweed to Melrose and Dryburgh, not then as now the cynosure of all possible tourists ; thence up the Ettrick to Selkirk, a small upland town, not yet made immortal by the sheriffship of Scott and the flourishing industry of the handsome woollen stuff called tweeds. Of the night spent in this interesting old town, the tourist finds a memorial in the shape of an inscribed marble tablet in the wall just beneath the West Port of the town, and close to the house where the gallant Montrose slept the night before the fatal battle of Philiphaugh ; and from this spot it was that Burns indited the letter to William Creech, his publisher, that appears in his works.[1] From

[1] Of the night spent by Burns and his fellow traveller at Selkirk, the following incident is told by Hogg :—"I have often heard Dr Clarkson tell, with a heavy heart, and a loss of all patience with himself, that when Mr Ainslie and Burns arrived in Selkirk that evening, they were just like ' twa drookit craws.' The doctor and other two gentlemen were sitting in Veitch's Inn, near the West Port, taking their glass,—for Selkirk has a West Port as well as Edinburgh. When the travellers arrived, the trio within viewed them from the window as they alighted, and certainly conceived no very high opinion of them. In a short time, however, they sent Mr Veitch to the doctor and his friends, requesting permission for two strangers to take a glass with them. The doctor objected, and asked Mr Veitch what the men were like. Mr Veitch said he could not well

Selkirk he proceeded up the Tweed to Innerleithen, through one of the most delightful passages of lowland scenery, afterwards made more familiar to the English public by the genius of Sir Walter Scott; and thence wheeling eastwards, he retraced his course to Duns, after a poetical visit to Earlston, the birthplace of Thomas Learmonth, one of the earliest of the Scottish minstrels. After a short stay at Berrywell, where the charming Miss Ainslie appears to the manifest damage of the poet's heart, he takes a peep at Dunbar; and then determines, being so near England, to seize an opportunity which might never recur, of taking a tramp on the soil once so dangerously occupied by Scotland's old enemies the Plantagenets. He crossed the Tweed, and visited Alnwick Castle and picturesque old Warkworth. Morpeth also, "a pleasant enough little town," he touched at; slept at Newcastle, and came through Hexham to Carlisle; and thence to Annan. On the opening days of June we find him in Dumfries; and on the eighth of the month, after a pleasant ride up the beautiful valley of the Nith, and by the old Castle of Sanquhar, a place notable in the history of the Covenanters, we find him in his own modest home at Mauchline. Here, after receiving the congratulations of his brother, his mother, and

say; the one spoke rather like a gentleman, but the other was a drover-looking chap; so they refused to admit them, sending them word that they were sorry they were engaged elsewhere, and obliged to go away. The doctor saw them ride off next morning; and i was not till the third day, that he learned it had been the celebrated Scotch poet whom they had refused to admit. That refusal hangs about the doctor's heart like a dead-weight to this day, and will do till the day of his death, for the bard had not a more enthusiastic admirer."

sisters, still the tenants of Mossgiel, he could not avoid calling on old Armour, to whom the care of his little daughter had been committed. This, of course, was a delicate affair for both parties; on the one hand, for the renounced and denounced husband of a woman whom he had tenderly loved; and on the other, for the father who had scorned to receive as a son-in-law, in his state of poverty, the man in whom he now beheld the pride of his country, and in a fair way to a distinguished social career. The change in the manner of the old gentleman, brought about by this change of circumstances, seems to have made a most unfavourable impression on the mind of the poet; and he expressed himself to one confidant as "completely disgusted at the mean servile compliance of Armour's family," and to another indulges himself in the following misanthropic outburst against the human species in general, and the individual called Robert Burns in particular :—

"I never, my friend, thought mankind very capable of anything generous; but the stateliness of the patricians in Edinburgh, and the civility of my plebeian brethren (who perhaps formerly eyed me askance) since I returned home, have nearly put me out of conceit altogether with my species. I have bought a pocket Milton, which I carry perpetually about with me, in order to study the sentiments, the dauntless magnanimity, the intrepid unyielding independence, the desperate daring, and noble defiance of hardship, in that great personage Satan. 'Tis true, I have just now a little cash; but I am afraid the star that hitherto has shed its malignant purpose-blasting rays full in my zenith,—that noxious planet, so baneful in its influences to the rhyming tribe, I much dread it is not yet beneath my horizon. Misfortune dodges the path of human life; the poetic mind finds itself miserably deranged in, and unfit for the walks of business; add to all, that thoughtless follies and hairbrained whims, like so many *ignes fatui*, eternally diverging from the right line of sober discretion, sparkle with step-bewitching blaze in the idly gazing eyes of the poor heedless bard, till pop, 'he falls like Lucifer, never to hope again.'"[1]

This is strong language, such as a lyrical poet of his temper is fond to indulge in; but cogitations of this hue do not come from pleasant causes, and have a strong tendency to produce unpleasant effects.

Having as yet no definite plan for his immediate settlement in life, and being in the neighbourhood of that grand country whence his Highland Mary had proceeded, our travelling bard, not perhaps in the sweetest humour, made a short side excursion into the West Highlands, in the course of which he left a somewhat querulous stanza against the good people of Inverary:—

> " There's nothing here but Highland pride,
> And Highland scab and hunger ;
> If Providence has sent me here,
> 'Twas surely in his anger ! "

And, with all the wild sportiveness which characterised him, we find him on the " Bonnie, bonnie, banks of Loch Lomond," indulging in singing and drinking, and dancing and racing, in a manner much more to his liking than the stately convivialities of literary Edinburgh. On the 23d July he appears again at Mauchline, making to his young Edinburgh friend, Robert Ainslie, the confession, " I was never a rogue, but have been a fool all my life; and, in spite of all my endeavours, I see now plainly that I shall never be wiser." This is, no doubt, a little exaggerated, as almost all his phrases are; but it has an ill-

---

[1] Chambers, II. 97.

omened clang about it, and leaves the just judge of
moral matters in a doubtful issue, whether he ought more
to pity or to condemn. On the 25th August, after a
short residence in Edinburgh, Burns set out on a Highland tour of larger sweep, with his friend William Nicol,
one of the masters of the Edinburgh High School, for
his fellow traveller; for the essential sociality of his
nature—contrary to what we find in not a few worshippers of the Muse—seems to have compelled him always,
even in the midst of the grandest solitudes of Nature,
never to travel alone. Of his fellow-traveller on this
occasion, Dr Currie says that he was a Dumfriesshire
man, of a descent, as schoolmasters often are in Scotland,
equally humble with the poet; and then adds, with a
significant antithesis, that, like the great man whom he
accompanied, he "rose by the strength of his talents,
and fell by the strength of his passions." *Arcades ambo,*
—quite the right thing apparently for mutual enjoyment,
but not perhaps for mutual benefit. Their first resting-
place was Linlithgow, where, in the atmosphere of one of
the oldest dwelling-places of Scottish loyalty, Burns makes
an æsthetical remark on Presbyterian churches as they
were in his day:—"What a poor pimping place is a
Presbyterian place of worship; dirty, narrow, and squalid,
stuck in a corner of old Popish grandeur such as Linlithgow. Ceremony and show, if judiciously thrown
in, are absolutely necessary for the great bulk of mankind, both in religious and civil matters."[1] Falkirk with
its Roman vallum, Stirling with its castled strength, and
Bannockburn with its glorious brook, passed in review;

[1] So Goethe, " The world is governed by wisdom, by authority,
and by *show.*"

not omitting "a dirty, ugly place called Borrowstouness," on the Firth, and here the house of his entertainment is boastfully pointed out to the present day. As little were the glowing fires of the Carron ironworks, or the green beauties of Dunipace, with the foamy windings of the Carron, neglected in his picturesque rambles. From Stirling, leaving his travelling companion for a day, he made a defection into Clackmannanshire, to pay a visit to a Mrs Chalmers at Harvieston, a widow lady, a relative of his Mauchline patron, Gavin Hamilton, who lived there with two charming daughters, with one of whom, Margaret, the poet had made acquaintance in Edinburgh at Dr Blacklock's. Here he was on the banks of the Devon, one of the most beautiful softly winding waters in Scotland, and in the bosom of a family distinguished by that combination of cultivated intellect and graceful simplicity, so attractive to a man of poetic sensibility. Returned to Stirling, he proceeded northward through Crieff and Glenalmond to beautiful Taymouth, where English softness and Highland grandeur combine to form a harmonious union of the beautiful and the sublime in landscape, certainly not surpassed in any most lauded district of the United Kingdom. Here the poet, in his customary fashion, left a rhymed memorial of his admiration on the chimney-piece of the inn at Kenmore, where he spent the night :—

> "Admiring Nature, in her wildest grace,
>   These northern scenes with weary feet I trace ;
>   O'er many a winding dale and painful steep,
>   Th' abodes of covey'd grouse and timid sheep,
>   My savage journey, curious, I pursue,
>   Till fam'd Breadalbane opens to my view.

> The meeting-cliffs each deep-sunk glen divides,
> The woods, wild-scatter'd, clothe their ample sides ;
> Th' outstretching lake, embosom'd 'mong the hills,
> The eye with wonder and amazement fills ;
> The Tay, meand'ring sweet in infant pride,
> The palace, rising on its verdant side ;
> The lawns, wood-fringed in Nature's native taste ;
> The hillocks, dropt in Nature's careless haste ;
> The arches, striding o'er the new-born stream ;
> The village, glittering in the noontide beam."

Thence, following the **course of the Tay, he came to** Aberfeldy, where he wrote the well-known song :—

> " Bonnie lassie, will ye go,
> Will ye go, will ye go ?
> Bonnie lassie, will ye go
> To the Birks o' Aberfeldy ? "

and, resting at Dunkeld, had the good **fortune to be** entertained **by** a hospitable Highland laird on the roman- tic banks of the Bran, to meet and hear Neil Gow, the celebrated violinist, whose name makes a **mark in the** history of Scottish song. Him Burns describes **as "a** short stout-built honest Highland figure, with greyish hair shed on his honest social brow ; an interesting face, marked by strong sense, kind open-heartedness, and un- mistrusting simplicity." **The roaring** falls of the Tum- mel at Bonskeid, and the fragrant wilderness of birches at Killiecrankie, could not fail to **form the next** point of attraction in his northern journey; and at the latter place, as a **matter** of course, he dropped one of **his tears of** loyal sentiment over **the** grave of **the** gallant Dundee. Thence **a** few miles brought him to Blair Athole, **where** he met his friend Professor Walker, and received **a most**

G

hearty Highland welcome from the Ducal family,—a
family still, and exceptionally distinguished for the
genuine Gaelic character of its breeding and culture.
Celtic joviality and poetical sensibility mingled here harmoniously together; and the poet, to testify his gratitude
for the kindness of the noble family, and the pleasure he
had received from such a select company of "honest
men and bonnie lasses," left behind him a rhymed lauda-
tion of one of the picturesque scenes of the neighbourhood, which was destined to receive a practical response
in a fashion of which the published wishes of a passing
son of the Muses had seldom been able to boast :—

> " My Lord, I know your noble ear
>   Woe ne'er assails in vain ;
> Embolden'd thus, I beg you'll hear
>   Your humble slave complain,
> How saucy Phœbus' scorching beams,
>   In flaming summer-pride,
> Dry-withering, waste my foamy streams,
>   And drink my crystal tide.
>
> The lightly-jumpin' glowrin' trouts
>   That thro' my waters play,
> If, in their random, wanton spouts,
>   They near the margin stray ;
> If, hapless chance ! they linger lang,
>   I'm scorching up so shallow,
> They're left the whitening stanes amang,
>   In gasping death to wallow.
>
> Last day I grat, wi' spite and teen,
>   As poet Burns came by,
> That to a bard I should be seen
>   Wi' half my channel dry ;

A panegyric rhyme, I ween,
  Even as I was he shor'd me:
But had I in my glory been,
  He, kneeling, wad ador'd me.

Here, foaming down the shelvy rocks,
  In twisting strength I rin;
There, high my boiling torrent smokes,
  Wild roaring o'er a linn:
Enjoying large each spring and well,
  As nature gave them me,
I am, although I say't mysel',
  Worth gaun a mile to see.

Would then my noble master please
  To grant my highest wishes,
He'll shade my banks wi' towerin' trees,
  And bonnie spreading bushes;
Delighted doubly then, my lord,
  You'll wander on my banks,
And listen mony a grateful bird
  Return you tuneful thanks."

At Blair he had the good fortune to meet Mr Thomas Graham of Balgownie, afterwards Lord Lynedoch, and his beautiful spouse, a daughter of Lord Cathcart, and sister of the Duchess of Athole, one of Gainsborough's beautiful ladies, and memorised in the history of her country by her short-lived connection with one of Wellington's most notable Peninsular heroes, who died at an advanced age of ninety-four, with the unhealed however, for her premature decease in his bosom. From yre, as his the poet continued his tour by Dalnacar ruminating whinnie, and Aviemore to Inverness. Here he shortly Foyers, so familiar to Highland tourists Leaving Peggie day, received his tribute of praise; Ochtertyre on the

foamy sweep of this headlong plunge of Celtic waters
excited his admiration, beside the dark cauldrons of the
Findhorn, with its rocky banks, he knew to mingle the
solemn impressions of mountain solitude with the tragic
memories of a murdered monarch, and the echoes of
weird incantation from Macbeth's blasted heath. Gordon
Castle, the seat of the jovial Duchess who had led the
brilliant revels in Edinburgh, was his next resting-place
as he travelled eastward. Here he was delighted with a
repetition of the same cordial hospitality that had charmed
him at Blair Athole ; but his pleasure was nipped in the
bud by the foolish conduct of his travelling companion,
who, in a fit of magisterial self-importance sometimes
found in schoolmasters, imagining himself to be neglected
by his now so mighty companion, saddled his horse, and
shot off in a huff, leaving the poet to follow him the best
way he could. Had Burns been a man of less cordial
humanity, he might justly have left the indignant pedagogue to drive to Aberdeen in stately indignation alone ;
but the poet, though proud, was kind, and so on this
occasion felt no hesitation in sacrificing the expected
genialities of the Duchess to the irritated sensibilities of
the dominie. From Fochabers his route led him first to
Banff, where he visited Duff House, the noble mansion
the Earl of Fife ; thence he proceeded to Aberdeen,
anite capital of the north, where he had the good
to meet a clerical gentleman of the Episcopal
on of the Rev. John Skinner, a gentleman who
Episcopal clergyman in a village a few miles
Peterhead, and was well known through
That the author of the jovial song " Tulloch-
Wi' pathetic ballad of " The Ewie wi' the

crooked horn." The son, of course, was only too proud
to give the poet an introduction to the father, which
shortly afterwards issued in a correspondence between
the two parties not without note in the history of Scottish song. From Aberdeen he proceeded southwards to
Stonehaven, the seat of his father's family, where he had
the happiness to find two of his old aunts, Jean and
Isabel, still alive and hale; and thence, to complete the
circle, after a glance at Montrose, Arbroath, Dundee,
Perth, and Kinross, he proceeded to Queensferry, and
on the 16th September was in Edinburgh.

One might have thought that the poet had now had
enough of picturesque touring and provincial lionising
for the year; but the plans for his future life not being
yet completed, and the demands from his Edinburgh
patrons being both frequent and flattering, we find him
again, early in October, with his friend Dr Adair, starting
on a short tour through Clackmannan and Perthshire.
Linlithgow, Carron, and Stirling were again visited; but
the real mark of the poet on this tour was Harvieston,
where the banks of the Devon and the accomplished
Margaret Chalmers had left upon him an impression
that longed for a renewal. When in this beautiful
region he visited Castle Campbell, an ancient seat of
the Argyle family, the famous cataract of the Devon
called the Cauldron Linn, and the Rumbling Brig, and
other incentives to picturesque song, which, however,
elicited no scenic strains from the poet's lyre, as his
heart was no doubt altogether occupied with ruminating
on the charms of Miss Chalmers, whom he shortly
afterwards immortalised as "Peggie." Leaving Peggie
in the meantime, he proceeded to Ochtertyre on the

Teith, the seat of Mr Ramsay, and to another Ochtertyre in Strathearn, the seat of Sir William Murray. Of
his residence at the latter of these two places he has
left two well-known memorials, in the verses entitled
"On scaring some water-fowl in Loch Turit," where he
indulges in a tender-hearted denunciation of the field
sports in which our British gentlemen take such large
delight ; and also in a well-known love song :—

> " Blithe, blithe, and merry was she,
> Blithe was she but and ben,
> Blithe by the banks of Earn,
> And blithe in Glenturit glen ; "

of which the heroine was Miss Euphemia Murray of
Lintrose, a lovely lass of eighteen, known in the district
under the familiar name of "The Flower of Strathearn."
From the laird of the other Ochtertyre he received the
following striking commendation, which appears in a
letter to Dr Currie, in the first edition of Burns's collected works :—

"I have been in the company of many men of genius," says Mr
Ramsay, "some of them poets, but never witnessed such flashes of
intellectual brightness as from him,—the impulse of the moment,
sparks of celestial fire ! I never was more delighted, therefore, than
with his company for two days' *tête-à-tête.* In a mixed company I
should have made little of him ; for, in the gamester's phrase, he
did not always know when to play off and when to play on. . . . .
I not only proposed to him the writing of a play similar to the *Gentle
Shepherd, qualem decet esse sororem,* but Scottish Georgics, a subject
which Thomson has by no means exhausted in his *Seasons.*"

After these excursions to the two Ochtertyres, the
poet returned to his dear friends in Harvieston ; and

thence, with no light heart, home by Kinross and Dunfermline. At this place, so dear to every patriotic Scot,
he knelt down and kissed with fervid devotion the two
broad flagstones which marked the final resting-place of
of the great hero-king, to whose persistent stand in the
face of overwhelming forces Scotland owes her independent name and place in the annals of European
nationalities.

After having thus gratified his patriotic curiosity, and
published his literary fame, by such extensive rambles
through his dear native land, the poet was now ready to
face the serious business of life in that sphere which birth
and habitude had pointed out as his own. And, indeed,
about the beginning of December all was ready for the
scene of his future activity, when a double accident took
place,—an accident to his body, and an accident to his
soul. At the house of an Edinburgh lady, Miss Nimmo,
Burns had been introduced to a lady named M'Lehose,
who, being a spinner of verses herself, and of warm
human sympathies, had naturally formed a desire to
make a more intimate acquaintance with the acknowledged greatest master of the Scottish lyre. The meeting produced its natural result,—a mutual recognition of
social and intellectual kinship on both sides. The lady
being of a frank and open character, and anxious to know
something personally of such an extraordinary genius
whom in his works she passionately admired, invited the
poet to visit her at her lodgings a few days after the
meeting. Burns agreed, and was to have taken tea with
Mrs M'Lehose in her lodgings on the evening of Saturday,
December 8 ; but the night before he was tumbled out
of a cab by a drunken coachman, and got home pain-

fully with a severe bruise on his leg. The tea of course
was suspended ; but a lively correspondence was immediately set a-going, in which, from the high-flown and
rapturous style of the poet, the lady had instant occasion
to remind him that she was a married woman with a
living husband, and he must address her only as a friend ;
—the fact being, that she had had the misfortune, at the
early age of eighteen, to have been united to a worthless
husband, a Glasgow merchant, from whom she was
legally separated, she residing in Edinburgh, while he was
holding his establishment beyond the sea in Jamaica.

But Burns was not a man to understand how friendship with a woman whom he greatly admired could be
cultivated without passing into love ; and so the lady
forthwith found herself in the delicate position of being
passionately admired by a man whose admiration she
cordially returned, and that a man whose headlong
impetuosity of temper was continually leading him to
overstep those bounds which, in the intercourse of the
sexes, are the shield of honour and the safeguard of
innocence. Feeling herself in this situation, it might have
seemed wise in a lady of religious principle and virtuous
habits—which Agnes M‘Lehose essentially was—to
have shut the door after the first interview with so perilous
an acquaintance; but her frank unconventional nature combined with her profound respect for the poet to prevent
this ; besides, she felt herself firmly fenced with the mail
of a severe creed, and, if she were able to maintain her
own position, as she did nobly, she might also hope to
use her moral influence effectively in restraining the
passions and guiding the counsels of her admirer. The
correspondence of these two remarkable persons, con-

tinued with little interruption for more than three months, is in the highest degree interesting, exhibiting perhaps even more strikingly, if not more classically, than his love-songs the leading features in the character of this wonderful genius. Love and religion certainly never were so strangely tossed together as in these impassioned epistles, from which we shall now make a few extracts. In the following letter, dated 21st December, after alluding to the strong terms in which the poet had expressed his admiration of her poetical talents, she goes on to say :—

"Take care; many a 'glorious' woman has been undone by having her head turned. 'Know you!' I know you far better than you do me. Like yourself, I am a bit of an enthusiast. In religion and friendship quite a bigot,—perhaps I could be so in love too ; but everything dear to me in heaven and earth forbids ! This is my fixed principle, and the person who would dare to endeavour to remove it I would hold as my chief enemy. Like you, I am incapable of dissimulation ; nor am I, as you suppose, unhappy. I have been unfortunate ; but guilt alone could make me unhappy. Possessed of fine children,—competence,—fame,—friends, kind and attentive,—what a monster of ingratitude should I be in the eye of Heaven were I to style myself unhappy ! True, I have met with scenes horrible to recollection—even at six years' distance ; but adversity, my friend, is allowed to be the school of virtue. It oft confers that chastened softness which is unknown among the favourites of Fortune ! Even a mind possessed of natural sensibility, without this, never feels that exquisite pleasure which nature has annexed to our sympathetic sorrows. Religion, the only refuge of the unfortunate, has been my balm in every woe. O ! could I make her appear to you as she has done to me ! Instead of ridiculing her tenets, you would fall down and worship her very semblance wherever you found it." [1]

---

[1] "Burns and Clarinda," by her Grandson, W. C. M'Lehose, Edinburgh, 1834, p. 96.

Here, and in some other communications, she reveals herself as the most gracious and opportune of preachers. Calvinism from such sweet lips would sound quite differently than when thundered from the throat of the Rev. Dr Auld of Mauchline, or any of his condemnatory brethren of the Evangelical type. From her elevated point of view, unsoiled by the mire through which her correspondent had sometimes dragged his eagle plumes, she saw clearly through his character, and interpreted the history of his religious experiences and moral aberrations, with that keenness and sureness of glance which belong to the moral superiority of the interpreter :—

"One thing alone hurt me, though I regretted many—your avowal of being an enemy to Calvinism. I guessed it was so by some of your pieces ; but the confirmation of it gave me a shock I could only have felt for one I was interested in. You will not wonder at this, when I inform you that I am a strict Calvinist, *one or two* dark tenets excepted, which I never meddle with. Like many others, you are so either from never having examined it with candour and impartiality, or from having unfortunately met with weak professors who did not understand it, and hypocritical ones who made it a cloak for their knavery. Both of these, I am aware, abound in country life ; nor am I surprised at their having had this effect upon your more enlightened understanding. I fear your friend, the captain of the ship, was of no advantage to you in this and many other respects." [1]

These earnest appeals and serious warnings of the good lady had the valuable effect of drawing from the poet his confession of faith in a more complete form than we find it in any other part of his works. A Calvinist cer-

[1] "Clarinda," as above, p. 117.

tainly Burns was not, and could not be ; but though, like all emotional persons, repelled rather than attracted by the dogmas of a systematic theology, and, though not unfrequently seduced by his passions from his loyalty to his principles, he was by no means an irreligious man ; and here follows his creed :—

"He who is our Author and Preserver, and will one day be our Judge, must be—not for His sake, in the way of duty, but from the native impulse of our hearts—the object of our reverential awe and grateful adoration. He is almighty and all-bounteous, we are weak and dependent ; hence prayer and every other sort of devotion. ' He is not willing that any should perish, but that all should come to everlasting life ;' consequently, it must be in every one's power to embrace His offer of ' everlasting life,' otherwise He could not in justice condemn those who did not. A mind pervaded, actuated, and governed by purity, truth, and charity, though it does not merit heaven, yet is an absolutely necessary pre-requisite, without which heaven can neither be obtained nor enjoyed ; and, by Divine promise, such a mind shall never fail of attaining ' everlasting life ;' hence the impure, the deceiving, and the uncharitable exclude themselves from eternal bliss, by their unfitness for enjoying it. The Supreme Being has put the immediate administration of all this—for wise and good ends known to Himself—into the hands of Jesus Christ, a Great Personage, whose relation to Him we cannot comprehend, but whose relation to us is a Guide and Saviour, and who, except for our own obstinacy and misconduct, will bring us all, through various ways and by various means, to bliss at last." [1]

Our limited space forbids to enter more largely into these revelations from the inner soul of this man of large intelligence, noble aspirations, and ill-regulated passions. The more intimate relations with Mrs M'Lehose, or Clarinda, as she is poetically baptized, were abruptly

[1] " Clarinda," p. 122.

broken off in March, when the poet left the metropolis for the scene of his early loves and rustic occupations in Ayrshire. A visit to Mauchline again brought Jean Armour to her old place in the front, and Jean Armour followed his fates when, in the month of June, shortly afterwards, he went to try his fortune as an honest Dumfries farmer on the banks of the Nith. What remains of the story of this pious and accomplished lady, after her escape from the tempestuous fascinations of the poet, will fall to be mentioned in the next chapter.

CHAPTER IV.—1788-1791.

ELLISLAND.

"Musa meas errare boves, ut cernis, et ipsum,
    Ludere, quæ vellem, calamo permisit agresti."
                                        —VIRGIL.

AFTER various communings with his own disturbed soul, and various good advices from esteemed friends, early in the spring of the year 1788 Burns had made up his mind to buckle to the sober business of life in his original capacity of a cultivator of the soil. On the 13th of March we find him legally installed as tenant of the farm of Ellisland, belonging to Mr Miller of Dalswinton, on the banks of the Nith, about five or six miles above Dumfries. He made his start under kindly auspices; his landlord was his personal friend, and a friend who had befriended him in a substantial way in the time of his need; the terms of the lease are described as favourable; and the profits of the Edinburgh edition of his poems, after paying all expenses incident to his life in Edinburgh and his tour round Scotland, had left him with clear cash to the amount of £400 in his pocket. The only unfavourable circumstance seems to have been that the soil of the farm, when Mr Miller bought it, had been left in a very exhausted condition; and it was of evil omen also, that of the three farms of which his kind landlord offered him the election, the poet-tenant chose, not the one which economically promised the most satisfaction, but the one which æsthetically offered the fairest feast for the eye to a lover of Nature. His feelings and purposes, in prospect of farming, are expressed in a letter to Mr Miller so early as October 1787, which contains the following passage :—

"I want to be a farmer in a small farm, about a plough-gang, in a pleasant country, under the auspices of a good landlord. I have no foolish notion of being a tenant on easier terms than another. To find a farm where one can live at all is not easy. I only mean living soberly, like an old-style farmer, and joining personal industry." [1]

Than this nothing could sound better. His destiny was now fixed. The brilliant blaze of metropolitan festivities, and the delicious rapture of poetical love-makings must now vanish, or at least operate mildly from a pale distance ; and a simple farm-steading on the banks of a quiet river was to be his workshop and home. He had left Edinburgh finally so early as the 18th February, but it is not till the middle of June that we find him fairly settled in his farm as a working tenant. In the interval three pieces of serious business had to be trans-acted in the west, for which purpose he resided in Ayrshire for about three months and a half after leaving Edinburgh. The first business was the least serious and the most easily settled ; finding that from bad seasons

[1] Paterson, IV. 291.

and other causes the farm at Mossgiel was not in a very
prosperous condition, he generously handed over to his
brother Gilbert and the family about £200 of the ready
money which he had lying in the bank at Ayr. The
next matter was serious, and not to be settled without an
adjustment of those contending motives whose spiritual
war forms one of the most severe struggles in a good
man's life. This was his relation to Jean Armour. At
the time when Burns was darting his shots of amorous
electricity into the breast of Clarinda, he had good reason
to consider himself neither legally nor morally bound
to that poor girl. He had been disowned and denounced
formally in that quarter, and had made up his mind to
that wisdom of life which recommends to " let the past
be past for ever." How entirely he was disenchanted of
her under the influence of the brilliant fascination of
Clarinda appears from two notable letters, one from the
poet to his Edinburgh enchantress, and the other to his
convivial friend Robert Ainslie. To Clarinda, from
Mossgiel, February 23, he writes :—

"Now for a little news that will please you. I, this morning, as
I came home, called for a certain woman. I am disgusted with her
—I cannot endure her ! I, while my heart smote me for the pro-
fanity, tried to compare her with my Clarinda. 'Twas setting the
expiring glimmer of a farthing taper beside the cloudless glory of
the meridian sun. *Here* was tasteless insipidity, vulgarity of soul,
and mercenary fawning ; *there*, polished good sense, Heaven-born
genius, and the most generous, the most delicate, the most tender
passion. I have done with her, and she with me." [1]

---

[1] Paterson, V. 94.

To Ainslie, on March 3, he writes from Mauchline:—

"I have been through sore tribulation, and under much buffeting of the wicked one, since I came to this country. Jean I found banished, like a martyr,—forlorn, destitute, and friendless,—all for the good old cause; I have reconciled her to her fate; I have reconciled her to her mother; I have taken her a room; I have taken her to my arms; I have given her a guinea; and I have embraced her till she rejoiced with joy unspeakable and full of glory. But—as I always am on every occasion—I have been prudent and cautious to an astounding degree; I swore her, privately and solemnly, never to attempt any claim on me as a husband, even though anybody should persuade her she had such a claim, which she had not, neither during my life, nor after my death. She did all this like a good girl." [1]

What are we to expect next? All this care of the poor girl ended in the most human way possible; she was at this time about, for the second time, to give to the poet pledges of their irregular love, and in prospect of this had by her stern father been literally banished from her home, and cast adrift through the cold of a Scottish spring. Burns, in such a case, could do nothing less than what he did, for the moment to escape by some act of kindly compromise from "sore tribulation and buffeting of the wicked one." On the 13th of the month Jean was delivered of twin girls, who lived only a few days. This pitiful event, and the consciousness of his own original guilt in having produced it, united with the essential human kindness of his nature, and the relaxation by distance of the bonds which bound him to his Edinburgh enchantress, seem to have produced a complete revolution in the mind of Burns as respects

---

[1] Paterson, IV. 331.

his relation to his misfortuned first love. In a letter to his friend Smith, dated Mauchline, 28th April 1788, we find him talking of "Mrs Burns" as a man talks of his wife; and on the 5th day of August we find the following remarkable entry in the kirk-session books of Mauchline :—

"1788, *August* 5.—Compeared Robert Burns, with Jean Armour, his alleged spouse. They both acknowledged their irregular marriage, and their sorrow for that irregularity, and desiring that the Session will take such steps as may seem to them proper, in order to the solemn confirmation of the said marriage. The Session, taking this affair under their consideration, agree that they both be rebuked for this acknowledged irregularity, and that they be solemnly engaged to adhere faithfully to one another as man and wife all the days of their life.

"In regard the Session have a title in law to some fine for behoof of the poor, they agree to refer to Mr Burns his own generosity. The above sentence was accordingly executed, and the Session absolved the said parties from any scandal on this account.

"(Signed)   WILLIAM AULD, *Moderator.*
ROBERT BURNS.
JEAN ARMOUR."[1]

Any honest-minded person, I presume, will agree with me in thinking that this document bears witness to the most honourable and wise act in the life of a great genius, always remarkable for honour, not always for wisdom. Honourable it certainly was, to give to an unfortunate young woman that social position as his lawful wife which, had it not been for his improprieties, she might long ago have received from another; wise also beyond doubt it was, to strike out from his picture of domestic life all the images of a higher and more cultivated

[1] Chambers, II. 277.

womanhood with which his Edinburgh sojourn had made
him familiar, and to unite himself in firm family bonds
with a plain country girl on the same social platform with
himself. How nobly and how justly he felt on this subject the following extract from a letter to his confidential
friend, Mrs Dunlop, will set in the clearest light :—

"ELLISLAND, 13 *June* 1788.

"Your surmise, Madam, is just : I am indeed a husband. . . .
To jealousy or infidelity I am an equal stranger. My preservative
from the first, is the most thorough consciousness of her sentiments
of honour, and her attachment to me ; my antidote against the last,
is my long and deep-rooted affection for her.

"In housewife matters, in aptness to learn and activity to execute,
she is eminently mistress ; and during my absence in Nithsdale, she
is regularly and constantly apprentice to my mother and sisters in
their dairy and other rural business.

"The Muses must not be offended when I tell them the concerns
of my wife and family, will, in my mind, always take the *pas;* but
I assure them their ladyships will ever come next in place.

"You are right that a bachelor state would have insured me more
friends ; but, from a cause you will easily guess, conscious peace in
the enjoyment of my own mind, and unmistrusting confidence in
approaching my God, would seldom have been of the number.

"I found a once much-loved and still much-loved female, literally
and truly cast out to the mercy of the naked elements, but I enabled
her to *purchase* a shelter ;—there is no sporting with a fellow-crea-
ture's happiness or misery.

"The most placid good nature and sweetness of disposition ; a
warm heart, gratefully devoted with all its powers to love me ;
vigorous health and sprightly cheerfulness, set off to the best advantage by a more than commonly handsome figure ; these, I think, in
a woman, may make a good wife, though she should never have
read a page but the scriptures of the Old and New Testament, nor
have danced in a brighter assembly than a penny pay wedding." [1]

---

[1] Chambers, II. 264.

The third piece of business which he had to transact
as preliminary to his commencing the serious work of
the game of life, was certain preliminary studies and
exercises which required to be made with a view to his
qualification for holding some position in the Excise, of
which he had got a promise from Mr Graham of Fintry,
and other influential gentlemen. This had long been a
favourite idea of the poet, not that he had any special
preference for the occupation, but because he knew from
his father and mother's experience that farming is a very
slippery business, and, as a wise man, in the face of such
experience, he felt himself bound to have two strings
to his bow. Of this business all that requires to be said
is, that he passed muster before the Board of Excise in
the spring of the year, and on 13th June we find him at
work on the banks of the Nith. The old farmhouse, or
steading as we call it in Scotland, being in disrepair, the
poet was obliged to lodge himself as he best could in an
extempore way till the new house should be ready.
This occasioned the detention of Mrs Burns in Ayr,
so that the domestic enjoyment so necessary to compose
the mind of the bard at this period received an uncom-
fortable break at the start. Jean did not appear on the
scene till December, when she came bringing her beautiful self along with cartloads of plenishing, and a four-
posted bed, a marriage gift from Mrs Dunlop, and a
faithful servant girl called Elizabeth Smith, over whose
conduct the poet was enjoined to keep special watch
and to see her duly instructed in the Catechism,
which in Scotland stands for the most approved com-
pendium of orthodox Bible doctrine. Unfortunate as
this belatedness in Jean's taking full possession of

her connubial seat of honour may appear, it brought
with it, as evil is often found to do, a great accompanying good.　It set the lonely young husband a-musing
and brooding over the beauties of his distant partner,
beyond the Ayrshire hills in the west, of which the
witness remains for ever embalmed in that most popular
song :—

> " Of a' the airts the wind can blaw,
> 　I dearly like the west,
> For there the bonnie lassie lives,
> 　The lassie I lo'e best ;
> There wild woods grow, and rivers row,
> 　And mony a hill between;
> But day and night my fancy's flight
> 　Is ever wi' my Jean.
>
> I see her in the dewy flowers,
> 　I see her sweet and fair ;
> I hear her in the tunefu' birds,
> 　I hear her charm the air :
> There's not a bonnie flower that springs
> 　By fountain, shaw, or green,
> There's not a bonnie bird that sings,
> 　But minds me o' my Jean."

And the accompanying classical piece, "Oh, were I on
Parnassus Hill," where Jean is described at full length :—

> " I see thee dancing on the green,
> 　Thy waist sae jimp, thy limbs sae clean,
> 　Thy tempting lips, thy roguish een,
> 　　By heaven and earth I love thee ! "

As a member of country society at Ellisland, we find
the poet performing his part in a very creditable way.

Early in the year 1789 he appears corresponding with
an Edinburgh bookseller for a supply of books for a local
library, in the conduct of which he took a warm interest.[1]
At his proper business, farming, he appears to have been
pretty regular, a good holder of the plough, a good master
to his servants, happy in his home, and not sharing in the
Bacchanalian convivialities of the district in any degree
beyond what the habits of the age and country, to a man of
warm human sympathies, rendered unavoidable.[2] Of his
occasional convivial potations, a notable record remains in
the humorous poem called " The Whistle," whereby hangs
a tale. When James VI. of Scotland was married to
Anne of Denmark in 1589, the Danish fair one brought
in her train a certain tremendous swashbuckler of a
fellow, with a big stomach and a gigantic capacity for
drink. This son of Silenus carried with him a little
ebony whistle, which, at the commencement of his
Dionysian worship, he laid on the table, with the declaration that whosoever had strength of brain and breath
sufficient to blow the whistle, after all the rest of the
company had fallen under the table, should carry off the

---

[1] It may not be without interest to mention the names of the
books for which he gave an order in this letter,—" The Spectator,"
" The Mirror," " The Lounger," " Man of Feeling," " Man of the
World," " Guthrie's Geographical Grammar," and some " Religious
Pieces." At Dumfries, a few years afterwards, we find him pursuing
the same good work of local enlightenment, and thus preceding, by
more than half a century, the earliest workers in the great cause of
educating our intelligent democracy, so characteristic of the present
day.—See Chambers, IV. 44.

[2] Of his habitual sobriety when at Ellisland, we have most reliable
testimonies, as Chambers, III. 76.

whistle as his lawful booty, and a triumphant testimony to his Bacchanalian prowess. The Dane, as from a country famous for drinking (see Shakespeare's Hamlet), came to Edinburgh, with certificates of his potatory invincibility from all the principal courts of continental Europe, and little dreamed that the rubicund glory of the star which had shone so brightly at Copenhagen, Warsaw, and Moscow, should be destined to pale its fires before the lesser light of a Scotch laird. But so it was. In the days of royal Jamie a gentleman appeared in the lists, Sir Robert Lawrie of Maxwelltown, in Dumfriesshire, who, after three days and three nights of stout-hearted potations, left the Dane beneath the table, and marched off with the whistle. When Burns resided at Ellisland, the whistle, by legitimate descent, was in the possession of Captain Riddell of Friar's Carse, the neighbour and friend of the poet ; and this gentleman, with the chivalrous feeling which belongs to the military profession, determined to hold the Bacchanalian trophy no longer as a historical heir-loom, but to prove his divine right to it by a renewed contest after the manner of its original holder. The contest took place at Friar's Carse, on Friday, October 16, 1789, and of the three brave gentlemen who entered the lists, Captain Riddell himself, Sir Robert Lawrie of Maxwelltown, a descendant of the original Scottish victor, and Mr Ferguson of Craigdarroch, the last remained longest on his legs, and his honourable achievement was celebrated by the bard of Ellisland in a poem of more than seventy lines ; too long, of course, for insertion here, and nothing better at best than an extravaganza of drinking, of which one verse may serve as a sample :—

" Six bottles a-piece **had well wore** out the night,
  When gallant Sir Robert, to finish the fight,
  Turn'd o'er in one bumper a bottle of red,
  And swore 'twas the way **that** their ancestors did."

To another carousal of the same extravagant **kind**, which
only a thin-blooded prig or a sour Pharisee will take for
an exhibition of the poet's familiar **habits**, belongs the
favourite drinking song, " Willie **brewed a peck o' maut**,"
with the humorous chorus :—

" We are na fou, we're nae that fou,
  But just a **drappie** in our e'e ;
  The cock may craw, the day may daw,
  And aye we'll taste the barley bree."

The occasion of this song was an entertainment given at
Moffat to **our** old pedagogic friend William **Nicol**,
whom we saw, in a sublime huff, rattling eastward with
his back to Gordon Castle. He was fond **of** drink, and
could not feel as he wished to **feel** beside an old friend,
without **getting for the evening into a** state of real or
imaginary intoxication.

It is but natural to conclude, that the bard whose
Muse could feel itself so grandly at ease in the composition of Bacchanalian **ballads**, should not feel equally
comfortable under the ministry of the severe Calvinists,
who, as **we have seen above,** then dominated in the
Scottish pulpits of the south-west of Scotland. The
unkindly and unhuman denunciations which issued from
the stern dogmatism and frosty sympathies of these
grim doctors, were a constant thorn in the side of the
genial human-hearted poet ; and he **had** not been long
in Ellisland before an occasion arose which **moved him**

to fling a bomb into the camp of the orthodox, if not
quite so classical in form, no less galling in effect, than
the "Holy Fair" and "Holy Willie's Prayer;" with
this difference, however, that while the Mossgiel artil-
lery was directed against the popular abuse of a great
religious ceremonial, "The Kirk's Alarm" was a direct
march into the domain of controversial theology. One
of the ministers of Ayr, by name M'Gill, had published
some theological works which, to the sharp noses of the
heresy-hunters of those days, seemed to give clear scent
of Socinian or Unitarian principles. A cry of heresy
was raised, such as we have seen again and again stir
the religious heart of Scotland ; and the unhappy man
whose genius for independent thinking had brought him
into an antagonistic position to the Church of which he
was an office-bearer, was dragged from Church court to
Church court, and his teaching formally condemned,—
a condemnation which did not, in his case, blossom into
a bright crown of martyrdom, but faded away somewhat
ingloriously into explanation and compromise. To Burns
the individual points at issue were of little consequence ;
in all likelihood he had never read the books against
which the bann of the Church was cast; but he knew
that the heretic belonged to the Moderate party, of
which he had formerly been the champion, and he felt
firmly that that party, whatever their defects might be,
were the party of common-sense and common humanity,
which to him were dear beyond all doctrines, whether
orthodox or heterodox. So he entered with his usual
fearless alacrity into the fray, and sent forth "The Kirk's
Alarm," in which the leading members of the orthodox
party were satirised individually with the most supreme

contempt, and the most uncomplimentary phrases. The personality, which was the sting of the satire at the time, now that the combatants are long gone from the scene, acts as a hindrance to the full enjoyment of the poem ; but it remains, like "The Holy Fair," as a significant feature in the history of a Church, which up to the present day has made itself equally notable for the virtue of popular efficiency and the vice of theological jealousy.

" Orthodox, orthodox, wha believe in John Knox,
    Let me sound an alarm to your conscience ;
There's a heretic blast has been blawn in the wast,
    That what is no sense must be nonsense.

Dr Mac, Dr Mac, you should stretch on a rack,
    To strike evil doers wi' terror ;
To join faith and sense upon any pretence,
    Is heretic, damnable error.

D'rymple mild, D'rymple mild, tho' your heart's like a child,
    And your life like the new driven snaw,
Yet that winna save ye, auld Satan must have ye,
    For preaching that three's ane an' twa.

Daddy Auld, Daddy Auld, there's a tod in the fauld,
    A tod meikle waur than the clerk ;
Tho' ye can do little skaith, ye'll be in at the death,
    And if ye canna bite ye may bark.

Calvin's sons, Calvin's sons, seize your spiritual guns,
    Ammunition you never can need ;
Your hearts are the stuff will be powder enough,
    And your skulls are a storehouse o' lead."

The poet, with his eager human sympathies, sent some flying shots also into the political strife of the hour ; but as political matters touched him only incidentally, and did not flow like his religious convictions from the inner fountain of his moral nature, we may let them pass.[1]

The student of Burns who casts his eye over these political and theological rhymes, will see that they will not take their place among the classical achievements of the Scottish Muse which secure to her an honoured position along with her divine sisters on the Greek Parnassus ; they are rather to be taken as testimonies to the strong pulsing vitality of the writer, and are in effect rather clever controversial pamphlets than gems of the purest poetical distillation. But Burns had too lofty a literary ambition to feel satisfied with brilliant occasional skits of this description. He wrote, no doubt, as he was wont to say, " for fun ;" but his fun was of the catholic description which can play with a kitten or wheel with an eagle, equally at home. Ellisland, among not a few other lyrical gems which appeared in the early numbers of Johnston's " Musical Museum,"[2] had the honour of giving birth to two poems which stand second to none in the witness of the general human heart, and which are as remarkable for diversity in their character as for perfection in their form. We mean " Tam o' Shanter " and " Highland Mary." In the year 1790 the distinguished English antiquary, Captain Francis Grose, paid a visit to

---

[1] In Chambers, III., 89 and 127, the reader will find all that is notable in the poetical issues of the poet's electioneering sympathies, viz., two poems, " The Five Carlines,"—*i.e.*, the five burghs, Dumfries, Annan, Kirkcudbright, Sanquhar, and Lochmaben,—and a poetical epistle to Mr Graham of Fintry.

[2] Of this publication there are six volumes, extending from 1787 to 1803.

Scotland, and was entertained with his usual hospitality
by Captain Riddell. Here, of course, he was introduced
to the farmer of Ellisland ; and in their convivial qualities
and good-humour the poet and the antiquarian straight-
way recognised one another as brothers. In the course
of their confabulations Burns took the opportunity of
suggesting to the archæologist that there was a fine old
ruined church at Alloway, on the banks of the Doon,
a region to which the poet owed his birth, and where his
father had found a burial ground ; and which was, moreover, the traditional scene of strange witch and warlock
stories, than which few things could be more interesting
to a genial antiquary like Grose. The Captain at once
took the hint, and promised to give special prominence
to Alloway Kirk in his book, if Burns would furnish a
witch story to give a rich seasoning to the pudding. The
poet's love of frolic, and his deep-rooted patriotism, at
once jumped to the proposal. A bargain was made, and
the Muse of Coila, in one of her most fervid moments,
visited the bard one forenoon as he was pacing up and
down his favourite walk on the banks of the Nith, and
before evening the great masterpiece of Scottish character, Scottish humour, Scottish witch-lore, and Scottish
imagination, "Tam o' Shanter," was produced at full
length, glowing from the anvil. Besides the glory of
having accidentally been the cause of the production of
this excellent witch-idyll, the Middlesex antiquary had
the good fortune to elicit from the poet a personal description of himself, which will make him more immortal
than all his antiquarian works put together :—

> " Hear, Land o' Cakes, and brither Scots,
> Frae Maidenkirk to Johnny Groat's ;

If there's a hole in a' your coats,
　　　　I rede you tent it ;
A chield's amang you, taking notes,
　　　　And, faith, he'll prent it.

If in your bounds ye chance to light
Upon a fine fat fodgel wight,
O' stature short, but genius bright,
　　　　That's he, mark weel,—
And wow ! he has an unco slight
　　　　O' caulk and keel." [1]

The other poem, " Highland Mary," in the author's best
style of chaste tenderness, was produced in the same
scene of so many thoughtful musings, as the poet, on
the birthday of one of his chastest loves, was looking
devoutly up to the lessening ray of the evening star,—a
moment equally favourable for the breathings of a devout
heart, and the memories of a chaste affection. He who
would know Burns at his best, must think on Highland
Mary there.

Towards the end of the year 1791, the fourth act of
Robert Burns's chequered and shifting life-drama came
not altogether pleasantly to a close. The farming business had not succeeded ; whether from the originally
exhausted condition of the soil, which is averred, only,
or from that combined with other causes, it is difficult
to say. Anything like neglect of his business, or general
mismanagement by the tenant of Ellisland, is not hinted.
One thing, however, seems quite certain, he had from
the beginning, as we have seen, a hankering after an

---

[1] Of the " fine fat fodgel wight," we have a characteristic portrait
in "The Land of Burns," Vol. II., p. 28.

appointment in the excise; and not long after his full possession of the new farm at Ellisland, we find him formally equipped as an exciseman or gauger, with an income of some £50 a year. This business, which would only remove him occasionally to short distances from his home, the poet imagined could be managed conjointly with the farm to the damage of neither, and with the great comfort of the sure possession of the very tangible aid of £50 per annum. But he was perhaps a little out of his reckoning here. It is always more difficult to ride on two horses than on one; "to be a whole man to one thing at one time," is Lord Thurloe's well-known advice to all who hope to do any substantial work in the world; and in the case of a poet-farmer, the exclusive devotion to minute matters of agricultural economy which a farm might demand, was liable to be interrupted by not always well-timed visitations of the Muse. Besides this, the exciseman was not long in finding that the conscientious performance of his fiscal duties necessitated his not unfrequently taking long rides, which fatigued him sorely, and sometimes laid him on his back from pure weariness and nervous exhaustion. Anyhow, at the expiry of the three years, the poet had made up his mind that the farming business, so far from being a gain, had been the means of sinking in utter loss the whole residue of his profits from the Edinburgh edition of his poems. He therefore resolved to accept the situation of excise officer for the district of Dumfries, with a salary of £70 a year, and the expectation of promotion to a supervisorship with £200 in a few years; and on this basis of a small independence for the present, and a fair outlook for the future, on the 19th November 1791 he got himself formally disengaged from his farming contract with the laird of Dalswinton, and transferred himself with his wife and family to a new sphere of action in Dumfries.

DUMFRIES.

"There was Maggie by the banks o' Nith,
A dame wi' pride eneugh."
                    —*The Five Carlines.*

THERE have been, **and there** still may be, **a class of** persons ready to cast sore blame **on the** people of Edinburgh for their treatment of our great national poet,— feasting him and lionising him in every possible way, and then, when their eyes were sated with the lust of gazing at the strange phenomenon of a Scottish **Pindar**, sending him to drag out a degraded existence **as a gauger of ardent spirits** in a small provincial town. Nothing could **be a greater** mistake. The citizens of Edinburgh had done more for him **in a pecuniary, a literary, and a social way, than he** could **have reasonably** anticipated; and when, after failing for a second time in his natural occupation as **a** farmer, he reverted to a favourite old idea of making his living as an officer in the Excise, it is hard to see what occupation could have suited **him better. In** this business he had plenty of open air, free converse with Nature, and large opportunity of meeting with all classes **of** men presenting those bold types of natural character always more dear to poets and painters than the smooth aspects of social respectability and conventional propriety. Besides, Burns, by the noble launch given him by his Edinburgh patrons, and by the power of his own masculine intellect and the fascination of his society, at Dumfries, as at Ellisland, and wherever he might show himself, was received on perfectly equal terms by the best society of the country ; and it was altogether his own fault if he did not prove worthy of the kindness they were ready to lavish on him. As to his salary, though small, according to our present standard, it was quite large enough to enable him and his Jean to live comfortably and cleanly in a small house ; and to a man who always expressed the greatest contempt for money and what money could buy, and who, no doubt, was full of the proud consciousness of the old song which says " My mind to me a kingdom is," this small house in a small street of a small town in the South Highlands was as good as a palace. His small income was sure, and not liable to the element of uncertainty which belongs not only to farming but to many other sources of subsistence, —a consideration of the utmost importance to the race of poets, who will not have their enjoyment in the happy inspirations of the hour interrupted by anxieties about the investment of money, or the rise and fall of prices in the market. Add to all this, that our poet, though without any direct ministerial patronage, had so many influential friends, and was looked upon by so many as an honour to his country, that advancement to some higher and more lucrative post was to be looked for in due course. On the whole, to a sober eye, this last act of his life-drama, when the curtain rose, looked anything but tragical. Nevertheless, the good here, as in other cases,

was not without its accompanying evil. Dumfries was a
small provincial **town.** **Small** provincial towns have
always been—in Scotland certainly—the focus to which
motley groups of idle or half-idle persons incline to
gravitate, and indulge in those convivialities where good
fellowship too easily passes into bad company. The
age, moreover, was eminently a convivial age, and Burns
predominantly a convivial man. So situated, he required
to put on the triple mail of that piety in which he had been
brought **up by** his excellent father, **and whose** praises
he had **so** feelingly sung in " The Cottar's Saturday
Night ; " **for** the temptations **were great, and he, as a**
strong **swimmer, was not the** man to keep himself in shallow water for fear of being sucked into the whirl of some
adjacent Maelstrom, but was tempted, and fell,—once **it**
may be, and again, and again, and again, as, with that noble
openness so characteristic of his nature, he has taken
care to inform us. Witness this note to his old Edinburgh friend Robert Ainslie, dated **November 1791** :—

" MY DEAR AINSLIE,—Can you minister to a mind diseased ?
Can you, amid the horrors of penitence, regret, remorse, head-ache,
nausea, and all the rest of the . . . hounds of hell, that beset
a poor wretch, who has been guilty of the sin of drunkenness—can
you speak peace to a troubled soul ?

" *Misérable perdu* that I am, I have tried every thing that used
to amuse me, but in vain ; here must I sit a monument of the vengeance laid up in store for the wicked, slowly counting every click
of the clock as it slowly—slowly numbers over these lazy scoundrels
of hours, who, d——n them ! are ranked up before me, every one
at his neighbour's backside, and every one with a burden of anguish
on his back, to pour on my devoted head,—and there is none to pity
me. My wife scolds me ! my business torments me, and my sins come

I

staring me in the face, every one telling a more bitter tale than his fellow." [1]

Sad! sad! But ought not, as in the case of King David, the deep sincerity of the sorrow be taken as no small compensation for the shamefulness of the sin? Burns was not a drunkard,—not a man that drank habitually for the mere gratification of an animal craving, or the drowning of a solitary sorrow,—but he drank only as the carnal seasoning of a rampant intellectuality, which made moderation appear folly, and intoxication a delight. Later on, in December 1792, a letter to his oldest and best female friend, Mrs Dunlop, reveals the state of the case with regard to his Dumfries drinking, in the following interesting words :—

"You must not think, as you seem to insinuate, that in my way of life I want exercise; of that I have enough, but occasional hard drinking is the devil to me. Against this I have again and again bent my resolution, and have greatly succeeded. Taverns I have totally abandoned—it is the private parties in the family way among the hard-drinking gentlemen of the county that do me the mischief; but even this I have more than half given over."

We pass from these sad confessions to a more genial subject in the poet's special occupation as the Laureate of Love, in the praises of fair women. And the first name that meets us here is the Clarinda of his last Edinburgh rapture. In the month of February 1792, Mrs M'Lehose, after due consideration of a proposal of reunion on the part of her husband, set sail from Leith to join him in Jamaica; but she had not been long there before, partly

[1] Paterson, VI. 2.

from the continued unkindly conduct of her worthless
mate, partly from the evil effects of the climate on her
constitution, she was obliged to return to Edinburgh,
where she lived and died at a ripe old age, beloved and
respected by all who knew her. To us she is interesting
now only as having given occasion by her voyage to two
of the most beautiful of the poet's love-songs, "Ae fond
kiss and then we sever," and "My Nannie's awa'." Even
to the latest hour of his Dumfries life the poet, when
called upon at convivial meetings to give the toast of a
married lady, regularly proposed Mrs Mac; and if the
toast on the roll was a fair lady, or an Arcadian shep-
herdess, he gave the toast of Clarinda, in both cases
keeping the full name of the object of his worship in-
violate from the rude stare of a promiscuous company.
But Burns was not a man to let his imagination pasture
vaguely on distant beauties, however charming. Four
new Venuses appear on the lyrical stage at Dumfries,—
Bonnie Lesley, Chloris, Lucy Oswald, and Mrs Riddell
of Woodley Park. Bonnie Lesley, the heroine of the
song containing the well-known verse,—

> " The Deil he could na scaith thee,
>   Or aught that wad belang thee ;
> He'd look into thy bonnie face,
>   And say, ' I canna wrang thee !' "

was a Miss Lesley Baillie, an Ayrshire lady, who visited
Burns in the month of August 1792, and excited in his
susceptible soul the following beautiful outburst of impassioned admiration :—

" To Mrs DUNLOP.

" Do you know that I am almost in love with an acquaintance of yours?—Almost! said I—I am in love, souse! over head and ears, deep as the most unfathomable abyss of the boundless ocean; but the word Love, owing to the *intermingledoms* of the good and the bad, the pure and the impure, in this world, being rather an equivocal term of expressing one's sentiments and sensations, I must do justice to the sacred purity of my attachment. Know then, that the heart-struck awe; the distant humble approach; the delight we should have in gazing upon and listening to a Messenger of Heaven, appearing in all the unspotted purity of his celestial home, among the coarse, polluted, far inferior sons of men, to deliver to them tidings that make their hearts swim in joy, and their imaginations soar in transport,—such, so delighting, and so pure, were the emotions of my soul on meeting the other day with Miss Lesley Baillie, your neighbour at Mayfield." [1]

Those who do not understand what Platonic love means, may get a better notion of it from this language of our ploughman bard than from all the dialogues of the great Athenian idealist. The real name of the lovely young woman to whom he attached the Greek name of Chloris, from her light flaxen hair ($\chi\lambda\omega\rho\iota\delta\kappa o\mu o\varsigma$), was Jean Lorimer, the daughter of a farmer who lived at Kemmis Hall, on the banks of the Nith, about two miles below Ellisland, a blonde young girl of fine features and great charm of manners, who had an unfortunate history. When visiting the Johnstons at Dumcrieff, near Moffat, she had the misfortune to meet with a Cumberland gentleman named Whelpdale, who fell in love with her, and plied her vehemently with an amorous suit, protesting that, if she did not take pity on him, he would in a moment of desperation be tempted to lay violent hands on himself. To these foolish ravings the inexperienced lassie was simple enough to give ear; started with

[1] Paterson, VI. 25.

her brave protester to Gretna Green, and returned to
Moffat his wedded wife. But the wifehood, as is apt to
be the case with damsels of such easy-hearted credulity,
was of short duration; after a month or two she discovered that the man who had sworn to be her protector
through life, had only prevailed to rob her of her
character. By loose living, or bad management, he got
into debt; and, to escape the just demands of the law,
decamped into his native nest besouth the Solway;
and, seeking safety only for himself, left the poor girl to
find shelter in her father's home, and sympathy from his
kindly neighbours. Among these the most prominen
and the most warm-hearted was Robert Burns. He was
indeed specially missioned by Providence to console an
injured young woman under such circumstances; for,
besides the sweet charm of her misfortuned beauty, he
could not but be conscious, that, if never in a heartless,
more than once in a thoughtless way he had himself
been the cause of not a little misery to the objects of
his impassioned admiration. He accordingly gave full
swing to the dictates of his nature, in making this
beautiful young woman serve as his model in a series of
some dozen love songs composed in the year 1794. As
a moral preacher, he comforts her for the loss of the
young zest of life in early love, by the greater value she
would now be led to set on the higher pleasures of the
intellectual and moral nature :—

> " Since life's gay times must charm no more,
>   Still much is left behind ;
> Still nobler wealth hast thou in store,
>   The comforts of the mind.

Thine is the self-approving glow
On conscious honour's part,
And dearest gift of Heaven below
Thy friendship's truest heart."

But as the preacher's tone was not natural to him, he speedily falls into the attitude of a lover, who, had circumstances permitted, would have been happy to show her how an ardent admirer might turn into a faithful husband. The following is one of the most popular of his songs to Chloris :—

CHORUS.

" Lassie wi' the lint-white locks,
Bonnie lassie, artless lassie,
Wilt thou wi' me tent the flocks,
Wilt thou be my dearie O ?

Now Nature cleeds the flowery lea,
And a' is young and sweet like thee ;
O wilt thou share its joys wi' me,
And say thou'lt be my dearie O ?
Lassie wi', &c.

And when the welcome summer shower
Has cheer'd ilk drooping little flower,
We'll to the breathing woodbine bower,
At sultry noon, my dearie O ?
Lassie wi', &c.

When Cynthia lights, wi' silver ray,
The weary shearer's hameward way ;
Thro' yellow waving fields we'll stray,
And talk o' love, my dearie O ?
Lassie wi', &c.

And when the howling wintry blast
Disturbs my lassie's midnight rest ;
Enclaspèd to my faithfu' breast,
    I'll comfort thee, my dearie O ?

Lassie wi' the lint-white locks,
    Bonnie lassie, artless lassie,
Wilt thou wi' me tent the flocks,
    Wilt thou be my dearie O ? "

The object of this Platonic admiration, in consequence of her father's failure in the farming business, after passing through various vicissitudes of life, found a situation as housekeeper to a gentleman in Newington, Edinburgh, in whose service she died in the year 1831, and found a last resting-place in the cemetery of the district. A third fair lady from whom he drew amatory inspiration in Dumfries was Mrs Lucy Oswald, of Auchencruive in Ayrshire, by birth a Miss Johnston of Hilton. In her honour the poet wrote the song beginning :—

" Oh, wat ye wha's in yon toun,
    Ye see the evening sun upon,
The fairest dame in yon toun
    The evening sun is shining on."

A fourth lady who figures on the scene of his Dumfriesshire life is Mrs Riddell of Woodley Park, a few miles to the south of Dumfries, whose husband was brother to the Captain Riddell of whose chivalry in the matter of the Scandinavian whistle we took note in our last chapter. This lady, like Clarinda, was a poetess and an authoress, and, from her sympathy with poetical genius, was ready to second her husband in welcoming

Burns to a frequent seat at his hospitable board; and
no doubt many "nights and suppers of the gods" they
had there, in the liberal interchange of flashing wit,
genial good humour, and sportive intelligence. But
there were dangers here, of which the poet, from previous
experience, should have been aware; there were not only
an ample flow of intelligent talk and floods of roaring good
humour, but there was drinking, not shallow, and not at
all given to recognise the point where the Aristotelian
mean takes its station between too little and too much;
and so it chanced that, when the gentlemen in the
spring-tide of heated blood went up to join the ladies
in the drawing-room, the bard, with that self-confidence
which was seldom absent from him, marched straight up
to the beautiful hostess, and inflicted on her lips, before
all the company, a bouncing smack. The consequences
were such as might have been expected. Not even
the indulgence shown to the genius of the greatest lyric
poet of the age, or the license of society in those days,
could excuse such a gross impropriety. The poet's
doom was sealed, not only with Mrs Riddell, but with
the respectable society of the county of Dumfries, from
that moment. He might be a genius, but he certainly
was not a gentleman. Next morning he indited to the
lady the following epistle, which may stand here without
comment, as a voice of ominous warning to all persons
who may be tempted, on any occasion, in Shakespeare's
phrase, "to put a thief into their mouth to steal away
their brains":—

"MADAM,—I dare say this is the first epistle you ever received
from the nether world. I write you from the regions of Hell,
amid the horrors of the damned. The time and manner of my

leaving your earth I do not exactly know ; as I took my departure in the heat of a fever of intoxication contracted at your too hospitable mansion ; but on my arrival here, I was fairly tried and sentenced to endure the purgatorial tortures of this infernal confine, for the space of ninety-nine years, eleven months, and twenty-nine days ; and all on account of the impropriety of my conduct yester-night under your roof. Here am I, laid on a bed of pitiless furze, with my aching head reclining on a pillow of ever-piercing thorns, while an infernal tormentor, wrinkled, and old, and cruel,—his name, I think, is *Recollection*,—with a whip of scorpions, forbids peace or rest to approach me, and keeps anguish eternally awake. Still, madam, if I could in any measure be reinstated in the good opinion of the fair circle whom my conduct last night so much injured, I think it would be an alleviation to my torments. For this reason I trouble you with this letter. To the men of the company I make no apology.—Your husband, who insisted on me drinking more than I chose, has no right to blame me ; and the other gentlemen were partakers of my guilt. But to you, madam, I have much to apologise. Your good opinion I value as one of the greatest acquisitions I had made on earth, and I was truly a beast to forfeit it. There was a Miss I—— too, a woman of fine sense, gentle and unassuming manners,—do make, on my part, a miserable wretch's best apology to her. A Mrs G——, a charming woman, did me the honour to be prejudiced in my favour ; this makes me hope that I have not outraged her beyond all forgiveness.—To all the other ladies please present my humblest contrition for my conduct, and my petition for their gracious pardon. O all ye powers of decency and decorum ! whisper to them that errors, though great, were involuntary—that an intoxicated man is the vilest of beasts—that it was not in my nature to be brutal to any one—that to be rude to a woman, when in my senses, was impossible with me—but— regret ! remorse ! shame ! ye three hell hounds that ever dog my steps and bay at my heels, spare me, spare me ! Forgive the offence, and pity the perdition of, madam, your humble slave.

R. B."[1]

---

[1] Paterson, VI. 115.

But the offence was not forgiven, could not be forgiven. The man who had sinned in this fashion once, and repented, might do so again, nothing the better for his repentance. Such a sinner required a severe lesson, and it was good for him that he should receive it with all severity.

The intelligent reader will scarcely fail to take note here of those fits of despondency and misery to which Burns was subject, and from which again and again in his correspondence he sends forth a heart-rending cry. No doubt a certain constitutional melancholy he brought with him into the world, as the natural ebb from the tremendous flow of his emotional nature; but the principal cause of those tortures of the damned which he experienced, was, to use his own language in the snatches of French which he was fond of using, *moi même*. Of the lamentable inconsistency of character, which led him at one moment to fling himself into the hands of the devil, and at another to betake himself to the Father of all good for healing and consolation, the literature of biography does not perhaps contain a more striking example than stands forth in the following epistle :—

"TO MR CUNNINGHAM.

"*25th February* 1794.

"Canst thou minister to a mind diseased? Canst thou speak peace and rest to a soul tossed on a sea of troubles, without one friendly star to guide her course, and dreading that the next surge may overwhelm her? Canst thou give to a frame, tremblingly alive to the tortures of suspense, the stability and hardihood of the rock that braves the blast? If thou canst not do the least of these, why wouldst thou disturb me in my miseries, with thy inquiries after me?

. . . .

For these two months I have not been able to lift a pen. My constitution and frame were, *ab origine*, blasted with deep incurable taint of hypochondria, which poisons my existence. Of late a number of domestic vexations, and some pecuniary share in the ruin of these d——d times; losses which, though trifling, were yet what I could ill bear, have so irritated me that my feelings at times could only be envied by a reprobate spirit listening to the sentence that dooms it to perdition.

"Are you deep in the language of consolation? I have exhausted in reflection every topic of comfort. *A heart at ease* would have been charmed with my sentiments and reasonings; but as to myself, I was like Judas Iscariot preaching the gospel; he might melt and mould the hearts of those around him, but his own kept its native incorrigibility.

"Still there are two great pillars that bear us up, amid the wreck of misfortune and misery. The ONE is composed of the different modifications of a certain noble, stubborn something in man, known by the names of courage, fortitude, magnanimity. The OTHER is made up of those feelings and sentiments, which, however the sceptic may deny them, or the enthusiast disfigure them, are yet, I am convinced, original and component parts of the human soul; those *senses of the mind*, if I may be allowed the expression, which connect us with, and link us to, those awful obscure realities—an all-powerful and equally beneficent God; and a world to come, beyond death and the grave. The first gives the nerve of combat, while a ray of hope beams on the field;—the last pours the balm of comfort into the wounds which time can never cure.

"I do not remember, my dear Cunningham, that you and I ever talked on the subject of religion at all. I know some who laugh at it, as the trick of the crafty FEW, to lead the undiscerning many; or at most as an uncertain obscurity, which mankind can never know any thing of, and with which they are fools if they give themselves much to do. Nor would I quarrel with a man for irreligion, any more than I would for his want of a musical ear. I would regret that he was shut out from what, to me and to others, were such superlative sources of enjoyment. It is in this point of view, and for this reason, that I will deeply imbue the mind of every child of mine with religion. If my son should happen to be a man of feeling, sentiment, and taste, I shall thus add largely to his enjoyments.   Let me flatter myself that this sweet little fellow who is just now running about my desk, will be a man of melting, ardent, glowing heart ; and an imagination, delighted with the painter, and rapt with the poet.   Let me figure him, wandering out in a sweet evening, to inhale the balmy gales and enjoy the growing luxuriance of the spring ; himself the while in the blooming youth of life.   He looks abroad on all nature, and through nature, up to nature's God.   His soul, by swift, delighting degrees, is wrapt above this sublunary sphere, until he can be silent no longer, and bursts out into the glorious enthusiasm of Thomson,—

> ' These, as they change, Almighty Father, these
> Are but the varied God.—The rolling year
> Is full of thee.'

And so on, in all the spirit and ardour of that charming hymn.

"These are no ideal pleasures ; they are real delights, and I ask what of the delights among the sons of men are superior, not to say, equal to them?   And they have this precious, vast addition, that conscious virtue stamps them for her own, and lays hold on them to bring herself into the presence of a witnessing, judging, and approving God."[1]

In addition to these mental tortures, there seems little doubt that, though in the prime of life, the poet was now beginning, in the shape of bodily weakness, to suffer for the excesses of his youthful career.   On the 25th June of this same year he writes from Castle-Douglas to Mrs Dunlop :—" I am afraid I am about to suffer for the follies of my youth.   My medical friends threaten me with a flying gout, but I trust they are mistaken."

So much for the sad side of the picture.   But we must not allow the bright sun of lyrical gladness that we contemplate in Burns to be overshadowed by these clouds

---

[1] Paterson, VI. 118.

of misery. They were clouds indeed, awfully black at
times, but they were passing. It is of the very nature of
lyrical genius to be swayed by the passion of the moment,
and to change from storm to sunshine with an emotional
subtlety which only song-writers know. All the while
that the mind of the poet was tossed with the bitter conflicts which these, and not a few other letters, reveal, he
was doing an amount of regular work, both as a literary
man and a man of business, that would have done credit
to the most orderly proser that ever earned an honest
penny by a hard day's work. Before coming to Dumfries he had, as we have seen, sent his lyrical effusions in
considerable numbers to Johnston's "Musical Museum";
but shortly after his settlement in the town, we find him
taken in tow and led forth gallantly into a great sea of
song, by an Edinburgh gentleman, of higher pretensions.
This was Mr George Thomson, holding the respectable
position of clerk in the office of the Board of Trustees
for the Encouragement of Manufactures in Scotland;
and being a person wise to pluck the bloom of all
rational pleasure, and especially, as a Scot, keen to enjoy
the rich heritage of popular music, which is Scotland's
chiefest boast, he determined to devote his leisure hours,
in conjunction with a company of musical amateurs, to the
publishing of a collection of Scottish songs, with more
refinement of taste and in greater elegance of form than
had hitherto been current. In this patriotic work he
could find no associate in the whole of Scotland who
could in any degree be compared to Burns. He accordingly wrote to the bard as early as September 1792, with
the programme of his scheme, requesting his aid in
the selection of the old songs and the contribution of

new ones; and the answer came forthwith, as was natural to expect, in the most hearty style of effective co-operation. Burns would do any amount of work for the Scottish Muse, on three conditions,—first, that he should not be goaded to forced work, "only don't hurry me; *De'il tak' the hindmost* is by no means the *cri de guerre* of my Muse." Then, again, he must not be expected to write English verses; for "whether in the simplicity of the ballad, or the pathos of the song, I can hope to please myself only in being allowed at least a sprinkling of our native tongue." And the third condition was, that he would take no pay for his work; for "in the honest enthusiasm with which I embark in the undertaking, to talk of money, wages, fee, hire, and such like, would be downright prostitution of soul." To the admirable manner in which he fulfilled the promise made, the pages of Mr Thomson's work bear the most noble testimony. Instead of some twenty or twenty-five songs, which was the utmost that the editor expected to receive from the poet, Burns supplied him with at least a hundred; and the correspondence, carried on during a course of four years, between the two parties, is rich in materials of which the importance, in any estimate of the history and genius of Scottish song, can scarcely be overrated.[1]

Let us now inquire how the exciseman gets on with the daily routine of his revenue prose, for no life can be all poetry any more than milk can be all cream, or a flower all blossom. Of the general course of his life in Dumfries, Mr Chambers has given an admirable sum-

---

[1] Mr Thomson's work, of which I possess a copy, was published in three parts, bearing date 1801-2, under the title of "Select Collection of Original Scottish Airs."

mary, which we cannot do better than transfer wholesale to our pages :—

"He has three small apartments, each with a window to the street, besides, perhaps, a small kitchen in the rear. The small central room, about the size of a bed-closet, is the only place in which he can seclude himself for study. On the ground-floor immediately underneath, his friend John Lyme has his office for the distribution of stamps. Overhead is an honest blacksmith called George Haugh, whom Burns treats on a familiar footing as a neighbour. On the opposite side of the street is the poet's landlord, Captain Hamilton, a gentleman of fortune and worth, who admires Burns, and often asks him to a family Sunday dinner. The Nith rolls within a hundred yards, but it is not here a shining, pebbly stream, as at Ellisland, with green, broomy banks, but a sluggish tidal river, admitting of small craft from Cumberland and Liverpool. It was professionally a busy time with Burns, so much so that one would have thought he had little time for dissipation. Nevertheless, he did not escape the snare.

"Dumfries was then a great stage on the road from England to the north of Ireland. The Caledonian Hunt occasionally honoured it with their meetings, and the county gentlemen were necessarily often within its walls. Its hotels were consequently well frequented, and when a party of strangers found themselves assembled there, with no other means of passing an evening, they were very apt to make an effort to obtain the company of Burns, the brilliant intellectual prodigy of whom fame spoke so loudly. Now, it certainly was a most unreasonable thing for such persons to expect that they were to draw Burns away from his humble home and his wife and little ones, to bestow his time, strength, and spirits merely for the amusement of a set of people whom he probably never saw before, and was never to see again. Equally absurd was it for Burns to yield to such invitations, and render himself up a voluntarily enslaved Samson to make sport for such a set of Philistines. Yet so it is, that gentlemen, or what were called such in those days, would send messages for Burns, bidding him come to the 'King's Arms,' the 'George,' or the 'Globe,' as it might be, and there drink with them. And equally true it is, though most lamentable, that Burns did not

feel called upon by any principle, either of respect to himself, or
regard for his gentle wife and innocent children, to reject these
unworthy invitations. Sure was he to answer on the spur of the
moment in some such good-humoured terms as these :—

> ' The King's most humble servant, I
> Can scarcely spare a minute ;
> But I'll be with you by-and-by,
> Or else the Devil's in it.'

And sure was he in time to make his appearance before the strangers,
meditating at first, of course, only a social hour, but certain to be
detained hour after hour, till perhaps the crow had given his first,
if not his second, accusing crow.

"According to all accounts, it was not a love of debauchery for
its own sake that rendered Burns the victim of this system. Nor
can we doubt that he felt himself in error in giving way to such
temptations. Why, then, could he not resist them? Need we
answer, that the first grand cause was his social, fervent temperament, his delight in that ideal abnegation of the common selfish
policy of the world which arises amongst boon-companions over the
bowl? He could not but know the hollowness of convivial friendship, yet he could not resist the pleasing deceit. Burns, moreover,
though a pattern of modesty amongst poets, was not by any means
so insensible to flattery as his more ardent admirers would in
general represent him. He would have been more than mortal if
he had been beyond all sensibility to distinction on account of his
extraordinary intellect. Notwithstanding, then, his great pride,
and the powerful self-assertion which he had sometimes shown, he
certainly felt no small pleasure in being so signalised by these
gentlemen-strangers, and in seeing himself set up amongst them as
a luminary. It was the ready compensation for that equality with
common functionaries, and that condemnation to a constant contact
with the vulgar, in which his professional fate condemned him to
spend the most of his time. A vigorous will might have saved him
from falling under this influence, but here again our poet was sadly
deficient. And yet he was occasionally sensible that his course
was a wrong one. Of this there is proof in a very interesting anec-

dote, preserved by the family of his neighbour, George Haugh. One summer morning this worthy citizen had risen somewhat earlier than usual to work. Burns soon after came up to his shop-door, on his way home from a debauch in the 'King's Arms.' The poet, though excited by the liquor he had drunk, addressed his neighbour in a sufficiently collected manner. 'Oh, George,' said he, 'you are a happy man. You have risen from a refreshing sleep, and left a kind wife and children, while I am returning a self-condemned wretch to mine.' And yet he would go sinning on." [1]

The reader has here the complete Burns before him as he lived and moved from day to day in the pleasant little provincial town,—a picture of Scottish life as true as the best Wilkie, or Harvey, or John Faed ever painted. There is no sentimental mist here to conceal, nor sacrosanct indignation to disturb the picture. The excise business, from all that we can learn, if not sternly was faithfully performed ; and it was not on business, but, as we shall presently see, on political grounds, that opposition was made from some quarters to his professional advancement. The usual routine of his excise work received a double variation on one notable occasion, in the shape of a sword-in-hand expedition and a song. We owe to Mr Lockhart a well-substantiated account of this adventure. On the 27th February 1792 a suspicious-looking brig was discovered in the Solway Firth, engaged, as it turned out, in a contraband traffic then carried on extensively on the coasts of Galloway and Ayrshire. When the ship got into shallow water she showed a stout front, and Burns, who was on guard on the spot, stood waiting till a body of dragoons should arrive from Dumfries sufficient to

[1] Chambers, III. 266.

enable him to proceed to active measures against the
armed smugglers. When the dragoons arrived, Burns,
without delay, eager in action as he was in word, put
himself at their head, waded sword in hand to the brig,
and was the first to board her. The crew soon found
that they had a man of nerve and purpose to deal with,
and, though superior in numbers to the assailing force,
were soon obliged to yield. The vessel was condemned,
and with all her arms and ammunition sold next day at
Dumfries. This was a stroke of business which did
good service for Burns with the public and with the
patrons of the Excise; but such an event could not
happen to a man like Burns without a stroke of poetry
being added. The poetry came, not in the heroic, but
in the humorous style,—not to the tune of the Iliad, but
to the "Battle of the frogs and mice." Before the dragoons
arrived, and when the guard on the shore was becoming
a little impatient at the delay, Burns suddenly broke out
into some harsh language against his personal friend and
brother-exciseman, named Lewars, who had been sent to
speed the dragoons on their mission, and seemed to
linger on the road. One of the guard, taking up the
keynote of his displeasure, told him jeeringly, as he could
not add spurs to the legs of his friend, the best thing
he could do was to put him in the pillory with a song.
So hinted, so achieved. With a few steps along the
weeds and shingles of the shallow shore, the poet shook
out from his wallet the well-known song "The Exciseman:"—

> " The deil cam' fiddling through the toun
> And danced awa' wi' the Exciseman,

And ilka wife cries—'Auld Mahoun,
  I wish you luck o' the prize, man !'
    The deil's **awa'**, the deil's awa',
      The deil's awa' wi' the Exciseman ;
    He's danc'd awa,' he's danc'd **awa'**,
      He's danc'd awa' wi' the Exciseman !

We'll mak' our maut, we'll brew our drink,
  We'll dance, and sing, and rejoice, man ;
And mony braw thanks to the meikle black deil
  That danc'd awa' wi' the Exciseman !
    The deil's awa', the deil's awa',
      The deil's awa' **wi'** the Exciseman ;
    He's danc'd awa,' he's danc'd awa',
      He's danc'd awa' wi' the Exciseman !

There's threesome reels, there's foursome reels,
  There's hornpipes and strathspeys, **man ;**
But the ae best dance e'er came to the land,
  Was—the deil's awa' wi' the Exciseman !
    The deil's awa,' the deil's awa',
      The deil's awa' wi' the Exciseman ;
    He's danc'd awa', he's danc'd **awa'**,
      He's danc'd awa' wi' the Exciseman ! "

Passing from professional duty to public life, we shall
not be surprised **to learn that Burns, who** was no moonish
dreamer, but **a** poet **with** backbone and flesh and blood,
and every inch a man, **took** his fair share in the political
conflicts **of** that excited **time ; and,** as formerly **in Ayr-**
shire, entered formally into the lists as political pamph-
leteer in rhyme. Of course, as was to be expected from
a man in **his** position, and with his temperament, he
was a Liberal, and opposed to the Tory government
that set its stamp of reprobation on the **revolutionary**
Liberalism that broke out at **Paris in 1789.** The whole

country was in a fever of excitement, of passionate par-
ticipation on the one side, and passionate denunciation
on the other.   A great lyrical poet may have many great
human virtues, but it is a great rarity when he can
boast of prudence; and of all his inordinate members,
that little member the tongue was the one on which
Robert Burns seldom or never condescended to lay any
judicious rein.   Accordingly, in the days when the air
was full of fever, and the streets and the taverns full of
spies, the poetical exciseman was among the boldest and
the loudest to proclaim his devotion to the cause of
freedom, whether in France or in America, and had no
scruple at a dinner-party, when called on for a toast, to set
up Washington against Pitt as a worthy object of a
patriotic bumper.   It needed only a little loud talk of
this kind in those days to mark a man in the public eye
as a disaffected person,—as a seditious man, looking out
for a congenial atmosphere in Botany Bay,—certainly
not as a person in any wise entitled to expect promotion in any branch of the government service; and
no man will be surprised to find, that unfavourable
reports of the poet's loyalty had been transmitted to the
Board of Excise, from whom he received a sharp repri-
mand for his past license of speech, and a wise warning
for the future.   This led the poet, in a letter to Mr
Erskine of Mar, dated 13th April 1793, to make a
defence against his accusers, and a declaration of his
political principles.   Writing as a friend to a friend, he
said that "there existed a system of corruption between
the executive powers and the representative part of the
legislature which boded no good to our glorious constitution, and which every patriotic Briton must wish to

see amended. But of this constitution he was a sincere
friend, and looked upon it as insanity to sacrifice it to
an untried visionary theory. These were his sentiments;
but as a public servant, in however humble a capacity,
he had considered it his duty to forbear taking any part,
either personally or as an author, in the present business
of Parliamentary reform." This was sensible, and notably
characteristic of the man, who, as a true Scot, with all
his genius, was never deficient in the great practical
virtue of common-sense; and at no period of life was
touched with such Utopian schemes as, in their early
manhood, possessed the dreamy imagination of Coleridge
and Southey. The cloud of fiscal disfavour that threatened to ruin our poet's worldly prospects at this juncture,
after such satisfactory explanations to influential persons,
passed away; and in two years afterwards we find him,
in all the dignity of kerseymere breeches, short blue
coat faced with red, and round hat, enrolled in the loyal
ranks of the Dumfries volunteers, and at their patriotic
banquets denouncing foreign invasion and home factions
in strains that would have done honour to the most
fervent admirers of Mr Pitt :—

" Does haughty Gaul invasion threat?
    Then let the loons beware, sir;
There's wooden walls upon our seas,
    And volunteers on shore, sir.
The Nith shall run to Corsincon,
    And Criffel sink in Solway,
Ere we permit a foreign foe
    On British ground to rally !
        Fall de rall, &c.

> O, let us not, like snarling tykes,
> 　In wrangling be divided ;
> Till slap come in an unco loon,
> 　And wi' a rung decide it.
> Be Britain still to Britain true,
> 　Amang oursels united ;
> For never but by British hands
> 　Maun British wrangs be righted.
> 　　　　Fall de rall, &c."

But Burns was not destined to see the end of the great contest of British independence against continental aggression which his Muse had so patriotically inaugurated. His own end was at hand. In the month of January 1796, forgetful of his self-denying vows made, as we have seen above, to his good counsellor, Mrs Dunlop, he stayed late over the whisky bottle in the Globe tavern with some jovial fellows, among whom it was his misfortune to be the most admired and the most brilliant compotator. On the way home, as persons heavy with drink will do, he sat down in the cold air, and fell asleep. When he awoke and walked sadly to his own home, it was found that, as a natural consequence, the cold had penetrated to the stronghold of life, and the unhappy victim of convivial excess was laid down on a sick-bed, suffering the racking pains of rheumatic fever. In ordinary circumstances, with a man of originally sound constitution, such an attack might have passed off in a few weeks and left no dregs; but the poet, as we have seen, had been through life anything but careful to avoid those excesses to which persons of his temperament are prone. This was not the first time that he had to suffer from illness, brought on, as he himself sus-

pected, from habitual want of wisdom in the art of living;
and so, though he was now only thirty-seven years old,
his vital frame was not strong enough to shake off the
fell distemper that had seated itself so deeply in his bones.
He lingered on, however, not without hope of recovery,
through the spring and the early months of the summer,
and even mustered strength enough to send some lyrical
communications to his metrical correspondent, Mr George
Thomson. Among the other effusions of this flickering
twilight of his tuneful life are the well-known verses,
"Oh, wert thou in the cauld blast," which was afterwards
honoured in being wedded to the worthiest melody by
the great German composer Felix Mendelssohn. The
heroine of this song was Jessie Lewars, the sister of the
exciseman above mentioned, and who attended the poet,
as women only can do, with faithful ministrations
through all the stages of his fatal illness. On July 4, the
disease showing no tendency to relax its grip, the poet,
under medical advice, was removed to Brow, a small
country place well near the sea-shore; and the next
day his old friend Mrs Riddell, then in bad health herself, and now softened in her sore displeasure against her
offending admirer, paid him a kindly visit, and has left
her last farewell to her dying friend recorded as follows :—

" I was struck," says this lady, in a confidential letter to a friend
written some time after, " with his appearance on entering the room.
The stamp of death was imprinted on his features. He seemed
already touching the brink of eternity. His first salutation was:
'Well, madam, have you any commands for the other world?' I
replied, that it seemed a doubtful case which of us should be there
soonest, and that I hoped he would yet live to write my epitaph.
He looked in my face with an air of great kindness, and expressed

his concern at seeing me look so ill, with his accustomed sensibility. At table he ate little or nothing, and he complained of having entirely lost the tone of his stomach. He had a long and serious conversation about his present situation, and the approaching termination of all his earthly prospects. He spoke of his death without any of the ostentation of philosophy, but with firmness as well as feeling, as an event likely to happen very soon, and which gave him concern chiefly from leaving his four children so young and unprotected, and his wife in so interesting a situation in hourly expectation of lying-in of a fifth. He mentioned, with seeming pride and satisfaction, the promising genius of his eldest son, and the flattering marks of approbation he had received from his teachers, and dwelt particularly on his hopes of that boy's future conduct and merit. His anxiety for his family seemed to hang heavy upon him, and the more perhaps from the reflection that he had not done them all the justice he was so well qualified to do. Passing from this subject, he showed great concern about the care of his literary fame, and particularly the publication of his posthumous works. He said he was well aware that his death would occasion some noise, and that every scrap of his writing would be revived against him to the injury of his future reputation ; that letters and verses written with unguarded and improper freedom, and which he earnestly wished to have buried in oblivion, would be handed about by idle vanity or malevolence, when no dread of his resentment would restrain them, or prevent the censures of shrill-tongued malice, or the insidious sarcasms of envy, from pouring forth all their venom to blast his fame.

"He lamented that he had written many epigrams on persons against whom he entertained no enmity, and whose characters he should be sorry to wound ; and many indifferent poetical pieces, which he feared would now, with all their imperfections on their head, be thrust upon the world. On this account, he deeply regretted having deferred to put his papers in a state of arrangement, as he was now quite incapable of the exertion." The lady goes on to mention many other topics of a private nature on which he spoke. "The conversation," she adds, "was kept up with great evenness and animation on his side. I had seldom seen his mind greater or more collected. There was frequently a considerable degree of vivacity in his sallies, and they would probably have had a greater share had not the concern and dejection I could not disguise damped the spirit of pleasantry he seemed not unwilling to indulge.

"We parted about sunset on the evening of that day (the 5th of July 1796); the next day I saw him again, and we parted to meet no more!"[1]

On the 18th of the month, the poet, little or nothing profited by the sea air, returned on tottering footsteps to his home. Mrs Burns being then in expectation of an addition to her family, had not accompanied her husband to his sea retreat; and on his return, with this additional big drop of apprehension to his already overflowing cup of sorrows, the dying man wrote this last epistle from his pen to the father of his Jean :—

"MY DEAR SIR,—Do, for heaven's sake, send Mrs Armour here immediately. My wife is hourly expecting to be put to bed. Good God! what a situation for her to be in, poor girl, without a friend! I returned from sea-bathing quarters to-day, and my medical friends would almost persuade me that I am better; but I think and feel that my strength is so gone, that the disorder will prove fatal to me. —Your son-in-law."[2]

The end was now come. For three days we see the fevered sufferer stretched on his death-bed, with the faithful Jessie Lewars ministering with sleepless tendance at his side. His children had been sent to the house of her mother for the quiet necessary no less to them than to their dying father. On the 21st the sufferer sank into a delirium; his children were called in to see a living father for the last time; and, after a short struggle, the last flicker of life passed over his brow, and he was gone.

The funeral of such a man, cut off in the full flush of his career as a loyal citizen and a national poet, was, of

[1] Chambers, IV. 202.　　　　[2] *Ibid.*, IV. 209.

course, of a public nature, and is thus described by Dr
Currie :—

"The Gentlemen Volunteers of Dumfries determined to bury
their illustrious associate with military honours, and every prepara-
tion was made to render this last service solemn and impressive.
The Fencible Infantry of Angusshire, and the regiment of cavalry of
the Cinque Ports, at that time quartered in Dumfries, offered their
assistance on this occasion ; the principal inhabitants of the town
and neighbourhood determined to walk in the funeral procession ;
and a vast concourse of persons assembled, some of them from a
considerable distance, to witness the obsequies of the Scottish bard.
On the evening of the 25th of July, the remains of Burns were removed from his house to the Town Hall, and the funeral took place
on the succeeding day. A party of the volunteers, selected to perform the military duty in the churchyard, stationed themselves in
the front of the procession, with their arms reversed ; the main
body of the corps surrounded and supported the coffin, on which
were placed the hat and sword of their friend and fellow-soldier ;
the numerous body of attendants ranged themselves in the rear,
while the Fencible regiments of infantry and cavalry lined the
streets from the Town Hall to the burial-ground in the Southern
Churchyard, a distance of more than half a mile. The whole procession moved forward to that sublime and affecting strain of music
the 'Dead March in Saul,' and three volleys fired over his grave
marked the return of Burns to his parent earth ! The spectacle was
in a high degree grand and solemn, and accorded with the general
sentiments of sympathy and sorrow which the occasion had called
forth."

Dr Currie adds, "It was an affecting circumstance that, on the
morning of the day of her husband's funeral, Mrs Burns was undergoing the pains of labour, and that, during the solemn service we
have just been describing, the posthumous son of our poet was
born. This child was named Maxwell, in honour of Dr Maxwell,
the physician who had attended Burns on his death-bed. He died
in infancy."[1]

---

[1] Currie, I. 224.

CHAPTER VI.

Genius and Character.

"Every extraordinary man has a certain mission which he is
called upon to accomplish. If he has fulfilled it, he is no longer
needed upon earth in the same form, and Providence uses him for
some other purpose."

—Goethe.

A WRITER on Burns, distinguished no less by his
imaginative sympathy than by his philosophical
subtlety, makes the remark that of him more literally
perhaps than of any other writer can it be said that his
writing *lives*,[1] that is to say, that in every line the man is
there completely and emphatically alive. And not only
so, but we may say also, that no great writer has more
completely and more effectively written out his life in his
writings than Robert Burns ; not that he is offensively
and protrusively personal, like Lord Byron, but whatever
is his subject for the nonce, you feel that the man is
always in the midst of the business, and that his song is
always the direct emphatic utterance of his honest self,
moved from the backbone to the finger tips with the
quick pulse of an alert and a genial vitality. There is

---

[1] Dr Hutchison Stirling, in the book quoted above.

nothing got up here, nothing for show. It may flow out, hot as a boiling geyser, or mild as summer dew, but it is always spontaneous. In whatever style, tenderly pathetic or wildly humorous, the poet is always the man. He is found on the Queen's highway with you and me, or any common treader of the causeway, without dress shoes; he hires no balloon from the Muses to career about in ethereal regions, far from human flesh and blood, nor even a poetical state coach, but he enters a cab or an omnibus, with a lawyer's clerk or a shopkeeper, and spins his song forth to the rattling of the wheels on the stones as cheerily as if it were the music of the spheres. Reality, the most intense human reality, substantiality of the most solid contents, is the stuff of which his verses are made. It is for this reason that whosoever wishes to understand the man must read his verses, as the most speaking feature of his biography; and it is for this reason also that, in as far as the narrow limits prescribed to the present writer allowed, he has everywhere put forth the man, whether in song or epistle, to speak for himself. So much the less occasion will there be for a formal critical judgment of his genius and estimate of his character in a separate chapter; nevertheless, where the materials are so rich, and the scenes that pass before the eye so various, something in the shape of a summary of results will naturally be expected, and may assist the reader to a profitable conclusion. I will therefore attempt to make an articulate statement of the most salient points of the human phenomenon that is before us, distinguishing carefully between the genius of the poet and the character of the man, two factors which, though perfectly distinct, must be brought to bear together in a just estimate, otherwise the **exclusive admiration of the** genius may blind **the eye** to the defects of the character, **while, on the other** hand, a regard **fixed with severe ex-** clusiveness on the defects of the character may **deaden** the sensibility to the charms of the genius.

In respect of genius, **I** think it **is now** universally admitted that our Ayrshire bard has gained for himself, **by** **the** number, the variety, and the brilliancy of his productions, a place in **the first rank** of the great singers of the intellectual world,—Pindar, **Chaucer, Horace,** Hafiz, Goethe, **Béranger,** Moore, **and if there be any others** who enjoy an equally wide recognition. **Whatever qualities** are necessary to make **a** lyric poet,—and **in the term** lyrical we include not only songs in the **proper sense** composed to be sung, **but, for** want of **a better word,** idylls, sketches of character, and, it **may be, satirical side-** shots, and other short poems meant to be read,—these qualities Burns possessed with a complete equipment; **and** in addition to these, he was distinguished by certain great human qualities, not always present in great singers, which **add the** stamp of a vigorous **and manly** intellect to the charm of a nice emotional sensibility. The fire and fervour without which lyrical **poetry is scarce worthy** of the name, Burns **possessed in a high** degree; but it was not merely **fire** from within, consuming itself **in the** glow of some special pet enthusiasm, **but** it was a fire **that** went out contagiously **and** seized on whatever fuel **it** might find **in** the motley fair of the largest human life. **If ever there** was a song-writer who could say with the most catholic comprehensiveness in the words of the old comedian, " *I am a man, and all things* **human are kin to** *me,*" it was Robert **Burns.** **In** this respect he is the

Shakespeare of **lyric** poetry. Some have thought, indeed, that in respect of the fine objective eye, and power of self-transmutation, **shown in** "The Jolly Beggars," **and not a few others** of his poems, had he lived his genius might have **risen** to the dignity of the regular drama. Possibly; but **I am** inclined **to** think that, however quick his eye for dramatic peculiarities of character, and however far he **was from being the votary of** a purely subjective sensibility, the action **of his mind was** deficient **in that** continuity of persistent **effort which enables a man to** build **up** into a **firm structure** the complex **materials of a drama.** In connection with his power **of** seizing the striking features of character, must be mentioned his tremendous force as a satirist,—for a **satirist of the** most pungent order unquestionably he **was,—too much,** in fact, for his **own** peaceable march through life, and too much sometimes, **as we have seen, for his own** pleasant **reflections on his deathbed, but not too much** for public **correction and reproof when, as in the case of** "Holy Willie" **and** "The Holy Fair," the lash was wisely and effectively wielded. His admiring friend Mr Ramsay of Ochtertyre, anxious that his genius might reap sweet fruit with as little of the bitter element as possible, wrote to him with an earnest admonition, "to keep clear of the thorny walk of satire, which makes a man a hundred enemies **for** one friend;"[1] and this was, no doubt, good advice. Only in the passionate love of the beautiful, and the reverential admiration of the sublime, can true poetry find its life-breath; but **a satirical** fling occasionally at dominant follies, **seasoned** with kindliness, is **perfectly**

[1] Currie, II. 92; dated 22nd October 1787.

within the province of the poet in a secondary way, when
touching on matters that cannot be avoided, and that
deserve no **better** treatment. A song-writer, as **we have**
said, must always be a warm-hearted man,—a cold song **is**
inconceivable; but he is not always a strong man,—he
may be weak, with all his warmth. Not so Burns. He was
emphatically a strong man; there was, **as** Carlyle says,
"a certain rugged sterling worth about him," which
makes his songs as good **as** sermons sometimes, and
sometimes as good as battles. And it **was this** notable
amount of backbone, and force of arm, sensibly felt in
his utterances, which gave to his pathos and his tenderness such healthy **grace, and** such rare **freedom from**
anything that savoured **of** sentimentality. **In Burns** the
most delicate sensibility to beauty was harmoniously combined with the firmest grip and the **most** manly stout-
heartedness. This sensibility, of course, showed itself
most largely in the electric power constantly exercised
over him by the presence of God's great masterpiece of
creative skill, a lovely woman; but the heather-bell,
and the field daisy, and every grassy slope and wooded
fringe **and** wimpling brook of bonnie Ayrshire, **were ever**
as dear to his heart **as they were near to his footstep.**
Nor was it the Platonic admiration of the **beautiful only**
that moved him to sing. The Christian element of pity
also had a deep fount in his rich human heart, and a tear
of common-blooded affinity was ever ready to be dropt,
not only over the sorrows of an injured woman, but over
the pangs of a hunted hare or the terror of a startled field-
mouse. Add **to all** this, extraordinary quickness of
apprehension, great vividness of imagination, and great
powers of rhythmical utterance, and you have in the Ayr-

shire ploughman every element that goes to equip a master-spirit in the noble craft of song-writing. But there were also in the composition of Burns certain grand general human qualities which, though not necessary to the highest excellence of the lyrical Muse, are of a nature to adorn and to commend what they cannot create, and to extort admiration from persons the furthest removed from anything that savours of poetical inspiration. First, of course, there came the commendation that he was a man of good personal aspect and manly presentment. He had none of the pale cast of countenance that men of action expect to find in the poet and the philosopher; he was healthy and robust, and could handle the plough or the flail as vigorously as the pen. Then, again, his general vigour of mind was as notable as his vigour of body; he was as strong in thought as intense in emotion. If inferior to Coleridge in ideal speculation, to Wordsworth in harmonious contemplation, and to Southey in book-learning, in all that concerns living men and human life and human society he was extremely sharp-sighted, and not only wise in penetrating to the inmost springs of human thought and senti·ment, but in the judgment of conduct eminently shrewd and sagacious; gifted, in the highest degree, with that fundamental virtue of all sound Scotsmen, common-sense, without which great genius in full career is apt to lead a man astray from his surroundings, and make him most a stranger to that with which in common life he ought to be most familiar. One notable feature in his genius—a feature which has not seldom been wanting even in the greatest of minds—is humour, a certain sportive fence of the soul delighting in the significant conjunction of con-

traries, a quality peculiarly Scotch, and which in Scotsmen
seems a counterpoise graciously provided by Nature to
that overcharge of thoughtfulness and seriousness which
so strikingly contrasts them with their Hibernian cousins
across the channel. Burns also was strong in wit, a
domain in which Scotsmen generally are weak,—kindred
qualities, no doubt, in their root, but in their expression
diverse, wit acting by points and by flashes, humour by a
general breadth of playful light in the moral atmosphere
of the man. Another quality Burns possessed in an
eminent degree, a quality which tended to make him the
idol of his countrymen, and that was patriotism, a virtue
which, as Carlyle remarks, was in the days of Hume and
Robertson and Blair anything but common in the literary
atmosphere of Scotland. The great Scottish writers of
those days, he remarks, had no Scottish culture, scarcely
even English ; it was almost exclusively French.[1] Finally,
let us note what in other walks of literature might have
operated as a serious disadvantage, viz., his peasant
breeding and rustic habitude ; for in the domain of
popular song, the familiar intercourse with nature and
the natural forms of human life, has a saving virtue to
keep a man free from that crop of splendid affectations
and dainty conceits, which the hot pressure of literary
competition in an age of highly stimulated culture seldom
fails to produce.

So much for his genius in the shaping force and

[1] On the dominance of French culture among the gentry of Scotland in the eighteenth century, see " Songstresses of Scotland," by
Sarah Tytler and J. L. Watson, London, 1871, Vol. I., p. 56, an
admirable book that ought to be familiar to every lover of Scottish
song.

dominant direction of his intellectual products. His
character is an altogether different affair. No doubt in
a true man like Burns, the life and literature spring out
of the same root, and are identical in their primary
tendencies ; but the literary product of a lyrical poet
depends on the sensibility of the moment, the character
on the continuity of the life ; and this continuity of
course demands a presidency of other, and, it may be,
higher qualities than those which are sufficient for the
production of a song. Let us consider then in a few
salient points how the greatest of Scottish lyrists presents
himself amongst men as men. And, in the first place, we
note that he possessed in a remarkable degree what
Crabb Robinson remarked in Goethe, a great zest of
life. We meet with persons every day who seem only
half alive,—alive it may be with the worser half of their
nature, certainly not in the outside display of their
nature. But Burns was alive all round ; hence the
universally felt charm of his social intercourse. Wherever he appeared, he brought with him a tremendous
discharge of social electricity ; and the fascination of
his talk, especially in the presence of women, is described as irresistible. Allied to this virtue, however, or
rather growing out of it, was a strong love for passionate
excitement, an affection than which none is more delicious in its start and more dangerous in its career.
Against this danger, which lies in the very nature of all
excitement, his Clarinda, as a faithful Mentor, did not
fail to warn him seriously. " Could you command your
too impetuous passions," she wrote, " it would be a more
glorious achievement than his who conquered the world,
and wept because he had no more worlds to conquer."

And Richter, whose wisdom is as pure as his wit is brilliant, felt himself forced to sing a second to Solomon, when he asks the question " whether seeking happiness by passionate excitement is not just like warming your hands at a burning-glass ? " Here unquestionably lay the great mistake of Robert Burns's life. He did not know where to stop. Hence the bitter self-reproaches that followed his jovial compotations in the Globe tavern at Dumfries, compotations in which no doubt the luxury of plashing in a sea of convivial enjoyment was not a little heightened by the gratification to his vanity in being what is called the cock of the company for the nonce. In the admiration of fair women, even more than in devotion to the convivial cup, he was constitutionally inclined to scorn the safety which Nature and Aristotle have combined to indicate as the golden mean ; and more than once allowed himself to break down the bounds which Divine law has set up between the reverence due to a noble ideal and the license claimed by a vulgar passion. To compensate for these aberrations, he was endowed with most of those qualities which make the native nobility of man. He was utterly incapable of anything like baseness. No man could be more jealous of his honour ; no man had a greater pride in being largely and loftily a man. " My beloved household gods," he says, in one of his letters, " are independence of spirit and integrity of soul." And in the full feeling of this Carlyle says : " Many poets have been poorer than Burns ; no one was ever prouder." This also, with the keen glance of woman's love, Clarinda perceived :—" I believe nothing were a more impracticable task than to teach you a little of genuine gospel humility." Of course this implies blame ; all the virtues of his high-strung lyrical nature tended to excess; but the excess of pride in his case acted generally as a safeguard from baseness, not as a spur to insolence. As the most effective expression at once of manly independence and honest pride in his character, we cannot do better than insert here in full the popular song of "For a' that and a' that," a composition which, as giving in a condensed rhythmical form the poetical truth which belongs to one aspect of the famous French shibboleth of "liberty, equality, and fraternity," is perhaps unequalled in the literature of the world :—

" Is there, for honest poverty,
    That hangs his head, and a' that !
The coward slave, we pass him by,
    We dare be poor for a' that !
For a' that, and a' that,
    Our toils obscure, and a' that ;
The rank is but the guinea's stamp,
    The man's the gowd for a' that.

What though on hamely fare we dine,
    Wear hoddin' grey, and a' that ;
Gie fools their silks, and knaves their wine,
    A man's a man for a' that.
For a' that, and a' that,
    Their tinsel show, and a' that ;
The honest man, though e'er sae poor,
    Is king o' men for a' that.

You see yon birkie, ca'd a lord,
    Wha struts, and stares, and a' that,
Though hundreds worship at his word,
    He's but a coof for a' that ;

For a' that, and a' that,
　　His riband, star, and a' that;
The man of independent mind
　　He looks and laughs at a' that.

A king can mak' a belted knight,
　　A marquis, duke, and a' that ;
But an honest man's aboon his might,
　　Guid faith, he mauna fa' that !
For a' that, and a' that,
　　Their dignities and a' that,
The pith o' sense, and pride o' worth,
　　Are higher ranks than a' that !

Then let us pray that come it may—
　　As come it will for a' that—
That sense and worth, o'er a' the earth,
　　May bear the gree, and a' that.
For a' that, and a' that,
　　It's comin' yet, for a' that.
That man to man, the warld o'er,
　　Shall brothers be for a' that ! "

Of course the high-souled independence, which is the
inspiration of this song, like every other virtue in a man
of his character, had a tendency to run into a vice. No
man in the complicated organism of society can plant
himself altogether independent of other members of the
organism, or even of their opinions ; much less can a
wise man make himself independent of the necessary
foundation to a *locus standi* in this material world, called
money ; and in this regard our poet has sometimes been
severely blamed for the very cavalier fashion in which
he refused all pecuniary remuneration for his contributions to Thomson's " Scottish Melodies " ; but it may well
be that he looked on this in the light rather of a

patriotic adventure than of a mercantile speculation, and if so, his refusal to allow any thought of the purse to enter into the transaction only adds another gem to his crown. Prudent in money matters, or indeed in any matter connected with the routine of life, he could not specially be said to be,—in this respect decidedly inferior to his great Hebrew prototype King David (1 Sam. xvi. 18); but, though he had the poet's proverbial contempt for money, and all that money can bring, it does not appear that he either foolishly squandered the little he had, or thoughtlessly got himself into debt. Though anything but a spendthrift, he was often generous where richer men would have been niggardly; and he was always more eager to express gratitude for a favour received, than to expect reward for a service performed.

There is a fashion in some quarters of talking about Burns in Arcadian phrase, as if he were merely a minstrel peasant, an inspired ploughman, flinging his "wood notes wild" about men or mice, fair women or mountain daisies, as the rustic whim might move him. But this is a very inadequate notion of his intellectual position. He was a peasant, certainly, born and bred, but a man of very fair school culture, as we have shown above; and what is more, as falls here to be specially noted, he was a man of great intellectual ambition. He was not content with giving shape to a pretty fancy, or a genial emotion, as the inspiration might come; he made himself familiar with no small portion of the current literature of the day, and gave himself great pains to acquire a mastery of the English language, as it dominates the cultivated society of these islands both in conversation and in books. To this honourable ambition he owed it,

that the moment he appeared in the intellectual arena of
the metropolis, he was not only recognised as a grand
rustic lion, worthy to be stared at for a season in the
parade of fashionable society, but forthwith felt to be a
great social power, an expert master in that sort of
intellectual fence in which the keen wits of the Parliament House and the trained intellects of the University
delighted to disport themselves. His epistles to persons
of all ranks, though here and there a little inflated by
passion, and occasionally, it may be, tainted with the lust
of fine writing, exhibit such force and tact in the use of
the English language, that some of his friends seriously
advised him to give up the use of his native Scotch, as
confining his influence to a narrow circle; while others
even went so far as to invite him to settle in the great
metropolis, and find a sphere for the display of his
fervid humanity and catholic citizenship, as Coleridge
did, in the pages of the *Morning Chronicle.* But Burns,
though quite capable of wielding the periodical pen
effectively, had too much sense to allow himself to be
decoyed into the position of a London literary man, the
adjunct of a London journalist; and he wisely determined rather to do what he could do on his own ground
with a natural grace, than to act a brilliant part on a stage
to which he was not bred and must be trained. As to
song-writing, no master of the English lyre could surpass
the purity of his lyrical phrase when he chose to use it;
but he wisely told Mr Thomson, that systematically to
Anglicise the Scottish songs would be systematically to
spoil them,—to rob them of that honest directness, pure
truthfulness, easy grace, and playful simplicity which is
their peculiar charm. Besides, though not skilled in

music, he had ear enough to know that the Scottish language,—or rather, as we ought to say, the Scottish dialect of our general English tongue,—besides having more of the breath of sentiment about it, is more musical in a technical sense, and, like Italian, richer in full vocal sounds than the more highly cultivated sister dialect. The first verse of the beautiful song of Gala Water :—

> "There's braw, braw lads on Yarrow braes,
>   That wander thro' the blooming heather ;
> But Yarrow braes, nor Ettrick shaws,
> Can match the lads o' Gala Water,"

is in no wise peculiar in the frequency with which the most musical of the vowels strikes the ear. There is hardly a Scottish song of any popularity in which this broad musical *a* is not dominant ; a sound by softening which into the sound of *a* in *vane* the English have deprived even English songs of their natural sweetness, and the Virgilian hexameters of their natural majesty. Scotch, in fact, in this view, bears exactly the same relation to English that Doric Greek did to Attic Greek, and ought to be cultivated for its lyrical excellence as a branch of musical education by the Saxon population of the island on both sides of the Tweed. But instead of this we find, oblivious of the noble example of Robert Burns and Walter Scott, the classical Scottish dialect becoming less and less familiar to Scottish ears every year, and the most glorious moral heritage of the country thrown aside as worthless, and even condemned as pernicious, in favour of the glittering novelty of the hour, the vanity of a foreign accomplishment, or the echo of a London notoriety.

Of the religion of Burns, no doubt one of the most interesting features in his character, so much has peeped out already in the extracts which we have given from his correspondence, that there is less need for going into detail here. I remember well the late genial and catholic-hearted Dr Guthrie, the apostle of the ragged schools, saying to me at a country manse in Fife, that Burns was naturally a religious man, and, if he had had the happiness at a certain point of his career to meet with an evangelist of the right sort,—like Dr Guthrie himself I interpolated,—he would never have started off from the rails of moral rectitude so grossly as he sometimes did. Certain it is that he has again and again recorded his religious convictions in the strongest terms. "Religion," he says, in one of his letters, "has ever been to me not only my chief dependence, but my dearest enjoyment. A mathematician without religion is a probable character; an irreligious poet is a monster." Then again in another place, "I am, I must confess, too frequently the sport of whim, caprice, and passion; but reverence to God and integrity to my fellow-men I hope I shall ever preserve." His religion was unquestionably a reality with a root in his character, not a mere senti- mental affectation; and, though he had a keen eye both for the nonsense of the theological dogmatism of his day, and for the illiberality of not a few so-called religious people, he saw too far behind the scenes, and was too much of a thoroughbred Scottish patriot, to prefer the courtly religiosity of Claverhouse and his swearing troopers to the earnest piety and the manly independence of the Covenanters :—

> " The Solemn League and Covenant
> Cost Scotland blood, cost Scotland tears :
> But faith seal'd freedom's sacred cause—
> If thou'rt a slave, indulge thy sneers."

Wherein then lay his defect? Simply in this, that, as
Cicero says of virtue, "*Virtutis laus omnis in actione
consistit*," so we must say of religion that its whole praise
lies not in sentiment but in action, not in "calling Christ
Lord, Lord ! but in doing the things which He says."
The religion of Burns lay more in an undercurrent of
emotion than in a commanding seat of control. His
piety, like all the rest of his noble virtues, so nobly
expressed in rhyme, suffered in practice from the weakness of his will. Without a strong will no man can be
a complete character, or great in action. A clever
fellow may do anything in this world, says Goethe, only
not allow himself to drift, " for in this sea of time the
rudder is given into the hands of man in his frail skiff,
not that he may be at the mercy of the waves, but that
he may follow the dictates of a will directed by intelligence." No man knew this better than Burns. He had
in fact made a special study of his inner self, and taken
the exact measure of his capacities and his tendencies in
a fashion that appears nobly strange in a creature of
such violent impulses and headlong plunges. If he did
not allow himself systematically to drift, he certainly did
not sail with a sure chart, or keep a good look-out, or
stand in critical moments steadily at the helm. Scarcely
anything in the tragic story of his later years is more sad
than the following confession, which appears so early as
the first Kilmarnock edition of his poems :—

" Is there a whim-inspirèd fool,
　Owre fast for thought, owre hot for rule,
　Owre blate to seek, owre proud to snool,
　　　　Let him draw near;
　And owre this grassy heap sing **dool**,
　　　　And drap a tear.

　Is there a bard of rustic song,
　Who, noteless, steals the crowds among,
　That weekly this arena throng,
　　　　O, pass not by!
　But, with a frater-feeling strong,
　　　　Here heave a sigh.

　Is there a man, whose judgment clear,
　Can others teach the course to steer,
　Yet runs, himself, life's mad career,
　　　　Wild as the **wave**;
　Here pause—and, through the startling tear,
　　　　Survey this grave.

　The poor inhabitant below
　Was quick to learn and **wise to know**,
　And keenly felt the friendly **glow**,
　　　　And softer flame;
　But thoughtless follies laid him low,
　　　　And stain'd his name!

　Reader, attend—whether thy soul
　Soars fancy's flights beyond the pole,
　Or darkly grubs this earthly hole
　　　　In low pursuit;
　Know, prudent, cautious, self-control,
　　　　Is wisdom's root! "

How strange, how sad! that the man who could write
this so truly when he was twenty-six years old, should

have nothing better to say of himself after ten additional years of the most open-eyed experience of manly life. Strange ; but so it is. The most brilliant flashes of wit are not seldom stored in the same arsenal with the greatest follies ; an important lesson, at once of humiliation to the sons of genius, and of consolation to the dunces.

With this genius and with this character, Burns had to execute his mission in life ; for every specially gifted son of Adam, as Goethe, with his usual catholic wisdom, has remarked, has a special mission, direct from heaven, to employ his gifts for the glory of the great All-father, and the good of his fellow-men. This mission which, in the case of the Ayrshire bard, plainly was to elevate, enlarge, put a classical stamp on, and give a world-wide celebrity to Scottish song, he performed successfully and triumphantly ; not however in such fashion as to enable him to claim the literary man's proudest boast, that he wrote no line which dying he could wish to blot. Any person who looks into a common collection of popular Scottish songs, will be struck with the wonderful richness and various excellence of the repertory, altogether independent of the contributions of Burns ; still it was Burns that, partly by the striking excellence of his own contributions, partly by the exquisite tact with which he handled and improved traditional materials, gave to Scottish lyrical literature a position in the estimation of intelligent Europe similar to that which Shakespeare holds in the literature of the drama. Those who understand the significance of such a success, and the value of such a triumph, will not allow their gratitude for a great public service to be stinted by the tear which they are forced to drop over the occasional follies or social indis-

cretions of the private man. They will feel that, whatever may have been his personal deflections from the
straight line of social rectitude, as the exponent of
national sentiment he was noble and wise, and studi-
ously careful to teach his fellow-citizens, whom he loved,
to beware of those unreined impulses and unreasoned
passions which had pierced his heart through with many
sorrows, and flung such unseemly blots on the pure lustre
of his fame. Of his faithfulness as a preacher of right-
eousness to the youth of his country, we cannot give a
more striking proof than the letter of good ˙ advice
which he wrote to the son of one of his many good
friends, a letter so stamped throughout with the genial
humanity, genuine kindliness, and shrewd practical wisdom of the man, that we cannot do better than insert it
here at length as the most suitable epilogue to our brief
sketch of his brilliant career :—

> " I lang hae thought, my youthfu' Friend,
>   A something to have sent you,
> Tho' it should serve nae other end
>   Than just a kind memento;
> But how the subject-theme may gang,
>   Let time and chance determine ;
> Perhaps it may turn out a sang,
>   Perhaps turn out a sermon.
>
> Ye'll try the world fu' soon, my lad,
>   And, Andrew dear, believe me,
> Ye'll find mankind an unco squad,
>   And muckle they may grieve ye :
> For care and trouble set your thought,
>   E'en when your end's attained ;
> An a' your views may come to nought,
>   Where ev'ry nerve is strained.

I'll no say men are villains a' ;
  The real, harden'd wicked,
Wha hae nae check but human law,
  Are to a few restricked ;
But och ! mankind are unco weak,
  An' little to be trusted ;
If self the wavering balance shake,
  It's rarely right adjusted !

Yet they wha fa' in fortune's strife
  Their fate we shouldna censure ;
For still the important end of life
  They equally may answer :
A man may ha'e an honest heart
  Though poortith hourly stare him ;
A man may tak' a neighbour's part
  Yet hae nae cash to spare him.

Ay free, aff hand your story tell,
  Whan wi' a bosom crony ;
But still keep something to yoursel'
  Ye daurna tell to ony.
Conceal yoursel' as weel's ye can
  Frae critical dissection ;
But keek through ilka ither man
  Wi' sharpened sly inspection.

The sacred lowe o' weel-placed love
  Luxuriantly indulge it ;
But never tempt the illicit rove,
  Tho' naething should divulge it ;
I waive the quantum o' the sin,
  The hazard o' concealing,
But, och ! it hardens a' within,
  And petrifies the feeling !

To catch dame Fortune's golden smile,
   Assiduous wait upon her ;
And gather gear by ev'ry wile
   That's justified by honour ;
Not for to hide it in a hedge,
   Nor for a train-attendant ;
But for the glorious privilege
   Of being independent.

The fear o' hell's a hangman's whip
   To haud the wretch in order ;
But where ye feel **your honour grip,**
   Let that aye be your border :
Its slightest touches, instant pause—
   Debar a' side pretences ;
And resolutely **keeps its laws,**
   Uncaring consequences.

The great Creator to revere
   Must sure become the creature ;
But still the preaching cant forbear,
   And e'en the rigid feature ;
Yet ne'er with wits profane to range,
   Be complaisance extended ;
An atheist's laugh's a poor **exchange**
   For Deity offended.

When ranting round in pleasure's ring,
   Religion may be blinded ;
Or if she gie a random sting,
   It may be little minded :
But when on life we're tempest driv'n,
   A conscience but a canker,—
A correspondence fix'd wi' Heav'n,
   Is sure a noble anchor !

Adieu, dear, amiable youth !
   Your heart can ne'er be wanting ;
May prudence, fortitude, and truth,
   Erect your brow undaunting !
In ploughman phrase, ' God send you speed '
   Still daily to grow wiser ;
And may you better reck the rede
   Than ever did th' adviser ! "

THE END.

INDEX.

A.

AINSLIE, Robert, 89.

Armour, Jean, 59–64, 66, 93, 116; Burns marries her, 111–114.

Athole, Blair, the Ducal family at, 98.

B.

Bruar, Falls of, 98.

Burnet, Miss, of Monboddo, 78, 79.

Burns, Gilbert, the poet's brother, 10, 30.

Burns, Robert, ancestry, 4, 5; his father and mother, 5–7; born at Doonholm, 5; removes to Mount Oliphant, 6; death of father, 6, 27, 28; education, 8; books, 9; at Kirkoswald, 11; his independence, 13; love of woman, 16–18; Tarbolton songs, 19, 20; patriotism, 20; founds debating society, 22; at Irvine, 23; "Poet's Welcome," 25; despondency, 26, 138; a prayer, 27; at his father's deathbed, 28; Mossgiel, 29; "Epistles to Davie," 31–34; letter to Dr Moore, 33; masonry, 35; personal piety, 41, 139; common-place book, 41; sides with Moderate party in Church, 42; "Holy Willie," 44; "Epistle to Rev. John M'Math," 47; "Holy Fair," 50; "Cottar's Saturday Night," 52; "Birthday Ode to George III.," 53–56; Dr Hornbook, 57; "Jolly Beggars," 57; love for bonnie Jean, 59; "Highland Mary," 64; first publication, 67, 69; first patrons, 71, 76; at Covington, 74, 75; at Carnwath, 75; lodges in Baxter's Close, 75; "Ode to Edinburgh," 79, 81; on the Edinburgh lawyers, 81; at Roslin, 82; poet-laureate of the Mason Lodge,

M

Edinburgh, 82 ; no Jacobite, 83 ; erects a memorial slab to Fergusson, 85 ; described by Walker, 85, 86 ; described by Scott, 86–88 ; new edition of poems, 88 ; tour with R. Ainslie, 89 ; at Duns, 89 ; at Coldstream, 90 ; at Kelso, 90 ; at Jedburgh, 90 ; at Selkirk, 91 ; in North of England, 92 ; misanthropic outburst, 93 ; at Inverary, 94 ; Highland tour, 95 ; at Linlithgow, 95 ; on church architecture, 95 ; at Borrowstouness, 96 ; at Harvieston, 96, 101 ; at Taymouth, 97 ; at Aberfeldy, 97 ; at Killiecrankie, 97 ; at Blair-Athole, 98 ; at Gordon Castle, 100 ; at Duff House, 100 ; at Aberdeen, 100 ; at Ochtertyre, 101 ; at Dunfermline, 103 ; passion for Clarinda, 104 ; his confession of faith, 107 ; his farm at Ellisland, 109, 110 ; marriage to Jean Armour, 113 ; examination by Board of Excise, 115 ; forms a local library at Ellisland, 117 ; celebrates the drinking match of "The Whistle," 117 ; a champion on polemical theology, 120, 121 ; Johnston's "Musical Museum," 122 ; Captain Grose, 122–124 ; Excise appointment, 125, 127 ; on intoxication, 129, 130 ; Mrs

Riddell of Woodley Park, 136 ; correspondence with G. Thomson, 141 ; contribution to "Scottish Melodies," 142 ; in Dumfries, 143–145 ; adventure with smugglers, 145 ; a political reformer, 147–149 ; reprimanded by Board of Excise, 148 ; joins the Dumfries Volunteers, 149 ; his last illness, 151 ; death, 153 ; funeral, 154 ; his genius as a lyric poet, 157 ; a satirist, 158 ; character as a man, 162 ; his intellectual culture, 167 ; his religion, 169 ; the bard's epitaph, 171 ; epistle to a young friend, 173.

C.

Caledonian Hunt, 76, 77.
Chalmers', The, at Harvieston, 96.
Chalmers, Miss Peggie, 101.
Chloris, 131, 132.
Church, Scottish, parties in the, 37 ; severe discipline in, 43.
Civilisation, its character and effects, 2.
Clarinda : Agnes M'Lehose, 103–108, 111, 130.
Covenanters, 170.

D.

Dumfries, its character and society, 129, 143.
Dumfries Volunteers, 149.
Dunlop, Mrs, 114, 115.

E.

Edinburgh lawyers, 81.
Edinburgh society, 75, 76, 90, 93.
Erskine, Harry, 78.

F.

Ferguson of Craigdarroch, 118.
Fergusson, Robert: Burns places
a stone over his grave, 84, 85.

G.

Glencairn, Earl of, 75, 76.
Gordon, Duchess of, 76, 77, 100.
Gow, Neil, 97.
Grose, Captain Francis, 123.

H.

Hamilton, Gavin, Burns's landlord, 29, 43.
Highland Mary, 64–66.

J.

Johnston's " Musical Museum,"
122.

K.

Kilmarnock edition of poems,
69.
" Kirk's Alarm, The," 120.

L.

Laurie, Sir Robert, of Maxwell-
town, 118.
Lesley, Bonnie, 131, 132.
Lewars, Jessie, 151, 153.
Lindsay, Miss, 90.
Lorimer, Jean, 132.

Love, 14
Lynedoch, Lord, 99

M.

Mackenzie, " The Man of
Feeling," 77.
M'Lehose, Mrs, 103–108, 111,
130.
Masonry, Free, at Tarbolton,
35; Lodge at Edinburgh, 82.
Miller of Dalswinton, 109.
Monboddo, Lord, 78.
Murdoch, teacher of Burns, 9, 11.
Murray, Miss Euphemia, 102.

N.

Nasmyth, the artist, 82.
Nicol, W., 95, 119.

O.

Oswald, Lucy, 131, 135.

P.

Poets, their mission, 3.

R.

Ramsay of Ochtertyre, 102.
Riddell, Captain, of Friars'
Carse, 118, 123.
Riddell, Mrs, of Woodley Park,
135, 151.

S.

Scottish language, its musical
character, 168.
Scott, Sir Walter, his account
of Burns, 87, 88.

Sillar, David, 31.

Skinner, Rev. John, 100.

SONGS—

" A man's a man for a' that,"
84, 164, 165.

" Behind yon hill where Lugar
flows," 17.

" Birks of Aberfeldy," 97.

" Blithe, blithe, and merry was
she," 102.

" Bonnie Lesley," 131.

" Highland Mary," 122, 124.

" It was upon a Lammas
night," 18.

" Lassie wi' the lint-white
locks," 134–135.

" Of a' the airts the wind can
blaw," 116.

"Oh, were I on Parnassus Hill,"
116.

" Oh, wert thou in the cauld
blast," 151.

" O, wat ye wha's in yon
toun," 135.

" The Deil's awa' wi' the
Exciseman," 146, 147.

Stewart, Dugald, 71.

Stodarts of Carnwath, 75.

T.

"Tam o' Shanter," 122, 123.

Thomson, George, his " Scottish
Melodies," 141.

W.

Walker, Professor, his account
of Burns, 85 ; at Blair-Athole,
97.

Wallace and the Leglen wood,
21.

GLOSSARY.

THE Scottish language is not a different language from English, as Italian is a different language from Latin; but it is merely the northern dialect of English, as Venetian or Milanese Italian is a dialect of the language used by Dante, Tasso, and the other Italian classics. It stands, in fact, in the same relation to classical English that the Doric dialect of Greece did to the generally acknowledged norm of good Attic prose, and should be used by all speakers of the English tongue exactly as the Doric dialect was used by the Attic Greeks in their tragic choruses. Like the Greek Doric, the Scotch form of English bears on its face the distinct evidence of a dialect formed under the influence of music and popular minstrelsy. It is, philologically considered, the musical and lyrical variety of the general English speech, and as such has a claim to be recognised in the higher education of all who speak the common English tongue, a recognition which it has unfortunately not generally received even from the native Scotch. In the following Glossary only such words have been inserted as might occasion difficulty to the English reader; such musical variations as *sma* for *small*, *snaw* for *snow*, *awa* for *away*, *warl* for *world*, *loe* for *love*, *haud* for *hold*, and others, being safely left to the linguistic instinct of the reader, and the plain indications of the context.

J. S. B.

A.

Aiblins, perhaps.

B.

Beet, feed the fire, to warm.
Birkie, a lively young fellow.
Blaud, to strike, drive violently.
Blellum, an idle talker.
Braw, beautiful, dainty, bonnie.
Byre, a cowhouse.

C.

Cannie, cautious.
Caulk and keel, chalk and ruddle.
Chap, a man, a fellow.
Chiel, a lad, a man.
Cleed, to clothe.
Coof, a silly fellow.

D.

Diddle, to shake, jog.
Dool, sorrow, grief.
Douce, sober, grave.
Drouth, thirst, dryness.

E.

Eerie, unearthly, witch-like.

F.

Fash, to trouble, vex.
Fier, healthy and strong.
Fodgel, squat and plump.

G.

Gear, wealth.
Geck, to toss the head freely.
Glower, to stare, gaze.
Gowan, daisy.
Gree, grade of excellence, superiority.
Gulravage, running wild.

H.

Heeze, to elevate.
Hizzy, low word for a young woman.
Hoddin-grey, a coarse woollen stuff.
Hooly, softly, cautiously.

J.

Jaud, a loose young woman.
Jink, move quickly and suddenly.

L.

Lear, lore, learning.
Leeze, dear to, pleased with.
Lowe, flame.
Lug, the ear.

M.

Mang, among.
Maun, must.
Mirk, murky, dark.
Muckle, much.

N.

Nieve, hand, fist.

O.

Owre, too.

P.

Pauchty, saucy, malapert.
Poortith, poverty.

R.

Raploch, coarse, rough.
Rax, stretch.

S.

Scouth, room, freedom.
Scrieve, glide quickly.
Shaver, a humorous fellow, a wag.
Shavie, a trick, prank.
Skellum, a blockhead.
Sklent, an oblique glance.
Snool, to duck under, cringe.

Spairge, to scatter, to sprinkle.
Spavie, spavin.
Speir, to ask.
Sprachel, to clamber.
Stook, a rick, or stack of corn.
Swith, quickly.

T.

Tent, mark, take heed.
Tentless, careless.

U.

Unco, strange, queer, odd, excessive.

W.

Waur, worse.
Widdle, wriggle, bustle.
Willyart, wild, shy.

BIBLIOGRAPHY.

BY

JOHN P. ANDERSON

(British Museum).

I. Works.

II. Poetical Works.

III. Prose Works.

IV. Selections.

V. Appendix—
Biography, Criticism, etc.
Songs set to Music, etc.
Magazine Articles.

VI. Chronological List of Works.

I. WORKS.

The Works of Robert Burns. With an account of his life and a criticism on his writings. To which are prefixed some observations on the character and condition of the Scottish Peasantry. [By J. Currie.] 4 vols. Liverpool printed, London, etc., published, 1800, 8vo.
——Second edition. 4 vols. London, 1801, 8vo.
A reprint of the preceding, with a few corrections.
——Another edition. 4 vols. Philadelphia, 1801, 12mo.
——Third edition. 4 vols. London, 1802, 8vo.

The Works of R. B. Fourth edition. 4 vols. London, 1803, 8vo.
——Another edition. 3 vols. Philadelphia, 1804, 12mo.
——Fifth edition. 4 vols. Belfast, 1805, 12mo.
——Fifth edition. 4 vols. London, 1806, 8vo.
A reprint of Dr. Currie's second edition.
——New edition. 4 vols. Belfast, 1807, 12mo.
A reprint of Dr. Currie's edition.
——Seventh edition. 4 vols. London, 1813, 8vo.
——Eighth edition. To which are now added the Reliques of R. B. [Edited by R. H. C.—*i.e.*, R. H. Cromek, with contribu-

tions from G. Burns ; and with woodcuts by T. Bewick.] 5 vols. London, 1814, 12mo.

——Another edition. [Edited by J. Currie.] 4 vols. London, Edinburgh [printed], 1815, 12mo.

——Another edition. 4 vols. London, 1815, 18mo.

——Another edition. 4 vols. Baltimore, 1815, 18mo.

——New edition, with additional pieces. 4 vols. Montrose, 1816, 12mo.

——Another edition. 4 vols. Edinburgh, 1818, 12mo.

——Another edition, illustrated by 24 plates by Burnet. 4 vols. Edinburgh, 1819, 8vo.

——Eighth edition. To which are now added some further particulars of the author's life, new notes and many other additions, by G. Burns. 4 vols. London, 1820, 8vo.

The Works of R. B., with many additional Poems and Songs. 2 vols. Montrose, 1819, 24mo.

The Works of R. B., etc. 3 vols. Edinburgh, 1820, 16mo.

The Works of R. B., etc. 4 vols. Edinburgh, 1820, 12mo.

The Works of R. B., including his Letters to Clarinda, and the whole of his suppressed poems ; with an Essay on his life, genius, etc. 4 vols. London, 1821, 12mo.

The Works of R. B., etc. A new edition. 2 vols. Montrose, 1823, 24mo.

Works of R. B., with an account of his life. 4 vols. New York, 1824, 18mo.

The Works of R. B., etc. A new edition. 2 vols. Montrose, 1824, 24mo.

The Works of R. B., with an account of his life and a criticism on his writings, by J. Currie. A new edition, etc. 2 vols. Edinburgh, 1825, 12mo

The Works of R. B., containing his Poems, Letters, etc. With life by Currie. 2 vols. London, 1826, 24mo.

Works ; with an account of his life and writings, etc., by J. Currie. Edinburgh, 1831, 8vo.

The Works of R. B., including his Letters to Clarinda, and the whole of his suppressed poems ; with an essay on his life, genius, and character. London, 1831, 8vo.

The Entire Works of R. B., with his life, and a criticism on his writings, etc. By James Currie. The four volumes complete in one, with an enlarged and corrected glossary. With 13 engravings. (*Diamond Edition.*) London, 1833, 16mo.

Frequently reprinted. The seventh edition is dated 1842, the tenth 1845.

The Works of R. B. With his life, by [the editor] A. Cunningham. 8 vols. London, 1834, 8vo.

The title-page to vol. i. reads "In six volumes." Each volume is illustrated by two landscape vignettes by D. O. Hill.

The Works of R. B., with his life. By Allan Cunningham. 4 vols. Boston [Mass.], 1834, 18mo.

The Works of R. B. Philadelphia, 1835, 8vo.

The Works of R. B., containing his Life, by John Lockhart, Esq., etc. New York, 1835, 8vo.

The Works of R. B., with selected notes of A. Cunningham, a biographical and critical introduction, and a glossary by Dr. A. Wagner, etc. Leipsic, 1835, 8vo.

The Poems, Letters, and Land of Burns, illustrated by W. H. Bartlett, T. Allom, and other artists, with a new memoir of the poet, and notices, critical and biographical, of his works, by Allan Cunningham. 2 vols. London, 1838, 4to.

The Works of R. B., with life by Allan Cunningham, and notes by Gilbert Burns, Lord Byron, Thomas Carlyle, etc. London, 1840, 8vo.

The Works of R. B. Edited by the Ettrick Shepherd [J. Hogg] and W. Motherwell. 5 vols. Glasgow, 1840, 41, 38, 39, 12mo.

The Entire Works of R. B., with an account of his life and a criticism on his writings. To which are prefixed some observations on the character and condition of the Scottish Peasantry. By J. Currie. Seventh diamond edition, with illustrations from original designs by Mr. Stewart. London, Edinburgh [printed], 1842, 16mo.
Forms part of a series entitled the "Diamond Cabinet Library." With a second title-page, engraved.

The Complete Works of R. B., containing his poems, songs, and correspondence, illustrated by W. H. Bartlett, T. Allom, and other artists. With a new life of the poet, and notices, critical and biographical, by A. Cunningham. London, 1842, 8vo.

The Complete Works of R. B., containing his poems, letters, songs, his letters to Clarinda, and the whole of his suppressed poems, with an essay on his life, genius, and character. London, 1843, 8vo.

The Works of R. B., with Dr. Currie's memoir of the poet, and an essay on his genius and character, by Professor Wilson; also numerous notes, annotations, and appendices, embellished by eighty-one portraits and landscape illustrations. 2 vols. Glasgow, Edinburgh, and London, 1843-4, 8vo.

The Works of R. B., containing his life by J. Lockhart; the poetry and correspondence of Dr. Currie's edition; biographical sketches by himself, G. Burns, Professor Stewart, and others; Essay on Scottish poetry by Dr. Currie; Burns's songs, etc. Boston [Mass.], 1846, 8vo.

The Works of R. B. With life by A. Cunningham, and notes. New edition. London, 1847, 8vo.

The Complete Works of R. B., with an account of his life and a criticism on his writings, etc. By James Currie. A new and complete edition. Aberdeen, 1848, 12mo.

The Works of R. B. With life by Allan Cunningham. New edition. London, 1850, 8vo.
The engraved title-page bears date 1842

The Life and Works of Robert Burns. Edited by Robert Chambers. (*Chambers's Instructive and Entertaining Library.*) 4 vols. Edinburgh, 1851-52, 8vo.

The Poetical and Prose Works of R. B. [With 16 illustrations on steel.] Hartford, 1855, 8vo.

The Life and Works of R. B. Edited by R. Chambers. . . .

Library edition. **4 vols.** Edinburgh [printed] **and London** [1856, 57], 8vo.

The Complete Works of R. B., containing his Poems, Songs, **and** Correspondence. With a new **life** of the poet ; and notices, critical and biographical, by Allan Cunningham. Elegantly illustrated. Boston [Mass.], 1858, 8vo.

The **Complete** Works of R. B., with an **account** of his life, **and** a criticism on his writings. To which are prefixed some observations on the character and condition of the Scottish Peasantry. By James Currie. Halifax, 1859, 8vo.

The Life and Works of R. B. Edited by R. Chambers. **4 vols.** London, 1859-60, 12mo.

The Works of R. B., containing his Poems, Songs, and Correspondence. With life and notes, critical and biographical, **by** Allan Cunningham ; and many **notes** by Gilbert Burns, Lord **Byron,** Thomas Campbell, etc. **With** illustrations on **steel. 2** vols. Edinburgh, 1865, 8vo.

The Complete Works of R. B., including his Correspondence, etc. With **a** memoir by W. Gunnyon. The text carefully printed and illustrated with notes. **With portraits and illustrations on wood by eminent artists. Edinburgh, 1865, 8vo.**

The Complete Works of R. B., etc. By James Currie. With an enlarged and corrected glossary, and eight engravings **on** steel. Halifax, 1865, 12mo.

The Illustrated Family **Burns,** with an original memoir [and portrait]. Glasgow [1866], 4to.

The Works of R. B., illustrated by an extensive series of Portraits and Authentic Views. With a complete life of the poet ; an essay **on** his genius and character, **by** Professor Wilson. **Numerous** notes, annotations, **and** appendices. 2 vols. **London, 1866, 8vo.**

Life and Works of **R. B. By P.** H. Waddell. **Enriched with** portraits and numerous illustrations in colour, etc. Glasgow, 1867 [-69], 4to.

The Complete Works of R. B., including **his correspondence, etc.** Illustrated **with portraits and numerous steel** engravings. 2 vols. **Glasgow,** 1867, 8vo.

The Globe edition. Poems, Songs, **and Letters, being** the complete **works of R. B.** Edited from **the best** printed and manuscript authorities ; **with** glossarial index and a biographical memoir by **A.** Smith. London, **1868, 8vo.**

The **Works and Correspondence of** R. B., including his Letters to Clarinda ; remarks **on** Scottish songs and ballads. Illustrated by historical and critical notes, biographical notices. . . . With an extensive glossary of the Scottish language ; a life of the author ; and an essay on his genius and writings, etc. Glasgow [1870], 8vo.

The Works of R. B., poetical and **prose.** The Household Illus**trated Edition.** Arranged **and edited** by "Gertrude" [*i.e.,* **Mrs.** Jane Cross Simpson]. 2 **vols.** Glasgow, 1870, 8vo.

The Works of R. **B.**, illustrated by an extensive series of portraits **and authentic** views, etc. **2 vols. Glasgow**, 1877, 8vo.

The Works of R. B. [Edited by **W. S.** Douglas.] **6 vols.** Edinburgh, 1877-79, **8vo.**

The National Burns. Edited by George Gilfillan, including the airs of all the songs, etc. 2 vols. London [1879-80], 4to.

The Complete Works of Robert Burns, with his life and letters. Illustrated, **etc.** (*People's Edition.*) **London [1886, etc.],** 4to.

II. POETICAL WORKS.

Poems, chiefly in the Scottish dialect. Kilmarnock, 1786, **8vo.**
Very scarce. There are two copies **in** the Library of the British Museum, one of which contains additional poems and notes in MS., with the names and places in the poems supplied in the hand-writing of Burns. This is the first edition of the poems published, 31st July 1786. Of the 612 copies printed, 350 were subscribed for before publication.

——Second edition. Edinburgh, **1787, 8vo.**
This is the first Edinburgh edition.

——Third edition. **London, 1787**, 8vo.
A reprint of the preceding. **The** first London edition.

——Another edition. **Belfast,** 1787, 12mo.
A pirated edition.

——Another edition, **to** which **are** added Scots Poems, selected from the works of R. Fergusson. New **Y**ork, 1788, 8vo.
A reprint of the Edinburgh edition, 1787.

——Another edition. Dublin, 1789, 12mo.
The Belfast edition, with a **Dub**lin publisher's name.

Poems.—Another edition. Dublin, 1790, 12mo.
Reprint of Belfast edition, **with** a Dublin publisher's name.

——Another edition. Edinburgh, 1790, 8vo.

——Another **edition.** Belfast, 1790, 12mo.
A reprint **of the** Belfast 1780 edition.

——Second [Edinburgh] edition, considerably enlarged. 2 vols. Edinburgh, 1793, 8vo.
This edition includes twenty additional poems.

——Another **edition. 2 vols.** Belfast, **1793, 12mo.**
The first volume is a reprint of the 1789 Belfast edition, and the second contains the additional poems in the 1793 Edinburgh edition.

——A **new** edition, considerably enlarged. **2 vols. Edinburgh,** 1794, 8vo.
The second Edinburgh edition, with new title-pages, and the last printed in the author's life-time.

——New edition, considerably enlarged. 2 vols. Edinburgh, **1797,** 8vo.
A reprint of the 1794 edition.

——Another edition. 2 vols. Philadelphia, **1797,** 12mo.
A reprint of the preceding edition.

——New edition. 2 vols. Edinburgh, 1798, 8vo.
A reprint of **the 1797 edition.**

——Another **edition, considerably** enlarged. **2 vols. Edinburgh,** 1800, 8vo.
A reprint **of** the 1798 **edition.**

——Another edition. **2 vols,** Berwick-**upon**-Tweed, **1801,** 12mo.
Each volume has a separate title-page, engraved.

——Another edition. [With a glossary]. 2 vols. Edinburgh, 1801, 16mo.
Vignettes and tail-pieces by Bewick, and illustrations by A. Carse.

Poems. — Another edition. To which are added several other pieces not contained in any former edition of his poems. [Life of R. B.] Glasgow, 1801, 12mo.

——Another edition, considerably enlarged. Glasgow, 1801, 12mo.

——Poems ascribed to R. B. not contained in any edition of his works hitherto published. Glasgow, 1801, 8vo.

——Another edition. 2 vols. Edinburgh, 1802, 32mo.

——Another edition. 2 vols. Paisley, 1802, 32mo.
    This edition was suppressed.

——Stewart's Edition of B.'s Poems, including a number of original pieces never before published. With his life and character. Embellished with engravings, etc. Glasgow, 1802, 18mo.

——Crerar's Edition of B.'s Poems; with his life and character. [Portrait and plates by R. Scott.] 2 vols. Kirkaldy, 1802, 18mo.

——Poems by R. B., with his life and character. Dundee, 1802, 18mo.

——The Poetical Works of the late R. B., with an account of his life. A new edition, etc. Newcastle-on-Tyne, 1802, 12mo.

——Another edition. 2 vols. Dublin, 1803, 12mo.

——A new edition, which included all the poems and songs in that printed at Edinburgh in 1787, etc. London, Arbroath [printed], 1803, 12mo.
    Reprinted, London, 1824.

——Another edition. 2 vols. Dublin, 1803, 32mo.

Poems.—Another edition, with a complete glossary and life of the author. 2 vols. London, 1803, 32mo.

——Another edition. 2 vols. Cork, 1804, 8vo.
    A reprint of the 1803 Dublin edition.

——Another edition, with his life and character. Edinburgh, 1804, 18mo.

——Another edition, with his life and character. Glasgow, 1804, 18mo.

——Another edition. Wilmington, 1804, 12mo.

——A new edition. Including the pieces published in his correspondence, with his songs and fragments. To which is prefixed a sketch of his life [by Alexander Chalmers]. 3 vols. London, 1804, 8vo.

——The Poetical Works of R. B., with the author's life written by himself. 2 vols. Philadelphia, 1804, 18mo.

——Poems, chiefly in the Scottish dialect. By R. B. With his life and character [and a glossary]. Edinburgh, 1805, 12mo.

——Another edition. London, 1806, 12mo.

——Another edition. Edinburgh, 1807, 24mo.

——The Poetical Works of R. B., collated with the best editions. By T. Park. 2 vols. London, 1807, 16mo.

——The Poetical Works of R. B., and history of his life. Philadelphia, 1807, 18mo.

——The Poetical Works of R. B., with his life. With engravings on wood by Bewick. 2 vols. Alnwick, 1808, 8vo.

The Poetical Works of R. B., collated with the best editions, etc. (*Park's Works of the British Poets*, vol. xl.) 2 vols. London, 1808, 16mo.

——The Poems of R. B. A new edition. Musselburgh, 1808, 32mo.

——Poems, Letters, etc., ascribed to R. B., the Ayrshire Bard, not contained in any edition of his works hitherto published. Embellished with an elegant frontispiece. London, 1809, 16mo.

——The Poetical Works of R. B., with a complete glossary and life of the author. 2 vols. London, 1810, 12mo.
Each volume has a second engraved title-page.

——Poems by R. B., with an account of his life [by Josiah Walker], and remarks on his writings. Containing also many poems and letters not in Currie's edition. [Plates by J. Burnet.] 2 vols. Edinburgh, 1811, 8vo.

——The Poetical Works of R. B., with a complete glossary and life of the author. 2 vols. London, 1811, 12mo.
A reprint of the preceding.

——The Poetical Works of R. B., etc. Philadelphia, 1811, 12mo.

——The Poetical Works of the late R. B., with an account of his life, etc. Newcastle-on-Tyne, 1811, 12mo.
A reprint of the 1802 edition.

——The Poetical Works of R. B., with his life. Engravings on wood by Bewick, from designs by Thurston. 2 vols. Alnwick, 1812, 12mo.

——A Collection of Songs in the Scotch Dialect, by the cele-brated R. B. [Illustrations by Bewick]. Newcastle-on-Tyne, 1812, 12mo.

——Poems chiefly in the Scottish Dialect, by R. B. With a life of the author, etc. Baltimore, 1812, 12mo.

——Poems and Songs by R. B., with a short sketch of the author's life, and a glossary. Edinburgh [1812], 24mo.

——Poems by R. B. 2 vols. London, 1812, 8vo.

—— Poems, chiefly Scottish. Perth, 1813, 12mo.

——Poetical Works of R. B. London, 1813, 24mo.
A reprint of the 1804 edition in one volume.

——Poetical Works of R. B. Edinburgh, 1814, 18mo.

——The Poetical Works of R. B. Newcastle, 1814, 8vo.

——The Poetical Works of R. B. London, 1814, 24mo.

——The Poetical Works of R. B., with his Songs and Fragments, to which is prefixed a Sketch of his Life. Edinburgh, 1815, 18mo.

——Poems chiefly in the Scottish Dialect. Baltimore, 1815, 18mo.

——The Poetical Works of R. B. Edinburgh, 1815, 18mo.

——The Poems of R. B., with a sketch of his life. Belfast, 1815, 32mo.

——The Poetical Works of R. B., including several poems not to be found in any other edition, etc. 2 vols. Salem [N.Y.], 1815, 24mo.

——The Poetical Works of R. B., with an account of his life, and a selection of his best letters, etc. Belfast, 1816, 8vo.

The Poetical Works of R. B., including all the Poetry contained in Dr. Currie's edition, etc. Glasgow, 1816, 12mo.

——The Poetical Works of the late R. B., with an account of his life, etc. Embellished with copperplates. Edinburgh, 1816, 12mo.

——Findlay's Edition of Burns's Poems, including a number of original pieces never before published. Dublin, 1816, 16mo.

——The Poetical Works of R. B. With a complete glossary, and life of the author. 2 vols. London, 1816, 12mo.
A reprint of the 1810 edition.

——The Poetical Works of R. B., etc. 2 vols. Edinburgh, 1817, 32mo.

——The Poetical Works of R. B., including the pieces published in his Correspondence and Reliques, with his Songs and Fragments, etc. London, 1817, 24mo.

——Poems. Kirkaldy, 1817, 8vo.

——The Poems of R. B., etc. Belfast, 1818, 18mo.

——The Poetical Works of R. B., etc. Embellished with eleven beautiful engravings. Newcastle-on-Tyne, 1818, 8vo.

——Poetical Works of R. B., etc. Embellished with cuts. Dunbar, 1818, 24mo.

——The Poetical Works of R. B., etc. 2 vols. Philadelphia, 1818, 18mo.

——The Poems of R. B. Edinburgh, 1819, 24mo.

——The Lyric Muse of R. B., etc. Montrose, 1819, 24mo.

——The Poems of R. B., etc. Dublin, 1819, 18mo.

Poems and Songs of R. B., etc. Edinburgh, 1819, 18mo.

——Poems and Songs of R. B., with a life of the author. To which is subjoined an appendix, consisting of a panegyrical ode, and a demonstration of Burns's superiority to every other poet as a writer of songs, by the Rev. H. Paul. Air, 1819, 12mo.

——The Poetical Works of R. B. Including several pieces not inserted in Dr. Currie's edition; exhibited under a new plan of arrangement; and preceded by a life of the author, and a glossary. 2 vols. London, 1819, 8vo.

——The Poetical Works of R. B., etc. A new edition. London, 1821, 16mo.

——The Poetical Works of R. B., etc. Glasgow, 1821, 12mo.

——The Poetical Works of R. B. 2 vols. Chiswick, 1821, 8vo.

——The Poems of R. B. (*British Poets*, vol. lxxv., lxxvi.) 2 vols. Chiswick, 1822, 12mo.

——The Poetical Works of R. B., with a life of the author. (*Sanford's Works of the British Poets*, vol. xxxviii., xxxix.) Philadelphia, 1822, 12mo.

——The Poetical Works of R. B., with his songs and fragments. To which are prefixed, A History of the Poems, by G. Burns, and a sketch of his life. [With a portrait.] 2 vols. London, 1822, 12mo.

——The Poetical Works of R. B., including the pieces published in his correspondence and reliques. . . . To which is prefixed a sketch of his life. [By

A. C.—*i.e.*, A. Constable.] 3 vols. London, 1823, 8vo.

——The Poetical Works of R. B., including several pieces not inserted in Dr. Currie's edition, etc. 2 vols. London, 1823, 24mo.

——The Poetical Works of R. B. A new edition, etc. Edinburgh, 1823, 12mo.

——The Poetical Works of R. B., etc. Philadelphia, 1823, 8vo.

——The Poetical Works of R. B., etc. Edinburgh, 1824, 24mo.

——The Poetical Works of R. B., etc. 2 vols. London, 1824, 24mo.

——The Poetical Works of R. B., the Ayrshire Bard ; including all the pieces originally published by Dr. Currie, with various additions. A new edition, with an enlarged and corrected glossary, and a biographical memoir of the author. London, 1824, 8vo.

——Poems, chiefly in the Scottish Dialect. London, 1824, 12m.

——The Poetical Works of R. B., with a glossary, etc. London, 1825, 32mo.

——The Poetical Works of R. B., etc. 2 vols. New York, 1825, 24mo.

——The Poetical Works of R. B. London, 1826, 12mo.
One of a series entitled : "**Dove's** English Classics."

——The Poetical Works of R. B., etc. Glasgow, 1828, 24mo.

——The Poetical Works of R. B., including several pieces not inserted in Dr. Currie's Edition ; with an enlarged glossary, and an original life of the author. 2 vols. London, 1828, 24mo.

The Poems and Songs of R. B., with a life of the author, and a glossary. [With woodcuts by T. Bewick.] Alnwick, 1828, 12mo.

——The Poetical Works of R. B., as collected and published by Dr. Currie, with additional poems, etc. London, 1829, 12mo.

——The Poetical Works of R. B. 2 vols. Chiswick, 1829, 18mo.

——The Poetical Works of R. B. (With a memoir by Sir Harris Nicolas.) 2 vols. London, 1830, 8vo.
Aldine Edition of the British Poets.

——The Poetical Works of R. B., with his life, a critique, glossary, etc. 2 vols. in one. London, 1830, 16mo.

——The Complete Poetical Works of R. B., with explanatory and glossarial notes, and a life of the author, by James Currie, M.D. Abridged. New edition. London, 1834, 24mo.

——The Poetical Works of R. B., etc. Edinburgh, 1832, 24mo.

——The Poetical Works of R. B., etc. Dunbar, 1834, 18mo.

——The Poetical Works of R. B., etc. A new edition. 2 vols. Dundee, 1834, 24mo.

——The Poetical Works of R. B., etc. Boston [Mass.]. 1834, 18mo.

——The Poetical Works of R. B., etc. 2 vols. Edinburgh, 1835, 24mo.

——The Poetical Works of R. B., comprising an entire collection of his poems, etc. London, 1836, 12mo.
One of a series entitled "The Magnet Edition of the British Poets."

Standard Library Edition. The Poetical Works of R. B., with a life of the author, etc. London, 1838, 8vo.

——The Poetical Works of R. B., to which are now added notes illustrating historical, personal, and local allusions. Edinburgh, 1838, 8vo.

——Poetical Works. (Memoir of Burns, by Sir Harris Nicolas.) 3 vols. London, 1839, 8vo.
This is the second edition of Burns's Poetical Works published in the "Aldine Edition of the British Poets." There is a copy on vellum in the Library, British Museum.

——The Poetical Works of R. B., with a life of the author, and an essay on the genius and writings of Burns, by A. Cunningham, etc. London, 1839, 32mo.

——The Poetical Works of R. B. A new and complete edition, etc. London, 1840, 12mo.

——The Poetical Works of R. B., with a memoir, etc. Halifax, 1840, 32mo.

——The Poetical Works of R. B., etc. Newcastle, 1841, 48mo.

——The Poetical Works of R. B., etc. London, 1843, 48mo.

——The Poetical Works of R. B., etc. Glasgow, 1845, 32mo.

——The Poetical Works of R. B. With the life and portrait of the author. (*Tauchnitz Collection of British Authors*, vol. xc.) Leipzig, 1845, 16mo.

——The Poetical Works of R. B., with a life of the author, etc. London, 1846, 32mo.

——The Complete Poetical Works of R. B., with explanatory and glossarial notes; and a life of the author by James

Currie. New edition. London, 1846, 24mo.

Poetical Works of R. B., complete. Edinburgh, 1847, 8vo.

——The Poetical Works of R. B. London, 1848, 8vo.

——The Poetical Works of R. B., as collected and published by Dr. Currie. (*Cabinet Edition of the British Poets*, vol. ii.). London, 1851, 8vo.

——The Poetical Works of R. B. (*The Universal Library*. Poetry, vol. ii.) London [1853], 8vo.

——The Poetical Works of R. B., with life, notes, and glossary, by A. Cunningham, with many illustrations on steel. Philadelphia, 1856, 12mo.

——The Poetical Works of R. B. With memoir, critical dissertation, and explanatory notes. By G. Gilfillan. 2 vols. Edinburgh, 1856, 8vo.

——The Poetical Works of R. B. Edited [with a memoir] by the Rev. Robert Aris Willmott. Illustrated by John Gilbert (*Routledge's British Poets.*) London, 1856, 8vo.

——The Poetical Works of R. B., with a memoir of the author's life, etc. Glasgow, 1856, 18mo.

——Poems and Songs. Illustrated with numerous engravings. London, 1858 [1857], 4to.

——The Poetical Works of R. B., with critical and biographical notes by A. Cunningham, and a glossary. Elegantly illustrated by Schmolze. Philadelphia, 1858, 8vo.

——Centenary Edition. The Poetical Works of R. B.; with memoir, prefatory notes, and a complete marginal glossary.

Edited by John and Angus Macpherson. With portrait and illustrations. Glasgow, **1859,** 12mo.

——The Poetical Works of R. **B.** [Illustrated.] London, 1859, 8vo.

——**In** this edition the more objectionable passages and pieces are omitted. The Poetical Works and Letters of R. B. With Life. Edinburgh [1859], 8vo.

——The Poetical Works of R. B., with a Memoir **of** the Author's Life, and a glossary. Halifax, 1860, 24mo.

——The Poetical Works of R. **B.** With a sketch of the Author's Life. 3 vols. Boston [Mass.], 1863, 8vo.

The Memoir of Burns is from the eighth edition of the *Encyclopædia Britannica.*

——The Poems of R. **B. London,** 1863, 8vo.

One of "Bell & Daldy's Pocket Volumes."

——**The Poems** of **R. B. London, 1864, 8vo.**

Another copy of the preceding, **with** a new title-page, and forms part of "Bell & Daldy's Elzevir Series of Standard Authors."

——The Poetical Works of **R. B.** With memoir, critical dissertation, and explanatory notes **by** the Rev. George Gilfillan. **The** text edited by Charles **Cowden** Clarke. 2 vols. Edinburgh, 1864, 8vo.

——**The** Poetical Works of R. **B. Edited** from the best printed and manuscript authorities, with glossarial index and a biographical memoir by A. Smith. **2 vols.** London [printed] and Cambridge, 1865, 8vo.

Forming part of the "Golden Treasury Series."

The Poetical **Works of R. B.** Edited by **the Rev.** Robert Aris Willmott. Illustrated by John Gilbert. New edition. London, 1865, 8vo.

Forms part of **"Routledge's** British Poets."

——The Poetical Works of R. **B.** With **a** memoir of the author's life, and a copious glossary. Glasgow, 1865, 24mo.

——The Complete Poetical Works of R. B. Edited by J. S. Roberts. With an original memoir by W. Gunnyon. With portrait and illustrations **on** wood **by eminent artists. Seventh thousand. Edinburgh [1866], 8vo.**

——**The Poetical Works of R. B.** Edited by **R. A. Wilmott.** New edition. **With** numerous additions [by P. A. N.]. London [Bungay printed], **1866,** 8vo.

——The Complete Poetical Works of R. B. and Sir W. Scott. Illustrated . . . and a facsimile of a letter of B.'s to Mrs. Riddell. New edition. 2 parts. London, **Glasgow** [printed], 1866, 8vo.

——**The** Poetical **Works of R. B.** New edition. **With a memoir** by **Sir** Harris **Nicolas.** 3 vols. London, 1866, **8vo.**

"Aldine Edition **of the British** Poets."

——The Poetical Works of R. B. With a memoir of the author's life, and **a** glossary. Halifax, 1866, 32mo.

——Poems, chiefly in the Scottish dialect. (Poems as they appeared **in** the early Edinburgh editions. Posthumous [sic] Poems—Songs.). [Edited by

J. MacKie.] **4** parts. **Kil**-marnock [1867]-1869, 8vo.

Part 1 is a fac-simile reprint of the original Kilmarnock edition, and part 2 of the first Edinburgh edition. Part 4 has on the verso of the title-page, "American Edition."

——The Poetical Works of R. B., with a memoir. **2 vols. New** York, 1867, 16mo.

——Poems and Songs by R. B. With illustrations by R. Herdman, W. H. Paton, T. Bough, G. Steel, D. O. Hill, J. M'Whirter, and other Scottish Artists. Engraved by R. Paterson. Edinburgh, 1868 [1867], **4to.**

——The Poetical Works of R. B., complete. **With numerous** illustrations. **London, 1870,** 8vo.

——The Poetical Works of R. B., re-edited from the best editions, with explanatory glossarial notes, memoir, etc. (*Chandos Classics.*) London [1871], 8vo.

——Kilmarnock Popular Edition. The Complete Poetical Works of R. B., arranged in the order of their earliest publication. . . . With a memoir of the poet and new annotations by W. S. Douglas. 2 vols. Kilmarnock, 1871, 8vo.

——The Poetical Works of R. B. Edited, with a critical memoir, by W. M. Rossetti. Illustrated by J. M. Smith. London, Edinburgh [printed, 1871], 8vo.

——The Complete Poetical Works of R. B. and Sir Walter Scott. (*Blackwood's Universal Library of Standard Authors.*) New edition. London [1872], 8vo.

——The Poetical Works of R. B. With memoir, critical disserta-tion, and explanatory notes. The text edited by C. C. Clarke. **2 vols.** London [printed], Paris **and** New York [1872], 8vo.

Forming part of "Cassell's Edition of the British Poets."

——Kilmarnock edition, revised and extended. The Complete Poetical Works of R. B., with **new annotations,** biographical **notices. Edited** by W. S. Douglas. **2 vols.** Kilmarnock, 1876, 8vo.

——The Poetical Works of R. B. Edited, with introductory biography and notes, by C. Kent. With illustrations. London [1878], **8vo.**

——Burns, Ramsay, **and** the earlier poets of Scotland, to which is added ancient ballads and songs of Scotland. Edited, with notes, critical and biographical, by A. Cunningham and C. Mackay. [With engravings.] **2 vols.** London [1878, 79], **8vo.**

——The Poetical Works of R. B. **London,** Perth [printed, **1878**], 8vo.

——The Poetical Works of R. B. Edited, with a critical memoir, by William Michael Rossetti. Illustrated by John Moyr Smith. (*Moxon's Popular Poets.*) London [1879], **8vo.**

——The Poetical Works of R. B. Edited, **with** glossarial index and a biographical memoir, by A. Smith. 2 vols. London, 1879, 8vo.

——The Poetical Works of R. B. Edited by R. A. Willmott. London [1880], 8vo.

Forming part of the "Excelsior Series."

Poems. With a glossary. 2 vols. London, Plymouth [printed], 1881, 32mo.

——The Poetical Works and **Letters of R.** B., with marginal **explanations** of the Scotch words, **and** life, etc. Edinburgh, London [1881], 8vo.
> Part of "The Landscape Series of Poets."

——The Poetical Works **of R.** B. Edited, with a critical **memoir,** by W. M. Rossetti. Illustrated by John **Moyr** Smith. London, Perth [printed, 1881], 8vo.

——The **Poetical** Works of R. B., with **memoir,** prefatory notes, and **glossary.** Edited by John and Angus Macpherson, etc. Glasgow [1883], 8vo.

——The Poetical Works of R. B. Edited, with notes, by C. Kent. (*The Blackfriars edition.*) London, 1883, 8vo.

——**The** Poetical Works of R. B. Pearl edition. Glasgow [1884], 32mo.

——The Poetical **Works** of R. B. Edited by **C. Kent.** London, 1885 [1884], 8vo.

——The Poetical Works of R. B. With a prefatory notice by Joseph **Skipsey.** (*Canterbury Poets.*) 2 parts. London, 1885, 8vo.

Poems of R. B. With a **glossary.** London [1886, etc.], 16mo.

The **Scots** Musical Museum. By James Johnson. 5 vols. Edinburgh, 1787-1803, 8vo.
> Included are 184 songs written or collected by Burns. Reprinted in 6 vols. in 1839, with notes by the late William Stenhouse, and illustrations [by David Laing]; and again in 4 vols. in 1853.

Illustrations of the Lyric Poetry and Music of Scotland, compiled to accompany the "Scots Musical Museum" [of J. Johnson], and now published separately, with additional notes and illustrations by William Stenhouse [and an introduction by D. Laing]. Edinburgh, 1853, 8vo.

The Caledonian Musical Museum; or, Complete Vocal Library of the best Scotch Songs. Embellished with a portrait, and containing upwards of two hundred songs by that immortal bard. The whole edited by his son [R. Burns]. London, 1809, 12mo.

Improved edition. The songs of R. B., etc. Liverpool, 1822, 16mo.

The Songs and Ballads of R. Burns: including ten **never** before published; with a preliminary discourse, and illustrative preface. London, 1823, 12mo.

Songs chiefly **in the** Scottish dialect. **London,** Chiswick printed, 1824, 12mo.

Burns's Songs, chiefly Scottish. London, 1825, 12mo.

The Songs of R. B., with his life, and a glossary. Glasgow, 1831, 32mo.

The Songs of Burns, with a biographical preface, notes, and glossary. London, 1834, 32mo.

——Second **edition.** The Songs of Burns, etc. Liverpool, 1834, 18mo.

The Scottish Keepsake; **or, Songs** of the Ayrshire Bard. **Mauch**line, 1844, 32mo.

The Songs of R. B., alphabetically arranged, etc. London, 1844, 32mo.

The Songs of R. B. Dumfries, 1848, 18mo.

The Songs and Ballads of R. B., including a number of pieces not to be found in any other copy. New and improved edition. Glasgow, 1857, 18mo.

Illustrated Songs of R. B., with a portrait after the original by Nasmyth. [Edinburgh] 1861, fol.

The Songs of R. B., with music. Centenary edition. Glasgow, 1859, 8vo.

The Songs of R. B. London, 1863, 16mo.
    One of "Bell & Daldy's Pocket Volumes."

The Principal Songs of R. B. translated into Mediæval Latin verse, with the Scottish version collated. By A. Leighton. *Eng.* and *Lat.* Edinburgh, 1862, 8vo.

The Ballads and Songs of R. B. With a lecture on his character and genius by T. Carlyle. [With illustrations.] London, Glasgow [printed], 1864, 18mo.

––––––

An Address to the Deil. With the answer by J. Lauderdale. [Edinburgh ?], 1795, 12mo.

––––Another edition. With explanatory notes. Illustrated by engravings after designs by T. Landseer. London, 1830, 12mo.

Alonzo and Cora, with other original poems, etc., by Elizabeth Scot. To which are added Letters in Verse by Blacklock and Burns. London, 1801, 8vo.

Alloway Kirk ; or Tam O'Shanter. With Life of Burns. Air, 1817, 8vo.

––––Alloway Kirk ; or, Tam O'Shanter. A tale in verse. Paisley, 1822, 16mo.

––––Tam O'Shanter : a tale. To which are added Observations on the statues [by J. Thom] of Tam O'Shanter and Souter Johnny now exhibiting. [London, 1829], 8vo.

––––Tam O'Shanter and Souter Johnny. Illustrated by T. Landseer. London, 1830, 12mo.

––––Tam O'Shanter. Illustrated by John Faed. For the members of the Royal Association for the Promotion of the Fine Arts in Scotland. [Seven plates.] Edinburgh, 1853, fol.

––––Tam O'Shanter, a Poem : The Statues of Tam O'Shanter and Souter Johnny, etc. Ayr [1853], 8vo.

––––Tam O'Shanter, with illustrations by E. H. Miller, etc. New York, 1868, 4to.

––––Tam O'Shanter, and Lament of Mary Queen of Scots. Photolithographed [from the original MSS.] by W. Griggs, etc. (*Sharman's Photo - Lithograph Fac-similes*, No. 1.) London [1869], fol.

––––Tam O'Shanter. With illustrations by George Cruikshank. London [1884], 4to.

––––Sculpture. Tam O'Shanter, Souter Johnny, the Landlord and Landlady, executed by J. Thom ; and illustrative of Tam O'Shanter, a tale, by R. B. [With the text.] London, 1830, 8vo.

Auld Lang Syne. By Robert Burns. Illustrated by George

Harvey, F.S.A. For the members of the Royal Association for the Promotion of the Fine Arts in Scotland. [Five plates.] Fol., 1859.

B.'s Farewell [to the Brethren of St. James's Lodge, Tarbolton]; together with The Voice of Labour (a chant of the Monster Meetings); and Highland Mary [by R. B.]. Waterford [1846 ?], 16mo.

The Calf [a satire, in verse, by R. B.]; the Unco Calf's Answer; Virtue—to a Mountain Bard; and the Deil's Answer to his vera worthy frien', R. B. [In verse.] [Edinburgh ?, 1787], 8vo.

The Cotter's Saturday Night. (*Roach's Beauties of the Poets, etc.*, vol. vi.) London, 1795, 12mo.

——Burns's Cotter's Saturday Night. Cupar Fife, 1804, 12mo.

——Cotter's Saturday Night—A Winter Night—To a Mountain Daisy—To a Mouse. (*Pratt's Cabinet of Poetry*, vol. vi.) London, 1808, 12mo.

——The Cotter's Saturday Night. Illustrated by John Faed. For the members of the Royal Association for the Promotion of the Fine Arts in Scotland. [Eight plates.] Edinburgh, 1853, obl. fol.

——The Cotter's Saturday Night, and Tam O'Shanter. London [1854 ?], 32mo.

——The Cotter's Saturday Night. Illustrated by F. A. Chapman. New York, 1867, 8vo.

——Burns. The Cotter's Saturday Night and the Twa Dogs. With life, etc. (*Chambers's*

Reprints of English Classics.) London, 1883, 8vo.

The Fornicator's Court. [A poem.] [Edinburgh ?, 1810 ?], 8vo.

Holy Willie's Prayer, etc. Edinburgh, 1801, 8vo.

——Another edition. Glasgow, 1801, 12mo.

The Jolly Beggars. Printed for the first time, from the author's MS. Glasgow [1800 ?], 12mo.

——The Jolly Beggars : a Cantata ascribed to the celebrated R. B. Newcastle-on-Tyne, 1804, 12mo.

——The Jolly Beggars ; or, Tatterdemalions : a Cantata. Edinburgh, 1808, 18mo.

——Fac-simile of Burns's celebrated poem, entitled The Jolly Beggars. From the original manuscript. [The "Advertisement" subscribed W. W.] Glasgow, 1838, 4to.

The Kirk's Alarm, a satire, and other pieces by R. B. Glasgow, 1801, 12mo.

The Robin's Yule Song. Extracted from Chambers's Popular Rhymes of Scotland. Illustrated by W. F. F. and E. C. F. [Attributed to R. B. in the preface.] London, Edinburgh [printed ? 1859], obl. fol.

The Soldier's Return, illustrated by John Faed. (Six plates.) Edinburgh, 1857, fol.

III. PROSE WORKS.

The Prose Works of R. B., containing his Letters and Correspondence, Literary and Critical, and Amatory Epistles ; including Letters to Clarinda, etc. ; with nine engravings. Newcastle, 1819, 8vo.

The Prose Works of R. B., with
the notes by Currie and Cromek, and many by the present
editor [Robert Chambers].
Edinburgh, 1839, 8vo.

The Complete Prose Works of
R. B. **Edinburgh** [1865], 8vo.

Reliques of R. B., **consisting**
chiefly of original letters, poems,
and critical observations on
Scottish Songs. Collected and
published by R. H. Cromek.
London, 1808, 8vo.
   Comprises 62 letters, with commonplace books, journals, fragments of poetry. etc.

——**Another** edition. Philadelphia, 1809, 12mo.

——Select Scottish Songs, ancient
and modern ; with critical
observations and biographical
notices by Robert Burns.
Edited by R. H. Cromek. 2
vols. London, 1810, 8vo.

——Reliques of R. B., etc.
Second edition. **London, 1813,**
8vo.
   A reprint of the 1808 edition.

—— Fourth edition. **London,**
1817, 8vo.
   A reprint of the 1808 edition.

The Letters of R. B., chronologi-
cally arranged. From Dr.
Currie's collection. 2 vols.
London, 1819, 8vo.

——**Letters** of R. B. 2 vols.
Boston [Mass.], 1820, 16mo.

——The Letters of R. B., **chron-**
ologically arranged ; compre-
hending the whole of Dr.
Currie's collection, and the
most valuable portion of Cromek's Reliques. [With portrait.]
Glasgow, 1828, 8vo.

Letters addressed to Clarinda,
etc. Glasgow, 1802, 16mo.

Letters **addressed to Clarinda, etc.**
A new edition. Belfast, 1806,
8vo.
   A reprint of the preceding.

——Letters addressed to Clarinda.
Philadelphia, 1809, 12mo.

——A new edition. Belfast, 1816,
8vo.

——**Another edition.** Glasgow,
1820, 8vo.

——**Another edition.** Belfast,
1826, 12mo.

——The Correspondence between
B. and Clarinda. With a
memoir of Mrs McLehose
(Clarinda). Arranged and
edited by W. C. McLehose.
Edinburgh, 1843, 12mo.
   There is also a second engraved
   title-page.

R. Burns's Commonplace Book.
Printed from the original manuscript of **J.** Adam, Esq.,
Greenock. [With a preface
by C. D. L.] Edinburgh, 1872,
8vo.
   Privately printed.

IV. SELECTIONS.

The Beauties **of Burns.** Air,
1802, 12mo.
   Contains Death and Dr. Horn-
   book, The Twa Brigs, the Cottar's
   Saturday Night, Halloween, and
   Songs.

Twenty Songs. **Glasgow** [1800],
12mo.

——Second edition, containing
eight songs **not** in the first.
Seventeen songs by R. B.
Glasgow, 1809, 12mo.

Seventeen favourite songs, by **the**
celebrated Scottish Poets, B.
and Tannahill, etc. [13 by R.
B., 4 by Tannahill.] Glasgow
[1815 ?], 12mo.

The Beauties of Burns's Poems: consisting of the most admired pieces of that celebrated Scots Poet. Falkirk, 1819, 18mo.

The Ceremony of Halloween displayed, to which is added First of April, Hunt the Gowk! or, All-fools' day. Compiled from B.'s works by W. Smith. [Edinburgh], 1825, 8vo.

The Beauties of Burns, consisting of selections from his poems and letters by Alfred Howard. London, 1826, 18mo.

A Series of Twelve Illustrations of the Poems of R. B. Engraved on steel by J. Shury from original paintings by W. Kidd. London, 1832, 8vo.

Selections from the Scottish Poems of R. B. Edinburgh, 1834, 12mo.

The Beauties of Byron and Burns, being a collection of poems by the above authors. Hull, 1837, 32mo.

Burns Songster [21 Songs]. New-castle-upon-Tyne [1850 ?], 12mo.

In Honorem. Songs of the Brave. Poems and Odes by Campbell, Wolfe, Collins, Byron, and Macaulay [and R. Burns]. London, 1856, 8vo.

Select Songs and Ballads of R. B. Glasgow, 1859, 32mo.

The Flowers and Plants of Burns, with their scientific names, and quotations from his works, etc. Paisley, 1875, 8vo.

Poems selected from the works of R. B. Edited, with life of the author, notes, and glossary, by A. M. Bell. (*English School Classics.*) London, 1876, 16mo.

Favorite Poems. Illustrated. Boston [Mass.], 1877, 16mo.

The Burns Birthday Book. [Edited by J. Gibson.] Ardrossan [1877], 16mo.

——Another edition. Ardrossan [1879], 16mo.

——Another edition. [London ? 1879], 16mo.

Auld Acquaintance: a Birthday Book of the wise and tender words of R. B., compiled by J. B. Begg. Edinburgh, 1879, 16mo.

The Select Songs of Burns and Tannahill chronologically arranged, with memoirs. Glasgow [1883], 8vo.

Birthday Chimes. Selections from Burns. Edinburgh, 1887 [1886], 16mo.

V. APPENDIX.

BIOGRAPHY, CRITICISM, ETC.

Adams, Francis. — Writings of Burns; being a discourse delivered at Banchory on the Burns Centenary. Aberdeen, 1859, 12mo.

Adams, W. H. D. — Wrecked Lives, or men who have failed. Two series. London, 1880, 8vo. R. Burns, Ser. 2, pp. 162-209.

Adamson, Archibald R. —Rambles through the Land of Burns. Kilmarnock, 1879, 12mo.

Ainslie, Hew.—A Pilgrimage to the Land of Burns; containing anecdotes of the Bard, and of the character he immortalised, with numerous pieces of poetry, original and collected. [By H. Ainslie.] Deptford printed, London published, 1822, 8vo.

Ainslie.—Scottish Songs, Ballads, and Poems. New York, 1855, 8vo.
  Contains—"Lines written on the Anniversary of Burns's Birth," "Lines to Alloway Kirk," "Farewell to the Land of Burns."

Alexander, W. L.—The Idolatry of Genius: a discourse delivered in Queen Street Hall, 6th February 1859. Edinburgh, 1859, 12mo.

Allan, Robert.—Evening Hours, Poems and Songs. Glasgow, 1836, 12mo.
  Contains—"Lines written for Burns's Anniversary."

American.—English and Scottish Sketches. By an American. London, 1857, 8vo.
  The Land of Burns, pp. 285-297.

Anderson, George, and Finlay, John.—The Burns Centenary Poems. A Collection of Fifty out of many hundred written on the occasion of the Burns Centenary Celebration, including the six recommended by the judges at the Crystal Palace Competition, etc. Selected and edited by G. A. and J. F. Glasgow, 1859, 4to.

Anderson, William.—The Scottish Nation. 3 vols. Edinburgh, 1863, 4to.
  Robert Burns, with portrait, vol. i., pp. 498-512.

Andrews, Samuel. — Our Great Writers; or, popular chapters on some leading authors. London, 1884, 8vo.
  Burns, pp. 158-187.

Argonaut.—Argonaut, edited by the Rev. E. Paxton Hood. London, 1877, 8vo.
  Robert Burns, by Emily Mewburn, vol. vi., pp. 53-63.

Austin, A.—An English version of the Cotter's Saturday Night. By A. Austin. London, 1859, 8vo.

Ayr. — Reminiscences of Auld Ayr. Edinburgh, 1864, 12mo.
  Contains a chapter on Burns' Cottage.

Balfour, Alexander.—Contemplation; with other poems. Edinburgh, 1820, 8vo.
  "To the memory of Robert Burns," pp. 104-115.

Ballantine, James.—Chronicle of the hundredth birthday of Robert Burns. Collected and edited by J. B. Edinburgh, 1859, 8vo.

Ballingall, William.—Burns, the Ploughman Poet: a Memorial Tribute. [Peckham, 1878], 8vo.

Balmanno, Mrs.—Pen and Pencil. [Pieces in verse and prose.] New York, 1858, 4to.
  Memoir of Mrs. Renwick, the "Blue-Eyed Lassie" of Burns, with his poems addressed to her, pp. 172-181.

Bayne, Peter.—Two Great Englishwomen, Mrs. Browning and Charlotte Brontë; with an Essay on Poetry, illustrated from Wordsworth, Burns, and Byron. London, 1881, 8vo.

Beard, John R.—Burns' Anniversary. The Religion of Robert Burns, with an estimate of his character, and extracts from his works. London, 1859, 12mo.

Bede, Cuthbert [i.e., Edward Bradley].—A Tour in Tartan-Land, etc. London, 1863, 8vo.
  Chapters xi., xii., and xiii.—Grave of Burns's Highland Mary, etc. The true story of Burns and his Highland Mary, The Ayrshire Don Giovanni, etc., pp. 119-151.

Bennett, D. M. — The World's Sages, Infidels, and Thinkers, etc. New York, 1876, 8vo.
  Robert Burns, pp. 642-648.

Bennoch, Francis.—The Storm,
and other **poems.** London,
1841, 12mo.
  Contains—"To the memory of
  Burns" and "Coila" to the same.

Bigmore, E. C.—Descriptive **List**
of a **Collection** of Original
Manuscript **Poems by** R. B.
[London], 1861, **8vo.**

Biographical Magazine.—Lives of
the Illustrious. (The Biographical Magazine.) London, 1854,
8vo.
  Robert Burns, **vol.** v., pp. 256-266.

British **Poets.** — Biographical
Sketches of eminent British
Poets, etc. Dublin, 1851, **8vo.**
  Robert **Burns,** pp. 473-495.

——Lives **of the** British **Poets,**
etc. Edinburgh [1866], 8vo.
  Burns, with portrait, pp. 229-328.

Brooke, Rev. Stopford A.—Theology in the English Poets.
Cowper, Coleridge, Wordsworth,
and Burns. London, 1874,
8vo.
  Burns comprises pp. 287-339.

Brown, **C. R.**— **Sanct** Mungo's
Centenary : Tribute to Scotland's Bard. By C. R. B.
Specially composed for the
great National Festival at Glasgow, etc. **Glasgow,** 1859, 4to.

Brown, James Harris.—Scenes **in**
Scotland, with sketches **and**
illustrations, etc. Glasgow,
1833, 8vo.
  The Widow of Burns—The Poet's
  Tomb, pp. 66-72; Robert Burns, pp.
  80-89.

Brown, Rev. Thomas.—Letter **to**
the Rev. T. B., occasioned by
some remarks on the Life and
Writings of Robert Burns ap-
pended to his late publication
on Family Devotion. Perth,
1825, 24mo.

Browne, Felicia D. — **Poems.**
Liverpool, 1808, 4to.
  A Tribute to the genius of Robert
  Burns, pp. 96, 97.

Buchanan, William.—A **Volume**
of Verses, serious, humorous,
and satirical. Edinburgh, 1866,
8vo.
  Robert Burns : a Centenary **Ode,**
  pp. 24-33.

Burnes, James. — Notes on his
Name and Family. Edinburgh,
1851, 8vo.
  Printed for private circulation.

Burns, Robert. — Burns's Calf
turn'd a Bull ; or, some remarks
on his attack of Mr.*****
when preaching from Mat. **iv.** 2.
To which is added, some **obser-**
vations on Dr. M'G—ll's [*i.e.*,
William MacGill's] **practical**
essay. By a rhymer. **[In**
verse.] [Edinburgh ?], **1787,**
8vo.

——The Cottager's Saturday
night : a poem. [Altered from
Robert Burns.] London [1800],
12mo.

——Another edition. **Lancaster**
[1818], 12mo.

——The Answer **to B.'s** Bonny
Jean. To **which** are added
Bold Maginnes from the County
Tyrone, Blithe was She, and
Sally and Robert's Courtship.
[Four Songs.] Glasgow [1810 ?],
12mo.

——Burnomania : **the celebrity**
of R. B. considered **in a dis-**
course, to which **are added**
epistles in verse **respecting**
Peter Pindar, Burns, etc. Edinburgh, 1811, 8vo.

——A Critique on the Poems of
Robert Burns, illustrated by
engravings [after designs by J.
Burnet]. Edinburgh, 1812,
8vo.

Burns, Robert.—Festival in commemoration of Robert Burns, and to promote a subscription to erect a national monument to his memory at Edinburgh, etc. [A programme.] London, 1819, 8vo.

——Burns's Monument. Account of the grand Masonic procession which took place at laying the foundation-stone of a monument to R. Burns. To which is added Tam O' Shanter, etc. Ayr, 1820, 16mo.

——History of R. Burns, the celebrated Ayrshire Poet. [Newcastle, 1820 ?], 12mo.

——A Parody on Bruce's Address before the Battle of Bannockburn (by B.). [With other satirical verses.] Dublin [1830 ?], 8vo.
Without title-page.

——The Widow of Burns: her death, character, and funeral. Dumfries, 1834, 16mo.
Originally appeared in the *Dumfries and Galloway Courier.*

——A Descriptive Sketch of Burns's Birthplace, Alloway Kirk, Monument and Slabs, and his haunts on the Ayr. Ayr, 1837, 8vo.

——Catalogue of the Burns Gallery: a series of paintings illustrative of the writings of the Scottish poet, by D. O. Hill, etc., now exhibiting, at Edinburgh. ——, 1841, 8 vo.

——Mausoleum and Memorials of Burns. Edinburgh, 1842, 8vo.

——Festival in honour of the Memory of our National Poet, Robert Burns, etc. Glasgow, 1844, 8vo.

——A Winter with R. Burns. Being Annals of his Patrons and Associates in Edinburgh during the year 1786-7, and the details of his Inauguration as Poet - Laureate of the Can [ongate] Kil [winning Mason Lodge]. Edinburgh, 1846, 12mo.

——Fac-Simile of the handwriting of R. B. Copied from his Family Bible by C. Mackie. London, 1847, fol.

——Robert Burns, the Representative of his Era. Glasgow, 1859, 8vo.

——Centenary Celebration of the Birth of Robert Burns, January 25th, 1859. The Prize Poem written in honour of the occasion, words of the songs to be sung, and an account of the relics. London, 1859, 12mo.

——Report of the Meeting held to celebrate the Centenary of the Birthday of Robert Burns, at the Revere House, Boston, January 25th, 1859. Boston [Mass.], 1859, 8vo.

——Report of the Proceedings at the Celebration of the Burns Centenary at Kirkcudbright, 1859. Liverpool, 1859, 12mo.

——One of the six hundred and twenty-one. A Burns centenary poem. London, 1859, 12mo.

——Burns Centenary. Are such honours due to the Ayrshire Bard? Glasgow, 1859, 8vo.

——Crystal Palace. The Burns Centenary: a Rejected Ode. London, 1859, 8vo.

——The Burns' Centenary: being an account of the proceedings and speeches at the various banquets and meetings throughout the kingdom. With a memoir and portrait of the poet. **Edinburgh**, 1859, 8vo.

——The Twa Dogs. A new version [of the poem of the same title by R. B.]. London [1870?], 8vo.

——Burns : an Essay for the Working Classes of Scotland. By a Member of the Literary Institute. Edinburgh, 1872, 8vo.

——Some account of the Glenriddell MSS. of B.'s Poems : with several poems never before published. Edited by 'H. A. Bright. Liverpool, 1874, 4to.

——The Burns Calendar: a manual of Burnsiana ; relating events in the poet's history, names associated with his life and writings, a concise bibliography and a record of Burns relics. Kilmarnock, 1874, 4to.

——Memorials of R. Burns and some of his contemporaries and their descendants. By the Grandson of R. Aiken (P. F. Aiken). With a numerous selection of his Poems and Songs, etc. London, Bristol [printed], 1876, 8vo.

——Caledonia, described by Scott, Burns, and Ramsay. With illustrations by John Macwhirter, engraved by R. Paterson. London, 1878, 4to.

——Burns's statue, Dumfries. Poetical garland for the proposed monument. Reprinted from the *Dumfries Standard* of 25th January 1879. Dumfries, 1879, 12mo.

——Robert Burns and the Ayrshire Moderates. A correspondence [between "Aliquanto Latior" and A. T. Innes] reprinted from *The Scotsman*, with re-

marks. Privately printed. **Edinburgh**, 1883, 4to.

Campbell, Hugh.—The Wanderer in Ayrshire, etc. Kilmarnock, 1817, 8vo.
  Coila's Bard, pp. **111-118.**

Campbell, Thomas.—Specimens of the British Poets, with biographical and critical notices, etc. 7 vols. London, 1819, 8vo.
  Robert Burns, vol. vii., pp. **230-274.**

——The Poetical Works of T. **C.** New edition. 2 vols. London, 1833, 12mo.
  Ode to the Memory of Burns, vol. i., pp. 204-209.

Carlyle, Thomas.—On **Heroes**, Hero-Worship, and the **Heroic** in History. London, **1841, 12mo.**
  The Hero as Man of Letters. **Johnson, Rousseau, Burns, pp. 249-315.**

——Burns. London, 1854, 8vo.
  Originally appeared in the *Edinburgh Review*, December 1828, as a review of Lockhart's "Life of Burns." Reprinted without alteration. Included in all the collected editions of Carlyle's works.

Carruthers, Robert.—The Highland Note-Book, etc. Edinburgh, 1843, 8vo.
  A Ramble among the Scenery of Burns, pp. 260-277.

Chambers, Robert.—The Picture of Scotland. 2 vols. Edinburgh, **1827,** 8vo.
  Numerous references to Burns.

——A Biographical Dictionary of Eminent Scotsmen. Originally edited by R. **C.** New edition by the Rev. **T.** Thomson. **3** vols. London, 1868, 8vo.
  Burns, with portrait, vol. i., pp. 253-261.

——Chambers's Cyclopædia of English Literature. Third edi-

tion. 2 vols. London, 1876, 8vo.
> Robert Burns, vol. ii., pp. 186-194.

Combe, George. — Phrenological Development of Robert Burns, from a cast of his skull moulded at Dumfries the 31st day of March 1834, with remarks by George Combe. Edinburgh, 1834, 8vo.
> Reprinted in 1859.

Corr, Rev. Thomas J.—Favilla : Tales, Essays, and Poems. London, 1887, 8vo.
> Robert Burns; a Reverie, pp. 78-96.

Corrodi, August.—Robert Burns und Peter Hebel. Eine literar-historische Parallele. (*Virchow's Sammlung* gemeinverständlicher wissenschaftlicher Vorträge, etc. Ser. viii., Hft. 182). Berlin, 1873, 8vo.

Cotton, Dr.—Domestic Happiness exhibited, in—I. Fireside, a poem by Dr. Cotton ; II. John Anderson, my Joe, improved. By Robert Burns. Glasgow [1800], 12mo.

Coutts, W. G.—The Games, a Nicht wi' Burns, and other poems. New York, 1860, 8vo.

Cox, Robert.—An Essay on the character and cerebral development of Robert Burns, by R. C. Edinburgh, 1859, 8vo.

Craig, Hugh.—Ayrshire Aspirations in verse and prose. Kilmarnock, 1856, 12mo.
> "Birthday Song in honour of Burns."

Craig, Isa.—The Burns Festival. Prize Poem, recited at the Crystal Palace, January 25, 1859. By Isa [Craig]. London, 1859, 8vo.

Craik, George L.—A Compendious History of English Literature,

etc. 2 vols. London, 1861, 8vo.
> Burns, vol. ii., pp. 398-425.

——A Manual of English Literature, etc. Ninth edition. London [1883], 8vo.
> Burns, pp. 440-456.

Crawford, John. — Doric Lays : being snatches of song and ballad. Second Series. Edinburgh, 1860, 8vo.
> The Gatherin' o' the Bards—Burns's Centenary, pp. 177-211.

Cunningham, Allan.—Landscape Illustrations to the first complete and uniform edition of the Life and Works of Robert Burns ; with original descriptions by A. C. London, 1835, 8vo.

Cunningham, George Godfrey.—The English Nation ; a history of England in the Lives of Englishmen. 5 vols. Edinburgh [1863-68], 4to.
> Robert Burns, with portrait, vol. iv., pp. 311-322.

Cunningham, Joseph.—The Centennial Birthday of R. Burns, as celebrated by the Burns Club of the City of New York, January 25th, 1859. Edited by J. C. [New York] 1860, 8vo.

Currie, James.—Views in North Britain [by J. S. Storer and J. Greig], illustrative of the works of Robert Burns. With descriptions, and a sketch of the poet's life. [Compiled from the life of Burns by J. C.] London, 1805, 4to.

Cuthbertson, John. — Complete Glossary to the Poetry and Prose of R. Burns, with illustrations from English authors. Paisley, 1886, 8vo.

Dennis, John.—Heroes of Literature. English Poets, etc. London, 1883, 8vo.
> Robert Burns, pp. 257-277.

Dodds, Rev. James. — Personal Reminiscences and Biographical Sketches. Edinburgh, 1887, 8vo.
The Family of Burns, pp. 193-198.

Dove, P. E. — A Biographical Sketch of Robert Burns. Glasgow, 1859, 8vo.
Reprinted from the *Imperial Dictionary of Universal Biography*.

Drake, Nathan. — Mornings in Spring. 2 vols. London, 1828, 8vo.
Chaucer, Dunbar, and Burns compared, vol. ii., pp. 1-36.

Drake, Samuel Adams. — Our Great Benefactors ; short biographies, etc. Boston, 1884, 4to.
Robert Burns, illustrated, pp. 111-115.

Drummond, Robert Blackley. — The Religion of Robert Burns, a lecture. Edinburgh, 1859, 8vo.

Dulcken, H. W. — Worthies of the World : a series of historical and critical sketches, etc. London [1881], 8vo.
Robert Burns, with portrait, pp. 353-368.

Dunbar, David. — Poems and Songs. Glasgow, 1859, 8vo.
"Robert Burns : a Centenary Poem," pp. 9-22 ; Song—"Burns," pp. 154-156.

Duncan, J. F. — Lights and Shadows ; or, episodes in the life of Robert Burns ; a dramatic sketch. Dundee, 1879, 12mo.

Dutton, W. H. — Celebration of the Hundredth Anniversary of the Birth of Robert Burns, by the Boston Burns Club. Boston [Mass.], 1859, 8vo.

Duyckinck, Evert A. — Portrait Gallery of eminent men and women, etc. New York [1875], 4to.
Robert Burns, with portrait, vol. i., pp. 204-217.

Elder, William. — Robert Burns as Free-thinker, Poet, and Democrat. A lecture, etc. Paisley, 1881, 12mo.

Emerson, Ralph Waldo. — Miscellanies. London, 1884, 8vo.
Robert Burns, pp. 363-369. Speech at the Celebration of the Burns Centenary, Boston, Jan. 25, 1859.

Encyclopædia Britannica. — Encyclopædia Britannica. Ninth edition. Edinburgh, 1876, 4to.
Burns, by Prof. Nichol, vol. iv.

English Writers. — Essays on English Writers, by the author of "The Gentle Life." [J. H. Friswell.] London, 1869, 8vo.
Burns, pp. 350-356.

Evans, W. Downing. — Ode composed for the centenary festival in honour of Robert Burns. London, 1859, 8vo.

Ferguson, Rev. Fergus. — Burns, and the lapse of a Hundred Years : a sermon, etc. Glasgow, 1859, 18mo.

——A Manual : containing a Discourse against the Christian Commemoration of the Birthday of Robert Burns, delivered by the Rev. F. Ferguson, Dalkeith ; together with a Report of Burns's Anniversary held in Jedburgh. Jedburgh, 1859, 12mo.

Fisher, M. — Scenes from Scripture, and other poems. Carlisle, 1859, 8vo.
"Burns Centenary," pp. 25-33.

Fraser, Thomas. — Prize Poems : written for the Baltimore Burns Club Centennial Celebration of the Birthday of Burns, etc. Baltimore, 1859, 8vo.

G. M. L. — Ode on Burns. London, 1859, 12mo.

Gairdner, M. S. — Robert Burns : an Inquiry into certain aspects of his Life and Character, and the moral influence of his poetry. London, 1887, 8vo.

Gall, Richard.—Poems and Songs. Edinburgh, 1819, 12mo.
Epistles addressed to Robert Burns, pp. 46-50, 54-57; Verses on Visiting the House in which Burns was born, pp. 58-60; On the Death of Burns, pp. 82-84.

Gibson, James.—R. Burns and Masonry. [Liverpool] 1873, 8vo.
Privately printed.

Giles, Henry. — Illustrations of Genius, etc. Boston [Mass.], 1854, 8vo.
Robert Burns, pp. 267-299.

Gilfillan, George. — Galleries of Literary Portraits. 2 vols. London, 1856, 8vo.
Burns, vol. i., pp. 54-64.

Gilfillan, Robert. — Poems and Songs. Fourth edition. Edinburgh, 1851, 8vo.
Land of Burns, pp. 357-358.

Gillespie, George W.—Poems and Songs. Edinburgh, 1827, 12mo.
Poem "On reading Burns's Poems."

Gillespie, Rev. William.—Tributes to Scottish Genius, etc. Second edition. Dumfries, 1827, 12mo.
The Anniversaries of Burns.

Gillis, Bishop.—A paper on the subject of Burns' Pistols: Read at a meeting of the Society of Scottish Antiquaries, on Tuesday, the 19th day of April 1859. By the Right Rev. Bishop Gillis. Edinburgh [1859], 8vo.

Glen, William.—The Poetical Remains of W. G., etc. Edinburgh, 1874, 16mo.
Poem "In Memory of Robert Burns."

Grant, Mrs.—Poems on various subjects. Edinburgh, 1803, 8vo.
Remarks on the character of Burns. Lines "On the Death of Burns," etc.

Gray, Charles.—Poems. Cupar, 1811, 16mo.
A Pastoral on the Death of Burns, pp. 42-44.

——Lays and Lyrics. Edinburgh, 1841, 12mo.
"Address to the Shade of Burns," pp. 33-37; "A Stramash among the Stars," written for the fourth anniversary of the Irvine Burns' Club, 1830, pp. 49-52; "Burns," pp. 98, 99.

Grinsted, T. P.—Relics of Genius: visits to the last homes of poets, etc. London, 1859, 8vo.
Robert Burns, with a view of the Mausoleum, Dumfries, pp. 260-266.

Hamilton, Walter.— Parodies of the Works of English and American Authors. Collected and annotated by W. H. London, 1886, 4to.
Robert Burns, vol. iii., pp. 48-71.

Hannay, James. — Satire and Satirists. London, 1854, 8vo.
Political Satire and Squibs—Burns, pp. 201-237.

Hartung, Gustav.—Ueber Robert Burns' poetische Episteln, etc. Wittstock [1868], 4to.

Hastings, James.—Robert Burns: a Commemorative poem, in twelve parts. Liverpool, 1859, 12mo.

Hawke, Hon. Annabella. — Babylon and other poems. London, 1811, 12mo.
Contains—"The Grave of Burns."

Hawthorne, Nathaniel.—Our Old Home. 2 vols. London, 1863, 8vo.
Some of the Haunts of Burns, vol. ii., pp, 45-79.

Hazlitt, William.—Lectures on

the **English** Poets. Second edition. London, 1819, 8vo.
On **Burns**, and the old English Ballads, pp. 245-282.

Heavisides, **Henry.** — The Minstrelsy of **Britain** ; or, a glance **at our** lyrical poetry and poets from the reign of Queen Elizabeth to the present time, including a dissertation on the genius and lyrics of Burns. Stockton, 1860, 8vo.

Henderson, James.—Glimpses **of** the Beautiful, and other poems. Glasgow, 1848, 8vo.
Contains "To the **Memory of** Burns."

Heron, Robert.—A Memoir **of** the Life of the late Robert **Burns.** Edinburgh, 1797, 8vo.

Hetrick, Robert. — Poems **and** Songs. Ayr, 1826, 12mo.
Contains an Elegy on the Death of Burns.

Hoffmann, Frederick A.—Poetry, **its origin,** nature, and history, **etc. London,** 1884, 8vo.
Burns, vol. i., pp. 507-521.

Holloway, Laura C.—The Mothers **of Great** Men and Women, etc. New York, 1884, 8vo.
The Mother **of** Burns, pp. **581-596.**

Howitt, William. — **Homes and** Haunts of the **most eminent** British Poets. **Third edition.** London, 1857, 8vo.
Robert Burns, pp. **229-268, with** two illustrations.

Hunter, William.—Burns as **a Mason** : a Lecture delivered **on the** 9th December 1858 before **the** Lodge of Journeymen **Masons.** Edinburgh [1859], 12mo.

Inglis, John.—Poems and **Songs. Edinburgh,** 1866, 12mo.
Contains "Lines to the Memory of **Burns," etc.**

Irving, David.—The Lives of the Scottish Poets, etc. 2 vols. Edinburgh, 1804, 8vo.
The Life of Robert Burns, vol. **ii.,** pp. 443-501.

——Another edition. **2 vols.** London, 1810, 8vo.

Irving, Joseph. — The West **of** Scotland in History : being brief notes concerning events, family traditions, etc. Glasgow, **1885, 4to.**
Burns and 'Highland Mary,' pp. 250-255.

Jamieson, Robert.—Burns in his youth, **and** how he grew **to be a** poet, etc. Papers read **before** the Belfast Burns Club. **Belfast,** 1878, 8vo.

Jeffrey, Francis. — Contributions to the Edinburgh Review. London, 1853, 8vo.
"Reliques of Robert Burns," Jan. 1809, pp. 423-439

Jerdan, William. — The autobiography of William Jerdan, etc. 4 vols. London, 1852, 8vo.
Robert Burns : a rather **Scotch** Chapter, vol. ii., pp. 110-123.

Jingleverb, Jock. — The Real Souter Johnny, etc. A Poem **;** with explanatory notes and an **appendix.** Maybole, 1834, 8vo.

Jones, Jacob. — A Century **of** Sonnets, etc. London, 1866, 8vo.
The Burns Commemoration **of** 1859, pp. 102-109.

Keats John.—Life, letters, and literary remains. Edited by R. M. Milnes. 2 vols. London, 1848, 8vo.
Two Sonnets ; one "On Visiting the Tomb of Burns," and the other written in the cottage where Burns was born, vol. i., pp. 156 and 159.

Kenney, J. H.—The Burniad ; an Epistle to a Lady, in the manner of Burns, with poetic miscellanies, etc. London, 1808, 8vo.

Kent, Hindham.—Burns: a Commemoration Poem. London, 1859, 8vo.

Kent, W. Charles.—Dreamland, with other poems. London, 1862, 8vo.
Burns at Mossgiel (16 verses), pp. 72-76.

Kent, Wyndham.—Burns. [A commemorative poem.] London, 1859, 8vo.

Kerr, Robert.—Memoirs of the life, writings, and correspondence of William Smellie. 2 vols. Edinburgh, 1811, 8vo.
Numerous references to Burns, with letters to and from Smellie and Burns.

Kidd, William. — A Series of Twelve Illustrations of the poems of R. B. Engraved on steel by J. Shury from original paintings by W. Kidd. London, 1832, 8vo.

Kingsley, Charles.—The Works of C. K. London, 1880, 8vo.
Robert Burns and his School, vol. xx., pp. 127-184.

Knight, Charles.—The Land we live in. A pictorial and literary sketch-book of the British Empire. [By C. Knight, J. Thorne, G. Dodd, etc.] Vols. 1-4. London [1847-50], 4to.
Ayrshire and the Land of Burns, vol. iii., pp. 153-184.

Lacy, Fanny E. — Centenary Tribute to R. Burns. London, 1859, 12mo.

Lang, Andrew.—Letters to Dead Authors. London, 1886, 8vo.
To Robert Burns, pp. 195-204.

Lee, G. A. B.—Elegiac Stanzas to the Memory of Burns. London, 1859, 4to.

Lemon, Mark. Robert Burns; a Drama. London, n.d., 4to.

Little, Janet. — The Poetical Works of J. L., the Scotch Milkmaid. Air, 1792, 8vo.
On a Visit to Mr. Burns, pp. 111-112; An Epistle to Mr. Robert Burns, pp. 160-163.

Livingston, Peter. — Poems and Songs: with lectures on the genius and works of Burns, etc. Ninth edition. Aberdeen, 1855, 12mo.

Lockhart, John Gibson.—Life of R. Burns. Edinburgh, 1828, 8vo.
——Third edition, corrected. (*Constable's Miscellany*, vol. xxiii.) Edinburgh, 1830, 12mo.
——Fourth edition. London, 1838, 12mo.
——Fifth edition. London, 1847, 12mo.
——New edition, with notes of the death of the poet's widow, and a memoir of the author. London [1871], 8vo.
——Enlarged edition. By W. S. Douglas. (*Bohn's Standard Library*.) London, 1882, 8vo.

Logan, Alexander Stuart. — On Robert Burns, an address: Judas the Betrayer—his ending, a political fragment. Edinburgh, 1871, 8vo.

Longfellow, Henry Wadsworth.—Ultima Thule. London, 1880, 8vo.
Robert Burns (9 verses), pp. 27-30.

Longmuir, John.—A Run through the Land of Burns and the Covenanters. Aberdeen, 1872, 12mo.

Lucas, R. C.—Tam O' Shanter. Fifteen Unique Illustrations by R. C. Lucas. Sculpture. ——, 1841, obl. fol.

Macaulay, James. — Poems on various subjects in Scots and English. Edinburgh, 1788, 12mo.
Rhyming Epistle to Mr. R * * * * * B * * * *.

M'Diarmid, John. — Picture of Dumfries, etc. Edinburgh, 1832, 4to.
R. Burns, pp. 30-37.

MacDowall, William.—Burns in Dumfriesshire: a sketch of the last eight years of the poet's life. Edinburgh, 1870, 8vo.

M'Kay, Archibald. — Burns and his Kilmarnock Friends, etc. Kilmarnock, 1874, 12mo.

MacKay, Charles.—Forty Years' Recollections of life, literature, and public affairs, from 1830 to 1870. 2 vols. London, 1877, 8vo.
The Burns' Festival at Ayr, vol. i. pp. 247-261.

M'Kie, James. — Bibliotheca Burnsiana. Life and Works of Burns, titlepages and imprints of the various editions in the private library of J. M'Kie prior to date, 1866, etc. Kilmarnock, 1866, 8vo.

——The Bibliography of Robert Burns, with biographical and bibliographical notes, etc. Kilmarnock, 1881, 8vo.

M'Lachlan, Kenneth. — Hope's Happy Home, and other poems. Second edition. London, 1869, 8vo.
Ode to the memory of Burns, pp. 71-79; Song—Robin Burns, pp. 175, 176.

Maclagan, Alexander. — Sketches from Nature, and other poems. Edinburgh, 1851, 8vo.
The Harp of Burns, pp. 82-84; Land of Burns, pp. 122, 123; Ode written for the Sheffield Burns' Club Anniversary, 1851, pp. 227-230.

Macphail, Myles.—Burns' vision of the future, a centenary poem. Edinburgh [1859], 8vo.

Macrae, David.—Robert Burns. Three Lectures. Dundee, 1886, 8vo.

Massey, Gerald.—Robert Burns; a centenary song, and other lyrics. London, 1859, 4to.

Maxwell, James.—Animadversions on some Poets and Poetasters of the present age; especially R——t B——s [*i.e.*, Robert Burns] and J——n L——k [*i.e.*, John Lapraik], with a contrast of some of the former age. [In verse.] Paisley, 1788, 12mo.

Mézières, L.—Histoire critique de la Littérature Anglaise, etc. Seconde édition. 3 tom. Paris, 1841, 8vo.
Burns—Lettres, Tom. iii., pp. 142-154.

Miller, Hugh.—Essays, historical and biographical, political and social, literary and scientific. Edinburgh, 1862, 8vo.
The Burns' Festival and Hero Worship, pp. 132-142.

Mitchell, John.—My Grey Goose Quill, and other poems and songs. Paisley, 1852, 12mo.
"Lines written after visiting Burns' Festival," "Six Poems written for Burns' Anniversaries," etc.

Moir, David M.—The Poetical Works of D. M. M. 2 vols. Edinburgh, 1852, 8vo.
Stanzas for the Burns' Festival, vol. ii., pp. 7-12.

Montgomery, James. — Lectures on poetry and general literature. London, 1833, 8vo.
Robert Burns, pp. 250-261.

Mudford, William.—Nubilia in search of a Husband, etc. London, 1809, 12mo.
A Conversation on Burns, pp. 240-257.

Mylne, James.—Poems consisting

of miscellaneous **pieces, and two** tragedies. **Edinburgh, 1790,** 8vo.
" To Mr. Burns, on his poems."

Neaves, Lord.—A lecture on cheap and accessible pleasures, with a comparative sketch of the poetry of Burns and Wordsworth, delivered at Haltwhisle, 1872. Edinburgh, 1872, 8vo.

Newbigging, Thomas.—Sketches and Addresses, political, social, literary. Manchester, 1887, 8vo.
Robert **Burns; Speech at the** Literary **Club, Manchester, Jan. 25,** 1886.

Nicholl, Robert. — Poems **and** Lyrics. Glasgow, 1852, 12mo.
" Stanzas on the Birthday of **Burns,"** and poem, " The Grave of **Burns."**

Nithsdale Minstrel.—The Nithsdale Minstrel : being original poetry, chiefly by the bards of Nithsdale. Dumfries, 1815, 8vo.
Verses on visiting the grave of Burns, in Jan. 1814, pp. 62-66; Verses delivered at the public dinner on occasion of laying the foundation-stone of Burns's Mausoleum, pp. 166-170.

Norton, Hon. **C. E. S.** — The Centenary Festival. Reprinted from *The Daily Scotsman.* [Verses in honour of Robert Burns.] [London, 1859], 4to.

Notes and Queries. — General Index to Notes and Queries. Five series. London, 1856-1880, 4to.
Numerous references to **Burns.**

Oliphant, Margaret O. — **The Literary** History of England, etc. **3** vols. London, 1882, 8vo.
Robert Burns, vol. i., pp. 98-167.

Ord, John Walker.—The Bard, **and** Minor Poems. Edited by

John **Lodge.** London, 1842, 12mo.

Page, H. A.—Literary Bye-Hours, etc. London, 1881, 8vo.
Robert Burns as a Celt, pp. 191-202.

Park, Andrew.—To the Memory of Burns. Centenary Ode. Glasgow, 1859, 8vo.

Parley, **Peter** [*i.e.*, Samuel Griswold Goodrich].—Famous Men of Modern Times, **etc.** (*Parley's Cabinet Library*, **vol. i.)** Philadelphia, 1846, 8vo.
Robert Burns, pp. 155-191.

Parton, James. — Some noted Princes, Authors, and Statesmen of our Time. Edited by J. P. New York [1886], 8vo.
A Grandson of Robert Burns, by Will Carleton, pp. 257-260.

Paterson, James.—The Contemporaries of Burns, **and** the more recent poets of Ayrshire, with selections from their writings. [By James Paterson]. Edinburgh, 1840, **8vo.**

Pebody, Charles. — Authors **at** Work. London, 1872, 8vo.
Robert Burns, pp. 86-114.

Peterkin, Alexander.—A **Review** of **the** Life of R. Burns, and **of various** criticisms on his **character and** writings. Edinburgh, 1815, 8vo.

Petrie, John.—Love Lyrics, **etc.** London, 1859, 12mo.
Ode on the Centenary of Robert **Burns, pp. 39-46.**

Phillips, **Maude G.**—A popular Manual **of** English Literature, **etc. 2 vols.** New York, 1885, 8vo.
Robert Burns (with portrait), the national poet of Scotland, vol. ii., pp. 165-216.

Picken, Ebenezer.—Miscellaneous Songs, etc. Edinburgh, **1813,** 12mo.

Contains "The Deil's Answer to his vera wordy friend, R * * * * * B * * * *," and "Verses on the Death of Robert Burns."

Poets.—Evenings with the Poets, etc. **London, 1860, 8vo.**
- Burns, pp. 285-290.

Prout, Father, [*i.e.*, the Rev. Francis Mahony].—The Works of Father Prout. London, 1881, 8vo.
Burns and Béranger, pp. 480, 481; reprinted from *Bentley's Miscellany*, May 1837.

Punch.—Punch for 1844. Vol. vii. London, 1844, 4to.
The Burns' Festival—"Repentant" Scotland, by Douglas Jerrold, pp. 81, 82.

——For 1859. London, 1859, 4to.
"The Bards of Burns. A Song of ye Crystalle Palace," vol. xxxvi., pp. 48, 49; "The Story of the Burns' Festival" (verses) by Shirley Brooks, p. 59; "Alexander upon Burns," p. 60. (13 verses.)

Rea, Thomas.—Coila over the Grave of Robert Burns. Newcastle-upon-Tyne, 1859, 8vo.

Reed, Henry.—Lectures on the British Poets. London, 1857, 8vo.
Burns, pp. 207-232.

——Lectures on the British Poets. 2 vols. Philadelphia, 1858, 8vo.
Burns, vol. ii., pp. 25-47.

Richardson, George.—Patriotism, in three cantos, etc. London, 1844, 8vo.
Contains "Verses for the Anniversary of Burns."

Richardson, Mrs. G. G.—Poems. Second Series. London, 1834, 8vo.
Contains "Lines for the Anniversary of Burns," pp. 120-124.

Robson, Joseph P. — Poems. Newcastle-on-Tyne, 1848, 12mo.

Contains "A Nicht wi' Burns," "The Vision of Robert Burns," "The Braw Sons of Burns," and "Robert Burns on earth."

Rogers, Charles. — The Modern Scottish Minstrel, etc. 6 vols. Edinburgh, 1856-57, 8vo.
The Influence of Burns on Scottish poetry and song, by the Rev. George Gilfillan, vol. iv., pp. v.-xv.

——Genealogical Memoirs of the Family of Robert Burns, and of the Scottish House of Burns, by the Rev. C. Rogers. Edinburgh, 1877, 8vo.

Rogerson, John B.—Musings in Many Moods. London, 1859, 8vo.
On the Anniversary of Burns, p. 297.

Rossetti, William Michael.—Lives of Famous Poets. London [1885], 8vo.
Robert Burns, pp. 189-200.

Rushton, Edward.—Poems by E. R. London, 1806, 12mo.
To the Memory of Robert Burns, pp. 75-82.

Russell, A. P.—Characteristics, Sketches and Essays. Boston [U.S.], 1884, 8vo.
Burns, pp. 132-159.

Russell, William.—Extraordinary Men : their boyhood and early life. London, 1853, 8vo.
Robert Burns, pp. 158-174.

Saure, Dr., and Weischer, Dr.— Biographies of English Poets. Leipzig, 1880, 8vo.
R. Burns, pp, 157-179.

Scherr, Dr. J.—A History of English Literature. Translated from the German. London, 1882, 8vo.
Burns, pp. 178-183.

Scotchwoman. — Robert Burns ; an enquiry into certain aspects of his life and character, and the moral influence of his poetry. By a Scotchwoman. London, 1886, 8vo.

——Cheap edition. London, 1887, 8vo.

Scottish Poets.—Lives of Eminent Scotsmen, by the Society of Ancient Scots. 3 vols. London, 1821, 12mo.
Robert Burns, vol. i., pp. 157-198. Signed A.S.

Semple, David. — The Tree of Crocstone, being a refutation of the fables of the courtship of Queen Marie and Lord Darnley of Crocstone Castle, under the Yew Tree; and of the poet, Robert Burns, carving his name on the Yew Tree. Paisley, 1876, 4to.

Shairp, John Campbell. — On Poetic Interpretation of Nature. Second edition. Edinburgh, 1877, 8vo.
Nature in Burns, pp. 213-219.

——Aspects of Poetry, being lectures delivered at Oxford. Oxford, 1881, 8vo.
Scottish Song and Burns, pp. 192-226.

——Robert Burns (English Men of Letters.) London, 1879, 8vo.

Shanks, Henry. — The Peasant Poets of Scotland, etc. Bathgate, 1881, 8vo.
Robert Burns: as a man and a poet, pp. 3-41.

Sinclair, George. — Intermittent Fountain, etc. London [1858]-63, 8vo.
The Birth of Burns, pp, 74-79.

Skinner, John.—Amusements of Leisure Hours, or poetical pieces, chiefly in the Scottish Dialect. Edinburgh, 1809, 12mo.
Contains letters from Burns to the author, "Rhyming Epistle to the Poet," etc.

Smith, John Campbell.—Writings by the Way. Edinburgh [1885], 8vo.

Burns and the Peasantry of Scotland, pp. 209-227. Two speeches reprinted from the Scotsman.

Stephen, Leslie. — Dictionary of National Biography. Edited by Leslie Stephen. London, 1886, 8vo.
Robert Burns, vol. vii., pp. 426-438. Written by Leslie Stephen.

Stephens, George.—The Rescue of Robert Burns, February 1759. A Centenary Poem. Cheapinghaven [Copenhagen, 1859], 8vo.

Sterling, John.—Essays and Tales, etc. 2 vols. London, 1848, 8vo.
Burns, vol. i., pp. 87-98.

Stevenson, Robert Louis. — Familiar Studies of Men and Books. London, 1882, 8vo.
Some aspects of Robert Burns, pp. 38-90.

Stewart, Robert. — Musings of Stray Hours. Glasgow, 1859, 12mo.
Contains "Lines on Robert Burns," and "Monody on the Burns' Festival."

Stirling, James Hutchinson. — Burns in drama [in five acts and in prose], together with stray leaves. Edited by J. H. S. Edinburgh, 1878, 8vo.

Storer, James.—Nineteen Views in North Britain, illustrative of the works of R. B. Drawn and engraved by J. S. and John Greig; accompanied by a sketch of the poet's life. London, 1805, 8vo.

Story, Robert.—The Alloway Centenary Festival. An ode recited at the above festival in Burns's Cottage, on the 25th January, 1859. London, 1859, 8vo.

Stuart, James Montgomery.—Reminiscences and Essays. London, 1884, 8vo.

The Ayrshire Ploughman and the Ettrick Shepherd, pp. 119-155.

Sylvan.—Sylvan's Guide to Coila, or the Land of Burns, with numerous illustrations, from original sketches by T. and E. Gilks. London, **1848**, 12mo.

Taine, H.—Histoire de la Littérature Anglaise. 4 tom. Paris, 1863-4, 8vo.

Robert Burns, tom. iii., pp. 427-458.

——History of English Literature. 4 vols. London, 1873-4, 8vo.

Robert Burns, vol. iii., pp. 389-412.

Tannahill, Robert.—The Soldier's Return, with other poems, etc. Paisley, 1807, 8vo.

Dirge on Burns' Funeral, pp. 44-45; Ode for Burns' birthday, 1805, pp. 55-58; Ode for Burns' birthday, 1807, pp. 109-112.

——The Poetical Works of R. T. London [1870], 8vo.

Ode to Burns, 29th Jan., 1810, pp. 38-39.

Taylor, John Ray.—The Burial of Burns. A poem. Glasgow, 1847, 8vo.

Taylor, W. C. — The Modern British Plutarch, etc. London, 1846, 8vo.

Robert Burns, pp. 23-30.

Thomson, Andrew. — Centenary Verses, descriptive of our national poet, Burns, etc. Dunfermline, 1859, 16mo.

Thomson, W. G. — A Poetical Address, delivered at the anniversary meeting of the Burns Club of Newcastle-upon-Tyne, January 31st, 1825. Newcastle-on-Tyne, 1825, 12mo.

Tillotson, John.—Lives of Eminent Men, etc. London, 1856, 8vo.

Contains a life of Burns.

Todd, Adam B.—Burns: or, the Ploughman Bard, a centenary poem. Kilmarnock, 1860, 12mo.

Todd, Adam B.—Poems, Lectures, and Miscellanies. Edinburgh, 1876, 8vo.

Contains "Burns; or the Ploughman Bard," a centenary poem; "The Memory of Burns," a centenary speech; and "Robert Burns," a lecture.

Tomlinson, John.—Three Household Poets — Milton, Cowper, Burns. With an introduction on poetry and song. London, 1869, 8vo.

Trovato, Ben [*i.e.*, Samuel Lover]. Rival Rhymes in honour of Burns; with curious illustrative matter. Collected and edited by B. T. London, 1859, 8vo.

Tuckerman, Henry T.—Thoughts on the Poets. Third edition. New York, 1848, 8vo.

Burns, pp. 193-204.

——Another edition. **London** [1852], 8vo.

Burns, pp. 162-174.

Tyler, Samuel.—Robert Burns; as a poet and as a man. Dublin, 1849, 12mo.

This is a reprint of an American edition published at New York in 1848.

Urquhart, Alexander Ross.—A Stone for the Poet's Cairn. Glorious Robert Burns, a panegyric on his life and genius. Glasgow, 1872, 8vo.

Vedder, David.—Poems, Lyrics, and Sketches. Kirkwall [1878], 8vo.

For the Anniversary of Burns, pp. 87-88; To Burns, p. 158; The Anniversary of Robert Burns, pp. 332-337.

Veitch, John.—The Feeling for Nature in Scottish Poetry. 2 vols. Edinburgh, 1887, 8vo.

Robert Burns, vol. ii., pp. 120-141.

Waddell, P. H. — Genius and Morality of Robert Burns; a Lecture; a Eulogy, with Chairman's Speech at the Cottage Festival, 25th January 1859. Ayr, 1859, 8vo.

Walker, Josiah.—An account of the Life and Character of R. B., with miscellaneous remarks on his writings. Edinburgh, 1811, 8vo.
> Appeared originally in the "Poems of R. B." 2 vols. Edinburgh, 1811.

Ward and Lock. — Ward and Lock's Penny Books for the People. The Life of Robert Burns, etc. London [1881], 8vo.

Ward, Thomas Humphrey.—The English Poets, etc. Edited by T. H. W. Second edition. 4 vols. London, 1883, 8vo.
> Robert Burns, by Dr. Service, vol. iii., pp. 512-571.

Waugh, Edwin.—Fourteen Days in Scotland. Manchester [1864], 8vo.
> Burns's Birthplace, etc., pp. 95-102.

Welsh, Alfred H.—Development of English Literature and Language. 2 vols. Chicago, 1882, 8vo.
> Burns, vol. ii., pp. 221-241.

White, James.—Robert Burns and Walter Scott. Two lives. London, 1858, 8vo.

——Robert Burns: a memoir. By the Rev. James White. London, 1859, 12mo.

Whittier, John Greenleaf.—The Complete Poetical Works of J. G. W. Boston [Mass.], 1876, 8vo.
> Burns, pp. 137-138.

Wilson, James Grant.—The Poets and Poetry of Scotland. London, 1876, 8vo.
> Burns, pp. 349-373.

Wilson, John.—The Works of Professor Wilson. Edinburgh, 1857, 8vo.

The Genius and Character of Burns, vol. vii., pp. 1-211. Speech of Professor Wilson at the Burns Festival, pp. 212-229.

Wilson, John, and Chambers, Robert.—The Land of Burns, a series of landscapes and portraits, illustrative of the life and writings of the Scottish poet. The landscapes from paintings by D. O. Hill. The literary department by Professor Wilson and R. C. 2 vols. Glasgow, 1840, 4to.

Wilson, Robert.—Poems, in the Scottish Dialect. Edinburgh, 1822, 8vo.
> Contains an Elegy on the Death of Burns.

Wilson, William. — Songs and poems on various subjects, etc. Kelso, 1810, 12mo.
> Contains a Song on the Death of Burns.

Wordsworth, Dorothy.—Recollections of a Tour made in Scotland, A.D., 1803. Edinburgh, 1874, 8vo.
> Contains—"Visit to the Grave of Burns," Poems "To the Sons of Burns," "At the Grave of Burns," etc.

Wordsworth, William.—A letter to a friend of Robert Burns [James Gray] occasioned by an intended republication of the account of the life of Burns by Dr. Currie, etc. London, 1816, 8vo.

——The Poetical Works of William Wordsworth. A new edition. 6 vols. London, 1882, 8vo.
> "At the Grave of Burns, 1803," vol. iii., pp. 2-5; "Thoughts suggested the day following, on the Banks of Nith, near the Poet's residence," pp. 6-8; "To the Sons of Burns," pp. 9-10.

Wylie, Robert.—History of the Mother Lodge, Kilwinning, etc. Glasgow, 1878, 8vo.

Yonge, Charles Duke. — Three Centuries of English Literature. London, 1872, 8vo.

> Burns, A.D. 1759-1796, pp. 460-476.

SONGS SET TO MUSIC, ETC.

The Scots Musical Museum. By James Johnson. 6 vols. Edinburgh, 1787-1803, 8vo.

> Included are 184 songs written or collected by Burns. Reprinted, with notes, in 1839, in 6 vols., by the late William Stenhouse, and illustrations [by David Laing]; and again in 4 vols. in 1853.

Illustrations of the Lyric Poetry and Music of Scotland, compiled to accompany the "Scots Musical Museum" [of J. Johnson], and now published separately, with additional notes and illustrations [and an introduction by D. Laing], by William Stenhouse. Edinburgh, 1853, 8vo.

A Select Collection of original Scottish airs for the voice . . . including upwards of one hundred new songs by Burns, etc. By George Thomson. 6 vols. London, 1793-1841, fol.

——New edition. The Melodies of Scotland, etc. 5 vols. London, 1838, fol.

The Jolly Beggars : Cantata by Burns, set to music by Henry R. Bishop. (Vol. v. of Thomson's Collection of Scottish Airs.) 1818.

The Caledonian Musical Museum, or complete vocal library of the best Scotch songs, ancient and modern. Embellished with a portrait and fac-simile of the handwriting of Burns, and containing upwards of two hundred songs by that bard. The whole edited by his son [R. B.]. London, 1809, 12mo.

The Scottish Minstrel. A selection of songs from Burns, Ramsay, etc. Edinburgh, 1814, 8vo.

Thomson's Collection of the Songs of Burns, Sir W. Scott, etc. 6 vols. London, 1822-5, 8vo.

The Miniature Museum of Scotch Songs and Music. Written by Ramsay, Crawford, Blacklock, Burns, etc. Edinburgh [1818], 8vo.

Centenary Edition. Thirty Scotch Songs. By R. B. With symphonies and pianoforte accompaniments by W. H. Montgomery. 3 Nos. *Musical Bouquet Office*, London, 1859, 4to.

> Consists of 3 Nos., with 30 songs in each.

Centenary Edition. The Popular Songs of Robert Burns. Words and music as sung by the most eminent vocalists and representatives of Scottish character. Glasgow, 1859, 18mo.

The Songs of R. B., with music. Centenary edition. Glasgow, 1859, 8vo.

Burns Album. Hundert Lieder und Balladen von Burns, herausgegeben von C. und A. Kissner. 4 Hfte. Leipzig, 1877, 8vo.

The National Burns. Edited by George Gilfillan, including the airs of all the songs, etc. 2 vols. London [1879-80], 4to.

Tam O'Shanter : a musical farce in two acts by Henry Robert Addison. London, 1834, 8vo.

Tam O'Shanter : a characteristic Cantata by Howard Glover, poetry by R. Burns. London, 1856, fol.

Select Songs of Robert Burns, with music. Glasgow [1883], 8vo.

Fourteen Songs to poems of Robert Burns. By Robert Franz. London, 1876, 8vo.

Ten Songs, the poetry by R. Burns. Music by George John Bennett. London [1885], 8vo.

Seven Songs by John Gledhill. The words by Shelley and Burns. London [1878], fol.

Six Songs by John Gledhill. Words by Burns, Moore, and Barry Cornwall. Brighton [1882], fol.

Six Songs, by Arthur Somervell. Words by R. Burns. London [1886], 4to.

Six Scottish Songs, by J. F. Simpson. The poetry selected from R. Burns. London [1872], oblong 4to.

Er und Sie. Fünf Lieder von R. Burns. Music by C. Reinecke, Leipzig [1883], fol.

Four part-songs for male voices, by C. Herman. The Words by R. Burns. London [1879], 8vo.

Two part-songs, by Mendelssohn, with English words by C. Jefferys and R. Burns. London [1854], fol.

————

"Adieu! a heart - warm fond adieu!" by J. A. Shaw, 1871.

"Ae fond kiss and then we sever," by G. Linley, 1854.

"And they're a' noddin," 1830.

"As I went down the water side" —*Call the ewes to the knowes*, by J. Bulmer, 1878.

"Behind yon hills," by T. Ebdon, 1794; W. Knyvett, 1810.

"Blithe hae I been on yon hill" —*Hopeless Love*, by T. W. Ellis, 1840.

"Bonnie wee thing, cannie wee thing," by H. C. Banister, 1869 and 1878; F. Dulcken, 1877; M. B. Foster, 1876; G. E. Fox, 1876.

"The Catrine woods were yellow seen"—*The Braes of Ballochmyle*, by J. Lodge, 1839; J. Ross, 1805.

"Come, let me press thee to my heart," by E. F. Fitzwilliam, 1845.

"Could aught of song relieve my pain," by H. B. Chapman, 1865; A. W. Pelzer, 1858.

"The day returns," by H. W. Goodban, 1847; R. de Muenck, 1847.

"Fairest flower, behold the lily," by T. Haigh, 1810.

"Fair the face of orient day"— *To Delia*, by E. Hecht, 1882.

"Fare the weel, thou first and fairest," by K. W. Mackinlay, 1881; J. Molineux, 1815; W. Shore, 1835; P. Urbani, 1801; J. Watlen, 1795.

"Farewell, thou bright day," by C. H. Elsley, 1850.

"Farewell, thou fair day," by J. W. Callcott, 1805; B. Hime, 1835.

"Fate gave the word" — *The Mother's Lament*, by H. J. Haycraft, 1844.

"Flow gently, sweet Afton"— *Afton Water*, by T. W. Ellis, 1843; J. Gledhill, 1874; A. Hume, 1876; W. W. Jones, 1860; Loder's Songs of the Poets, No. 2, 1844.

"From thee, Eliza, I must go," by T. Miles, 1818; P. Urbani, 1801.

" From the white-blossomed sloe"
—*The Thorn*, by L. Jansen,
1825 ; W. Shield, 1800.

" Hark the Mavis evening song "
—*Ca' the Yowes to the Knowes*,
by A. Sartoris, 1859.

" Here awa, there awa"—*Wandering Willie*, by W. Knyvett,
1806.

"Here's a health to them that's
awa," by J. E. Murdoch, 1864.

" Hey, the dusty Miller," by G.
Fox, 1880.

" A Highland lad my love was
born," by G. F. Kemp, 1843.

" How bank and brae are clothed
in green "—*The Bonnie blink
o' Mary's e'e*, by Robert Anderson (Home Songs, No. 21),
1877.

" How pleasant the banks "—
The Maid of Devon, by J.
Barnett, 1835.

" I gaed a waeful gate"—*The
Blue-Eyed Lassie*, by J. Clarke,
1800 ; H. J. Haycraft, 1844 ;
M. Hinckesman, 1825 ; W. C.
Macfarren, 1856.

" Jockie's taken the parting kiss,"
by G. Fox, 1879.

" John Anderson, my Jo," by G.
F. Kemp, 1843.

" The Jolly Beggars," by G.
Linley, 1862.

" Is there for honest poverty "—
A Man's a Man for a' that, by
A. Lee, 1856.

"It's nae thy bonnie face," by
E. Lassen (Sechs Lieder, Op.
66, No. 6), 1879.

" It was the charming month of
May," by J. Bruell, 1878 ; W.
Spark, 1857.

" It was upon a Lammas night"
—*The Rigs o' Barley*, by J.
Bruell, 1878.

" Loud blaw the frosty breezes"—
Castle Gordon, by W. S. Bennett (Six Songs, etc., No. 4),
1855.

"Loudon's bonny banks and
braes," by H. Little, 1825.

"Musing on the roaring ocean "
—*Talk of him that's far awa'*,
by T. Chantrey, 1850; A. W.
Pelzer, 1858.

" My Chloris, mark how green
the groves," by J. Bulmer,
1878.

" My heart is sair"—*For the sake
of Somebody*, by L. Caracciolo,
1881 ; F. Hiller. (Three Songs,
etc.), 1852 ; A Zimmermann,
1863.

" My heart is sair"—*My heart's
in the Highlands*," by R. Schumann. (Six songs, etc., No. 2,
4), 1853.

" My heart's in the Highlands,"
by W. Eavestaff, 1833 ; N. W.
Gade. (Eight duettinos, Op. 9,
No. 3), 1849 ; C. Oberthuer,
1851 ; D. Paterson, 1851 ; H.
Phillips, 1835 ; A. Reichardt,
1864 ; R. Schumann, 1872.

" My Nannie's Charming "—*My
Nannie O!* 1806.

" Now nature hangs her mantle
green "—*Lament of Mary Queen
of Scots*, by T. S. Smith, 1876.

" Now rosy May comes in with
flowers "—*Dainty Davie*, by G.
Fox, 1878 ; J. J. Jones, 1820.

"O gin my love were yon red
rose," by K. U. Mackinlay,
1881.

" Oh ! I am come to the low
Countrie "—*Highland Widow's
Lament*, by J. P. F., 1866.

" Oh ! lovely Polly Stewart. "—
Charming Polly, by H. Glover,
1862.

"O Mary at thy window be "— *Mary Morison*, by Sir A. S. Sullivan, 1874.

"O mirk, mirk is the midnight hour," 1860.

"O my love's like a red red rose "—*The Red Rose*, by B. Harwood (Six songs No. 2), 1885; W. Knyvett, 1808; F. W. Kuecken, 1850; T. Thompson, 1818 and 1825.

"O stay, sweet warbling Woodlark "—*To the Woodlark*, by W. Moodie, 1879; J. B. Robinson, 1859.

"Oh steer her up and haud her gaun "—*The Miller's Lassie*, by G. A. Macfarren, 1886.

"O thou pale orb that silent shines," by E. Silas, 1855.

"O were my love yon lilac fair," by H. B. Ellis, 1879; J. Gledhill (Seven songs, No. 5), 1878 : C. Hause, 1871.

"Oh wert thou in the cauld blast," by F. C. Atkinson (Six songs, No. 8), 1876; C. Krebs, 1848 and 1860; Mendelssohn (Six two-part songs, Op. 63, No. 5), 1854.

"O Willie brew'd a peck o' maut," by A. Masterton, 1874; W. Shore, 1876.

"Oh! wilt thou go wi' me "— *Tibbie Dunbar*, by C. Reinecke, 1881; E. M. Tucker, 1880.

"O'er the mist-shrouded cliffs "—*My Mary's no more*, by G. Linley, 1873; H. Spencer, 1862; J. Thomas (Six songs, No. 3), 1858.

"Of a' the airts the wind can blaw "—*The Bonnie Lassie*, by J. M. Miles, 1830.

"On a bank of flowers "—*Blooming Nelly*, by E. Bally, 1872.

"Philly and Willy," by W. Knyvett, 1812.

"Powers celestial, whose protection," by B. Harwood (Six songs, No. 6), 1885.

"A rosebud by my early walk," by T. Attwood, 1817; J. Clarke, 1805; J. Hunter (Three canzonets, etc.), 1816; J. T. Trekell, 1858.

"Scots wha hae wi' Wallace bled "—*The Battle of Bannockburn*, by G. F. Kemp, 1843; P. Urbani, 1797.

"She's a winsome wee thing "— *The Winsome Wee Wife*, by L. Jansen, 1825; B. Luetgen, 1880; Mrs. J. M. Miles, 1825 and 1858.

"Should auld acquaintance be forgot "—*Auld Lang Syne*, by J. D. George, 1881.

"Sing on, sweet thrush," by A. M. Smith, 1857.

"The smiling spring comes in rejoicing," by S. C. Domett, 1849; M. Higgs, 1860.

"Stay, my charmer, can you leave me," by Sir W. S. Bennett (The last set of four songs, No. 4), 1875; L. M. Gottschalk, 1864.

"Tam O'Shanter," by J. Smith, 1830.

"Their groves of sweet myrtles," by J. Ambrose, 1800; S. Porter, 1810.

"There's nought but care on every hand "—*Bonnie Lassies O!* by W. Shore, 1849.

"There were three kings into the east," by J. Blewitt, 1858.

"Thine am I, my faithful fair," by G. Goltermann, 1865.

"Thou ling'ring star with less'ning ray "—*To Mary in Heaven*, by Sir G. A. Macfarren, 1883.

"To sigh yet feel no pain," by J. T. Trekell, 1859.

"Turn again, thou fair Eliza," by A. H. Wehrhan, 1849.

"Twas on a simmer's afternoon," 1855.

"Wee, modest crimson-tipped flow'r "—*The Mountain Daisy*, by J. Blewitt, 1810.

"When I sleep I dream," by J. Mount, 1878.

"When o'er the hills the eastern star," by M. V. White, 1879.

"When wild **war's**," etc.—*The Soldier's Return*, by P. Urbani, 1801.

"While larks with little **wing**," by J. T. Trekell, 1859.

"Will ye gang to the ewe bughts, Marion?" by J. Parry, 1825.

"Willie Wastle dwelt on Tweed," by W. Moodie, 1879.

"Wilt thou be my dearie?" by C. J. Duchemin, 1870; J. Hoffmann, 1880; W. Knyvett, 1805; A. W. Pelzer, 1859; R. Tyrrell, 1800.

"The Winter it is past "—*Parted*, by F. E. Bache, 1867.

"Ye banks and braes, and streams around the Castle o' Montgomery "—*Highland Mary*, by J. Ross, 1805.

"Ye flow'ry banks of bonny Doon," by Sir G. A. Macfarren, 1886.

"Ye little birds that chaunt of love," by J. L. Roeckel, 1870.

MAGAZINE ARTICLES, ETC.

Burns, **Robert**. Universal Magazine, vol. 80, 1787, pp. 352-355.—European Magazine, vol. 30, 1796, pp. 78, 79, 266-270. —Quarterly Review, by Sir W.

Burns, **Robert**.

Scott, vol. 1, 1809, pp. 19-36.— Methodist Magazine, vol. 33, 1810, pp. 24-27.—Mirror, vol. 4, 1824, pp. 225, 226, 338, 422, 440.—Edinburgh Review, by T. Carlyle, vol. 48, 1828, pp. 267-312. — Edinburgh Literary Journal, 1829, pp. 349-352, 384-386. — Saturday Magazine, vol. 2, 1833, pp. 102-104. — Southern Literary Messenger, by J. F. Otis, vol. 2, 1836, pp. 238-244.—North American Review, by O. W. B. Peabody, vol. 42, 1836, pp. 65-75.—Revue des Deux Mondes, tom. 9, 1837, pp. 585-627.— Blackwood's Edinburgh Magazine, vol. 46, 1839, pp. 256-271. —Penny Magazine, vol. 10, 1841, pp. 353-355, 389-392.— Southern Literary Messenger, by H. T. Tuckerman, vol. 7, 1841, pp. 249-252.—Southern Literary Messenger, vol. 10, 1844, pp. 543-544. — Dublin University Magazine, vol. 25, 1845, pp. 66-81 and 289-305.— Literary Aspirant Magazine, vol. 1, 1846, pp. 1-20, 205-223.— Knickerbocker, vol. 32, 1848, pp. 206-214.—Scottish Review, vol. 1, 1853, pp. 25-40.— Knickerbocker, vol. 41, 1853, pp. 25-28.—Chambers's Edinburgh Journal, vol. 18, N.S., 1853, pp. 118-120. — British Educator, June and September 1856, pp. 145-148, 289-299.— West of Scotland Magazine, January 1859, pp. 266-272.— Blackwood's Edinburgh Magazine, vol. 111, 1872, pp. 140-168; same article, Eclectic Magazine, vol. 15, N.S., pp. 513-535, and Littell's Living

Burns, Robert.

Age, vol. 113, pp. 3-24.—Dublin University Magazine, vcl. 94, 1877, pp. 94-105.—Baptist Magazine, vol. 74, 1882, pp. 193-202.—Nuova Antologia, by G. Chiarini, vol. 86, 1886, pp. 209-228. — English Illustrated Magazine, by James Syme, Feb. 1887, pp. 323-339.

—— *Address written for the Anniversary of Birthday.* (Poem.) Scots Magazine, vol. 10, N.S., 1822, pp. 70-71.

——*and Béranger.* Nineteenth Century, by C. Mackay, vol. 7, 1880, pp. 464-485.

——*and Byron.* Portfolio, vol. 18, 4th Series, 1824, pp. 386-393.—Ayrshire Inspirer, No. 9, 1839, pp. 129-133. — Mirror, vol. 4, 1824, pp. 121-123, 157-159 (from the *London Magazine*).

——*and Cowper, Lecture on.* Tait's Edinburgh Magazine, by Ebenezer Elliott, vol. 9, N.S., 1842, pp. 357-363.

——*and Crabbe.* Dublin University Magazine, vol. 3, 1834, pp. 489-503.—Monthly Review, vol. 3, 1834, pp. 87-115.

——*and his Ancestors.* Hogg's Weekly Instructor, vol. 6, N.S., 1851, pp. 185-189.

——*and his School.* North British Review, by C. Kingsley, vol. 16, 1851, pp. 149-183 ; same article, Eclectic Magazine, vol. 25, pp. 114-133, and Littell's Living Age, vol. 31, pp. 529-542.

——*and his Works.* St. James's Magazine, by J. K. Nixon, vol. 7, 4th Series, 1830, pp. 127-133.

Burns, Robert.

——*and Robert Ferguson.* Canadian Monthly, by David K. Brown, vol. 4, 1880, pp. 63-73.

——*and Scotch Song before him.* Atlantic Monthly, by J. C. Shairp, vol. 44, 1879, pp. 502-513.

——*and Sir Walter Scott.* Macmillan's Magazine, by H. Bartle G. Frere, vol. 26, 1872, p. 168. —Eclectic Magazine, vol. 14, N.S., 1871, pp. 626-629.

——*and the Ettrick Shepherd.* Blackwood's Edinburgh Magazine, vol. 4, 1819, pp. 521-529.

——*Anniversaries of.* Edinburgh Theological Magazine, vol. 1, 1826, pp. 142-147.

——*Anniversary Poem on.* Once a Week, by S. Whiting, vol. 1, N.S., 1866, p. 92.

——*Art of.* Our Corner, by J. Robertson, vol. 4, 1884, pp. 152-159.

——*at Work.* Gentleman's Magazine, by Charles Pebody, vol 6, N.S., 1871, pp. 593-607.

——*Birthday of, Verses on.* New Scots Magazine, vol. 1, 1829, pp. 120, 121.

——*Birthday and Bowl.* Once a Week, vol. 6, 1862, pp. 286-289.

——*Centenary.* Chambers's Journal, vol. 11, 1859, pp. 129, 130.— Oddfellows' Magazine, vol. 2, 1860, pp. 81-87.

——*Chambers's Life and Works of.* Chambers's Edinburgh Journal, vol. 18, N.S., 1853, pp. 230-234.—Dublin University Magazine, vol. 41, 1853, pp. 169-184.

——*Character of.* Ayrshire Inspirer, No. 6, 1839, pp. 81-85.

Burns, Robert.

——*Characteristics of*. Ben Brierley's Journal, March 20, 1880, pp. 91-92.

——*Correspondence with Clarinda*. Appleton's Journal of Literature, vol. 10, 1873, pp. 679-682. —Monthly Review, vol. 1, N.S., 1844, pp. 144-147. — Tait's Edinburgh Magazine, vol. 10, 2nd Series, 1843, pp. 749-764, and vol. 11, pp. 28-35.

——*Cunningham's Life of*. Fraser's Magazine, vol. 9, 1834, pp. 400-410.

——*Death of Burns* (Poem). Scots Magazine, by William Roscoe, vol. 59, 1797, pp. 197-198.

—— ——*Elegy on Death of*. Scots Magazine, vol. 62, 1800, pp. 629, 630.

—— ——*Pastoral Elegy on Death of*. Scots Magazine, vol. 59, 1797, pp. 689, 690.

——*Family of*. Leisure Hour, 1872, pp. 327-328. — Dublin University Magazine, vol. 87, 1876, pp. 726-736.

—— *Festival*. Blackwood's Edinburgh Magazine, vol. 56, 1844, pp. 370-398.—Tait's Edinburgh Magazine, vol. 11, N.S., 1844, pp. 545-553.—Littell's Living Age, vol. 60, 1859, pp. 740-749.

——*Festival at Sheffield*, 1849. People's Journal, 1845, pp. 109-111.

——*Genius and Character of*. Monthly Review, vol. 1, N.S., 1841, pp. 261-276.

——*Grave of* (Song). Scots Magazine, vol. 72, 1810, p. 207.

——*Haunts of*. Atlantic Monthly, by N. Hawthorne, vol. 6, 1860, pp. 385-395.

Burns, Robert.

——*Highland Mary*. Chambers's Edinburgh Journal, vol. 14, N.S., 1850, pp. 1-4 ; same article, Eclectic Magazine, vol. 21, 1850, pp. 203-208.

—— ——*Poem to "Highland Mary."* Blackwood's Edinburgh Magazine, vol. 67, 1850, pp. 309-312.

——*His First Bosom Friend*. Broadway, by Robert Buchanan, vol. 1, 1868, pp. 746-752.

——*Home of*. Lippincott's Magazine of Literature, by J. G. Wilson, vol. 1, 1868, pp. 657-665.

——*Horace and Béranger : the three Lyrists*. Cornhill Magazine, vol. 17, 1868, pp. 150-167 ; same article, Littell's Living Age, vol. 97, pp. 3-13.

——*Influence of Scenery on his Character*. London Magazine, vol. 4, 1821, pp. 250-252.

——*Land of*. Harper's New Monthly Magazine, by W. H. Rideing, vol. 59, 1859, pp. 180-191.—Dublin University Magazine, vol. 18, 1841, pp. 509-523, 711-723. — Macmillan's Magazine, by Thomas Dykes, vol. 54, 1886, pp. 287-295.

——*Life and Character of*. Spirit and Manners of the Age, vol. 1, 1826, pp. 193-197.

——*Life and Poetry of*. Blackfriars Magazine, by H. C. Somers, vol. 3, 1886, pp. 110-118, and 178-184.

——*Life and Writings of*. Scots Magazine, vol. 59, 1797, pp. 3-8 ; vol. 63, 1801, pp. 663-666 ; vol. 64, 1802, pp. 131-133, 300-303.

——*Lockhart's Life of*. Blackwood's Edinburgh Magazine, by

Burns, Robert.

Professor Wilson, vol. 23, 1828, pp. 667-712.—London Magazine, vol. 1, 3rd Series, 1828, pp. 161-170.—Edinburgh Review, by T. Carlyle, vol. 48, 1828, pp. 267-312.

——_Loves of._ Belgravia, by Percy Fitzgerald, vol. 2, 2nd Series, 1870, pp. 421-437.

——_Memoir of._ Monthly Magazine, by R. Heron, vol. 3, 1797, pp. 213-216, 552-562.

——_Memorial Poem to._ Scots Magazine, vol. 59, 1797, pp. 51, 52.

——_New York and Dundee Statue of._ Art Journal, 1881, pp. 71, 72.

——_Ode to._ Scots Magazine, by Robert Tannahill, vol. 72, 1810, p. 127.

——_Phrenological Delineation of._ Phrenological Magazine, with portrait, vol. 2, 1881, pp. 20-22.

——_Pilgrimage to the Land of._ Christian Teacher, vol. 4, N.S., 1842, pp. 115-129.

——_Poem on._ Harper's New Monthly Magazine, by Henry W. Longfellow, vol. 61, 1880, pp. 321-323.

——_Poems, chiefly in the Scottish Dialect._ Edinburgh Magazine, vol. 4, 1786, pp. 284-288, 366-368, 371-375.

——_Poetry of._ Lounger, by Henry Mackenzie, vol. 3, 1787, pp. 278-289. — Southern Literary Messenger, by J. T. Otis, vol. 2, 1836, pp. 238-244. — St. James's Magazine, by T. Bayne, vol. 5, 4th Series, 1879, pp. 493-505.—Catholic Presbyterian, by David Sime, vol. 5, 1881, pp. 256-267.

Burns, Robert.

——_Recent Discoveries concerning._ Chambers's Journal, 1875, pp. 193-196.

——_Recollections of._ London Magazine, vol. 10, 1824, pp. 117-122.

——_Reliques of._ Quarterly Review, by Sir W. Scott, vol. 1, 1809, pp. 19-36.—Monthly Review, vol. 60, N. S., 1809. pp. 399-409. — Edinburgh Review, by F. Jeffrey, vol. 13, 1809, pp. 249-276 ; same article, Selections from Edinburgh Review, vol. 2, pp. 166-189.—Eclectic Review, vol. 5, 1809, by James Montgomery, pp. 393-410.— Scots Magazine, vol. 71, 1809, pp. 198-203.

——_Some Aspects of._ Cornhill Magazine, vol. 40, 1879, pp. 408-429; same article, Appleton's Journal of Literature, vol. 7, N.S., 1879, pp. 516-528.

——_Songs of._ Blackwood's Edinburgh Magazine, vol. 46, 1839, pp. 256-271.

——_Sonnet to._ European Magazine, vol. 79, 1821, p. 260.

——_Stanzas to the Memory of._ Monthly Magazine, vol. 3, 1797, pp. 53, 54.

——_Tam O'Shanter._ London Magazine, vol. 3, 3rd Series, 1829, pp. 557-560.

——_Tyler's._ Princeton Review, by M. B. Hope, vol. 21, 1849, pp. 251-259.

——_Unpublished Common-place Book._ Macmillan's Magazine, by William Jack, vol. 39, 1879, pp. 448-460, 560-572 ; vol. 40, pp. 32-43, 124-132, 250-261.

——_Unpublished Remains of._ Edinburgh Literary Journal,

Burns, Robert.

Nov. 21, 1829, pp. 349-352, Dec. 5. pp. 384-386.

——*Visits to Birthplace of.* Eclectic Review, vol. 2, N.S., 1859, pp. 182-192.—Century, vol. 26, 1883, pp. 752-761.

——*Walk with, on his birthday.* Scottish Monthly Magazine, vol. 2, 1837, pp. 147-152.

Burns, Robert.

——*Wordsworth's Letter on.* Blackwood's Edinburgh Magazine, vol. 1, 1817, pp. 261-266, and vol. 2, pp. 65-73, 201-204.

——*Works.* British Critic, vol 16, 1800, pp. 366-379 ; vol. 17 pp. 416-422.—Analyist, vol. 1, 1834, pp. 130-138.

VI. CHRONOLOGICAL LIST OF WORKS.

Poems, chiefly in the Scottish Dialect. (Kilmarnock Edition) . . . 1786

—— (Edinburgh Edition, with additions) . . 1787

—— (Second edition, includes twenty new pieces) 1793

Scots Musical Museum (Contributed 184 songs) . . . 1787-1803

Select Collection of Original Scottish Airs (Contributed) . . . 1793-1805

Letters addressed to Clarinda 1802

Reliques collected by R. H. Cromek 1808

Printed by WALTER SCOTT, *Felling, Newcastle-on-Tyne.*

www.ingramcontent.com/pod-product-compliance
Lightning Source LLC
Chambersburg PA
CBHW030101030726
47498CB00007B/2210